## THE RUNAWAY BRIDE

Dawn went swiftly across the hall to the door of her own room, which she had left so joyously a short hour before. Then she girded herself to carry out the resolution she had formed.

On the big white bed lay her bonnet and mantle. It was the work of but a moment to put them on, though her fingers trembled as she did so.

She paused an instant in the middle of the room and swept it with her eyes. Then with a little tragic wave of renunciation, she went swiftly into the room beyond.

The open desk caught her attention. She stopped and, taking up pen, wrote on a sheet of paper:

**Goodby. I had to go.**

—Dawn

# GRACE
# LIVINGSTON
# HILL

# DAWN OF THE
# MORNING

BANTAM BOOKS
TORONTO · NEW YORK · LONDON

*This low-priced Bantam Book
has been completely reset in a type face
designed for easy reading, and was printed
from new plates. It contains the complete
text of the original hard-cover edition.*
NOT ONE WORD HAS BEEN OMITTED.

DAWN OF THE MORNING
*A Bantam Book / published by arrangement with
J. B. Lippincott Company*

*PRINTING HISTORY*
*Lippincott edition published 1939*
*Bantam edition / December 1975*
*2nd printing ... October 1976    3rd printing .... August 1977*
*4th printing*

ISBN 0-553-11329-1

*Published simultaneously in the United States and Canada*

Bantam Books are published by Bantam Books, Inc. Its trade-
mark, consisting of the words "Bantam Books" and the por-
trayal of a bantam, is registered in the United States Patent
Office and in other countries. Marca Registrada. Bantam
Books, Inc., 666 Fifth Avenue, New York, New York 10019.

PRINTED IN THE UNITED STATES OF AMERICA

# WINGS OF THE MORNING

"The morning hangs its signal
    Upon the mountain's crest,
While all the sleeping valleys
    In silent darkness rest;
From peak to peak it flashes,
    It laughs along the sky
That the crowning day is coming, by and by!
We can see the rose of morning,
    A glory in the sky,
And that splendor on the hill-tops
    O'er all the land shall lie.
Above the generations
    The lonely prophets rise,—
The Truth flings dawn and day-star
    Within their glowing eyes;
From heart to heart it brightens,
    It draweth ever nigh,
Till it crowneth all men thinking, by and by!
The soul hath lifted moments
    Above the drift of days,
When life's great meaning breaketh
    In sunrise on our ways;
From hour to hour it haunts us,
    The vision draweth nigh,
Till it crowneth living, *dying,* by and by!
And in the sunrise standing,
    Our kindling hearts confess
That 'no good thing is failure,
    No evil thing success!'
From age to age it groweth,
    That radiant faith so high,
And its crowning day is coming by and by!"

*William C. Gannett*

v

# CHAPTER I

In the year 1824, in a pleasant town located between Schenectady and Albany, stood the handsome colonial residence of Hamilton Van Rensselaer. Solemn hedges shut in the family pride and hid the family sorrow, and about the borders of its spacious gardens, where even the roses seemed subdued, there played a child. The stately house oppressed her, and she loved the sombre garden best.

Her only friend in the old house seemed a tall clock that stood on the stairs and told out the hours in the hopeless tone that was expected of a clock in such a house, though it often took time to wink pleasantly at the child as she passed by, and talk off a few seconds and minutes in a brighter tone.

But the great clock on the staircase ticked awesomely one morning as the little girl went slowly down to her father's study in response to his bidding.

She did not want to go. She delayed her steps as much as possible, and looked up at the kindly old clock for sympathy; but even the round-eyed sun and the friendly moon that went around on the clock face every day as regularly as the real sun and moon, and usually appeared to be bowing and smiling at her, wore solemn expressions, and seemed almost pale behind their highly painted countenances.

The little girl shuddered as she gave one last look over her shoulder at them and passed into the dim recesses of the back hall, where the light came only in weird, half-circular slants from the mullioned window over the front door. It was dreadful indeed when the jolly sun and moon looked grave.

She paused before the heavy door of the study and

held her breath, dreading the ordeal that was to come. Then, gathering courage, she knocked timidly, and heard her father's instant, cold "Come."

With trembling fingers she turned the knob and went in.

There were heavy damask curtains at the windows, reaching to the floor, caught back with thick silk cords and tassels. They were a deep, sullen red, and filled the room with oppressive shadows in no wise relieved by the heavy mahogany furniture upholstered in the same red damask.

Her father sat by his ponderous desk, always littered with papers which she must not touch.

His sternly handsome face was forbidding. The very beauty of it was hateful to her. The look on it reminded her of that terrible day, now nearly three years ago, when he had returned from a journey of several months abroad in connection with some brilliant literary enterprise, and had swept her lovely mother out of his life and home, the innocent victim of long-entertained jealousy and most unfounded suspicion.

The little girl had been too young to understand what it was all about. When she cried for her she was forbidden even to think of her, and was told that her mother was unworthy of that name.

The child had declared with angry tears and stampings of her small foot, that it was not true, that her mother was good and dear and beautiful; but they had paid no heed to her. The father had sternly commanded silence and sent her away; and the mother had not returned.

So she had sobbed her heart out in the silence of her own room, where every object reminded her of the lost mother's touch and voice and presence, and had gone about the house in a sullen silence unnatural to childhood, thereby making herself more enemies than friends.

Of her father she was afraid. She shrank into terrified silence whenever he approached, scarcely answering his questions, and growing farther away from him every day, until he instinctively knew that she hated him for her mother's sake.

When a year had passed he procured a divorce without protest from the innocent but crushed wife, this by aid of a law that often places "Truth forever on the scaffold, Wrong forever on the throne." Not long after, he brought to his home as his wife a capable, arrogant, self-opinionated woman, who set herself to rule him and his household as it should be ruled.

The little girl was called to audience in the gloomy study where sat the new wife, her eyes filled with hostility toward the other woman's child, and was told that she must call the lady "Mother."

Then the black eyes that held in their dreamy depths some of the gunpowder flash of her father's steely ones took fire; the little face darkened with indignant fury; the small foot came down with fierce determination on the thick carpet, and the child declared:

"I will *never* call her mother! She is *not* my mother! She is a bad woman, and she has no right here. She cannot be your wife. It is wicked for a man to have two wives. I know, for I heard Mary Ann and Betsey say so this morning in the kitchen. My mother is alive yet. She is at Grandfather's. I heard Betsey say that too. You are a wicked, cruel man, and I hate you. I will not have you for a father any more. I will go away and stay with my mother. She is good. *You* are bad! I hate you! I hate you! *I hate you! And I hate her!*"—pointing toward the new wife, who sat in horrified condemnation, with two fiery spots upon her outraged cheeks.

"Jemima!" thundered her father in his angriest tone.

But the little girl turned upon him furiously.

"My name is not Jemima!" she screamed. "I will not let you call me so. My name is Dawn. My mother called me Dawn. I will not answer when you call me Jemima."

"Jemima, you may go to your room!" commanded the father, standing up, white to the lips, to face a will no whit less adamant than his own.

"I will not go until you call me Dawn," she answered, her face turning white and stern, with sudden singular likeness to her father on its soft round outlines.

She stood her ground until carried struggling upstairs and locked into her own room.

Gradually she had cried her fury out, and suc-

cumbed to the inevitable, creeping back as seldom as
possible into the life of the house, and spending the time
with her own brooding thoughts and sad plays, far in
the depths of the box-boarded garden, or shut into the
quiet of her own room.

To the new mother she never spoke unless she had
to, and never called her Mother, though there were many
struggles to compel her to do so. She never came when
they called her Jemima, nor obeyed a command prefaced
by that name, though she endured in consequence many
a whipping and many a day in bed, fed on bread and
water.

"What is the meaning of this strange whim?" demanded the new wife, with set lips. Her position was
none too easy, nor her disposition markedly that of a
saint.

"A bit of her mother's sentimentality," explained
the chagrined father. "She objected to calling the child
for my grandmother, Jemima. She wanted it named for
her own mother, and said Jemima was harsh and ugly,
until one day her old minister, who was fully as sen-
timental as she, if he was an old man, told her that
Jemima meant 'Dawn of the Morning.' After that she
made no further protest. But I had no idea she had
carried her foolishness to this extent, nor taught the child
such notions about her honest and honorable name."

"It won't take long to get them out of her head,"
prophesied the new-comer, with the sparkle of combat in
her eye. Yet it was now nearly three years since the little
girl had seen or heard from her mother, and she still refused to answer to the name of Jemima. The step-mother
had fallen into the habit of saying "you" when she wanted
anything done.

Of the events which preceded her father's summons
this morning, Dawn knew nothing.

Three days before he had received an urgent message from his former wife's father, stating that his daughter was dead, and demanding an immediate interview. It
was couched in such language that, being the man he
was, he could not refuse to comply.

He answered the summons immediately, going by
horseback a hard six-hours ride that he might catch an

earlier stage than he could otherwise have done. He was the kind of man that always did what he felt to be his duty, no matter how unpleasant it might be. It was the only thing that saved his severity from being a vice. His father-in-law had laid this journey upon him as a duty, and though he had no definite idea of the reason for this sudden demand, he went at once.

No one but his Maker can penetrate the soul of a man like Hamilton Van Rensselaer to know what were his thoughts as he walked up the rose-bordered path to the fine old brick house, which a few years before he had trod with his beautiful young bride leaning upon his arm.

With grave ceremony, the old servant opened the door into the stately front room where most of Van Rensselaer's courting had been done, and left him alone in the dim light that sifted through partly drawn shades.

He stood a moment within the shadowed room, a sense of the past sweeping over him with oppressive force, like a power that might not be resisted. Then as his eyes grew accustomed to the half-darkness, he started, for there before him was a coffin!

His father-in-law's message had not led him to expect to see his former wife. He had gathered from the letter that she might have been dead some weeks, and that the matter to be discussed was of business, though probably painfully connected with the one who was gone.

While the news of her death had given him a shock which he had not anticipated, he had yet had time in his long journey to grow accustomed to the thought of it. But he was in no wise prepared to meet the sight of her lying there in her last sleep, so still and white.

Strangely moved, he stepped nearer, not understanding why he felt thus toward one whom he firmly believed had made utter wreck of his life.

She lay in a simple white gown like the one she used to wear when he first knew her. In her hand was one white rose. It might have come from her wedding bouquet. The soft fragrance of it floated up and smote him with keen and unexpected pain. The rose had reached where a sword could not have penetrated.

Death had kindly erased the deep lines of suffering

from Mary Montgomery's beautiful face, and told no tales of the broken heart; but to see what he had once loved, pure and lovely as it used to be, with no trace of the havoc he had wrought upon it, spoke louder to the conscience of the man than a sorrowful face could have done; for then he might have turned from her with a hardened heart, saying it was all her own fault and she had got only what she deserved. But to see her thus was as if God's finger had touched her and exonerated her from all blame. The sight shook the very foundations of his belief in her disgrace.

He was filled with conflicting emotions. He had not supposed that he could feel this way, for he had thought that his love for Mary was dead; yet it had raised its dishonored head and given him one piercing look, while it had seemed to say to his heart, "You are too late! You are too late!"

The sound of footsteps coming down the hall recalled him to himself. It came to him that this was what he had been brought here for, this dramatic effect of Mary's death, perhaps for revenge, perhaps to try to make him acknowledge that he had been in the wrong.

He stiffened visibly and turned toward the door. His heart, so accustomed to the hardening process, grew adamant again, and he was ready with a haughty word to greet the father, but the dignity of the white-haired man who entered the room held him in check.

Mr. Montgomery went over to the window, merely giving his visitor a grave bow in passing, and pushed up the heavy shades. The sunlight burst joyously in upon the solemnity of the room, unhindered by the sheer muslin curtains, and flung its golden glory about the sweet face in the coffin, making a halo of light above the soft, dark waves of hair.

The younger man's eyes were drawn irresistibly to look at her once more, and the sight startled him more than ever, for now she seemed like a crowned saint, whose irreproachable life was too sacred for him to come near.

The old man came over and stood in the pathway of light from the window, though not so as to hinder its falling on the dead face, and turned toward his former son-in-law.

Then and not till then did the visitor notice that the old man held in his arms a beautiful boy between two and three years old.

Proudly the grandfather stood with the chubby arm around his neck and the dimpled fingers patting his cheek.

The sunlight fell in a broad illumination over the head and face of the child, kindling into flame the masses of tumbled curls which showed the same rich mahogany tint that had always made Hamilton Van Rensselaer's head a distinguished mark in any company. The baby's eyes were a wonderful gray, which even now held flashes of steel—albeit flashes of fun and not of passion. As the man looked, they mirrored back his own startlingly. In the round baby cheeks were two dimples strikingly placed, the counterpart of two that daring Nature had triflingly set in the otherwise stern countenance of the man. The likeness was marvellous.

In sheer astonishment the man gazed at the child, and then as he looked the baby frowned, and he saw his own face in miniature, identical even to the sternness which was the prevailing expression of his countenance.

Suddenly the man felt that he stood before God and was being judged and rebuked for his treatment of the dead. The awful remorse that stung his soul burst forth in a single sentence which was wrung from him by an unseen force:

"Why did you never tell me?"

He flashed the rebuke at the old man, but the dark eyes under the heavy white brows only looked at him the more steadily and did not flinch, as if they would tell him to look to himself for an answer to his question.

The steady gaze did its work. It was the Nemesis before which his pride and self-esteem fell. His glance went from the righteous face of the old man to the pure and beautiful eyes of the boy, now frowning with disapproval, and he dropped into a chair with a groan.

"I have been wrong!" he said, and bowed his head, the last atom of his pride rent away from him. There beside the dead, great scorching tears of bitterness found their way to his eyes, washing away the scales of blind conceit, and bringing clearer vision. Mary Montgomery was vindicated in the eyes of the man who had wronged her.

But the baby frowned and cried softly:

"Hush, bad man! You go away! You wake my pitty muvver! She's 's'eep!"

The strong man shrank from the child's words as from a blow, and looked up with almost a pleading on his usually cold face. But the old man watched him sternly.

"Yes, it is enough. You may go. There is nothing more to be said. Now you understand. This is why I sent for you. It was her right."

"But," said the stricken man, and looked toward the sleeping one in the coffin, "may I not wait until——"

"You have no right," the old man answered sternly, and the young man turned away with a strange wild feeling tearing his throat like a sob.

"No, I have no right."

Then with a sudden movement he turned toward the child as if he would claim something there, but the baby hid his face and clung to his grandfather's neck.

"I have no right," he said again. One last look he gave the sweet dead face, as though he would ask forgiveness, then turned and went unsteadily from the room.

The old father followed him silently, as though to complete some ceremony, and, closing the door softly behind him, spoke a few words of explanation, facts that had they been brought forth sooner might have made all things different. It was Mary's wish that no word should be spoken in her vindication while she lived. If her husband could not trust what she had told him when he first came home, it mattered not to her what he believed. The hope of her life was crushed. But now that she was beyond further pain, and for the boy's sake, her father had sent for him that he might know these things before the wife he had wronged was laid to rest.

Then Van Rensselaer felt himself dismissed, and with one last look at the huddled figure of his little son, who still kept his face hid, he went down the path again, his pride utterly crushed, his life a broken thing.

After him echoed the sound of a baby's voice, "Go away, bad man!" and then the great oak door closed quickly behind him for the last time.

He trod the streets of the village as in a nightmare, and knew not that there were those in his way who would have tarred and feathered him if it had not been for love of the honored dead and her family. Straight into the country he walked, to the next village, and knew not how far he had come. There he hired a horse and rode to the next stage route, and so, resting not even at night, he came to his home. But ever on the way he had been attended by a vision, on the left a sweet-faced figure in a coffin, with one white rose whose perfume stifled him, and on the right by a bright-haired boy with eyes that pierced his very soul. And whether on horseback or by stage, in the company of others or alone in a dreary woodland road, they were there on either hand, and he knew they would be so while life for him should last.

He reached home in the gray of a morning that was to become a gray day, and sent up word that his little daughter should come down to his study when her early tasks were finished.

He had not said a word to his wife as yet, though she had suspected where he was going when he told her that Mary Montgomery was dead. It lifted a great load from her shoulders to know that the other wife was no longer living. She had been going about these three days with almost a smile upon her hard countenance, and the little girl had had no easy time of it with her father away.

It was very still in the study after Dawn sat down in the straight-backed chair opposite her father. She could hear the old clock tick solemnly, slowly. It said, "Poor-child! Poor-child! Poor-child! Poor-child!" until the tears began to smart in her eyes.

Her father sat with his elbow on the desk, and his handsome head bowed upon his hand. He did not raise his head when she entered. She began to wonder if he was asleep, and her heart beat with awe and dread. Nothing good had ever come to her out of these interviews in the study. Perhaps he was going to send her away, too, as he had sent her mother. Her little face hardened. Well, she would be glad to go. What if he should send her to her mother! Oh, that would be joy!—but he never would.

She was a beautiful child as she sat there palpitating with fear and hope. Her face was like her mother's, fair, with wild-rose color, and eyes that were dark and dreamy, always looking out with longing and appeal. Her hair, like her father's only in its tendency to curl, was fine and dark, and fell about the little troubled face. It had been the cause of many a contention between her and her step-mother, who wished to plait it smoothly into braids, which she considered the only neat way for a child's hair to be arranged. Failing in that, she had tried to cut it off, but the child had defended her curls so fiercely that they had finally let her alone. It was wonderful what care the little girl took of them herself, for it was no small task to keep such a head of hair well brushed. But Dawn could remember how her mother loved her curls, and she clung to them. When she lifted the dark lashes there was a light in her eyes that made one think of the dawn of day. Such eyes had her mother.

At last Dawn looked up tremulously to her father, and he spoke. He did not look toward her, however, and his voice was cold and reserved.

"I have sent for you, my daughter—"

Dawn was glad he did not use the hateful name "Jemima."

"—to tell you that your mother was a good woman."

"Of course," said the child, with rising color. "I knew that all the time. Why did you ever say she wasn't?"

"There was a terrible mistake made." The father's voice was shaken. It gave Dawn a curious feeling.

"Who made the mistake?" she asked gravely.

The room was very still while this arrow found its way into the father's heart.

"I did." His voice sounded hoarse. The little girl felt almost sorry for him.

"Oh! Then you will bring her right back to us again and send this other woman away, won't you?"

"Child, your mother is dead!"

Dawn's face went as white as death, and she sprang to her feet, clasping her hands in horror.

"Then you have killed her!" she screamed. "You have killed her! My beautiful mother!" and with a wild cry she flung herself upon the floor and broke into a passion of tears.

The strong man writhed in anguish as his little child set the mark of Cain upon his forehead.

The outcry brought the step-mother, but neither noticed her as she entered and demanded the reason for this scene. She tried to pick the child up from the floor, but Dawn only beat her off with kicks and screams, and they finally went away and left her weeping there upon the floor. Her father took his hat and walked out into the woods. There he stayed for hours, while the wife went about with set lips and a glint in her eye that boded no good for the child.

Finally the sobs grew less and less frequent, and the old clock in the hall could again be heard in her ears, as she sobbed herself slowly to sleep: "Poor-child! Poor-child! Poor-child! Poor-child!"

It was after this that they sent her away to school.


CHAPTER II


HER father placed her on a Hudson River steamer in charge of the captain, whom he knew, and in company with two other little girls, who were returning to the school of Friend Isaac and Friend Ruth after a short vacation.

Dawn, attired in the grave Quaker garb of the school, leaned over the rail of the deck, inconsequently swinging by its ribbons her long gray pocket containing a hundred dollars wherewith to pay her entrance fee and provide necessities, and watched her unloved father walk away from the landing.

"Thee and thou and thy long pocket!" called out a saucy deck-hand to the three little girls, and Dawn turned with an angry flash in her eyes to take up the work of facing the world single-handed.

She did not drop the pocket into the water, nor fall overboard, but bore herself discreetly all through the journey, and made her entrance into the new life demurely, save for the independent stand she took upon her arrival:

"My name is Dawn Van Rensselaer, and my mother wishes me to wear my curls just as they are."

Her two fellow-travellers had given her cause to believe that there would be an immediate raid made upon her precious curls, and her determined spirit decided to make a stand at the start, and not to give in for anything. The quiet remark created almost a panic for a brief moment, coming thus unexpectedly into the decorous order of the place. Friend Ruth caught her breath, and two faint pink spots appeared in her smooth cheeks.

"Thee will wear thy hair smoothly plaited, child, as the others do, unless it be cut close," she said decidedly, laying her thin pink lips smoothly together over even teeth. "Thee will write to thy mother that it is our custom here to allow nothing frivolous or worldly in the dress of our pupils."

One glance at the cool gray eye of her oppressor decided Dawn to hide in her heart forever the fact that the mother whose wish she was flaunting was no more in this world, nor longer had the legal right to express her wishes concerning her child. With ready wits she argued the matter:

"But it isn't worldly. God made my curls, and it is just as bad to plait them up and take out the curl as it would be to go to work and curl them on an iron if they were straight. My curls aren't frivolous, and I take care of them myself. My mother loves them, and I must do as she says."

Friend Ruth looked at the determined little face set in its frame of dark curls, and hesitated. She was not used to logic from a child, yet there seemed to be reason in the words. Besides, Friend Ruth was a great advocate of honor to parents. It was a complicated question. She decided to temporize.

"I will speak to Friend Isaac about the matter, but

thee will have to wear them in a net. It is untidy to have curls tumbling about thy face."

That was the end of the matter. Dawn wore her curls without further question, albeit in a plain, dark net. Though outwardly the little girl was docile, except upon occasion, Friend Ruth learned to avoid any crossing of swords with the young logician, for she nearly always got the worst of it.

Dawn took to learning as a bird to the air, having inherited her father's brilliant mind and taste for letters, combined with her mother's keen insight and wide perceptive faculties. Her lessons were always easily and perfectly learned, and she looked with contempt upon the plodders who could not get time from their tasks for the fun which she was always ready to lead.

The pranks she played were many. On one occasion she led an expedition of the entire school in a slide down a newly made straw-stack, thereby damaging its geometrical shape and necessitating several hours' work by the farmhands. As a punishment, she was remanded to the garden alone to write a composition on the beauties of Nature. It began:

*A great green worm come cameing down the populo tree with great tribusence.*

Friend Ruth read the finished composition with the dismay of a hen which has a duck on its hands, and handed it over to Friend Isaac.

"The child has an original mind, and is going to be a brilliant woman," he remarked gravely.

"Yes, Isaac, but thee will not tell her so," said Friend Ruth quickly.

Six years had passed since Dawn, a child of ten, had come to the school, and she had never gone home. It had been her own wish, and for once her father and stepmother were willing to accede to her. To both, the sight of her and the thought of her were painful. Her father had visited her every year and brought with him a full supply of the modest wardrobe that the school allowed, and Dawn had money to meet all her necessary expenses.

She lived a sort of triple life—one in the world of her studies, in which she sometimes took deep delight, often going far ahead of her classes because she wanted to see what came next; one in the world of play, where she was leader in all sorts of mischief, getting the older ones into endless difficulties with the teachers, and protecting the little ones, even to her own detriment at times; the third life was lived alone in the fields or the woods, where she might sit quietly and look up into the blue sky, listening to the music of the winds and the birds or the sad chirp of a cricket, taking a little grasshopper into her confidence, talking to a friendly squirrel on the maple bough overhead—here was where she really lived. On the walls of her memory were hung strange, sad pictures of the past. Always on such occasions the mother all in white, with starry eyes, hovered over her, and seemed to listen to the wild longing that beat in her young heart, and to pour a benediction upon her.

She could not think of her father except sadly or bitterly, and so as much as possible she put him out of her thoughts. By degrees, as she came to see on his annual visits how old and careworn he was grown, how haunted and haggard were his eyes, she grew to pity him, but never to love, for her mother had been her idol, and he had killed her mother. That the girl could not forget, though as she grew older she felt with a kind of spiritual instinct that she must forgive. She felt it was his own blindness and stupidity that had done it, and that he was suffering some measure of punishment for his deed. She never actually put these thoughts before her in so many words. They were rather a sort of growing undertone of consciousness in her, as her mental and spiritual faculties developed.

In one year more she would be through with the school course. For some time she had been dreading the thought, and wondering what would come to her next? If she might go somewhere and "teach school,"—but she felt certain her father would never allow that. He was proud and held ideas about woman's sphere. Though she could scarcely be said to know him well, still she felt without asking that he would never consent. Sometimes she even entertained vague thoughts of running away when she should be through school, for the idea of dwelling under her father's roof again, under control of the woman who had usurped her mother's place, she could not abide.

It was therefore with trepidation that she received a message in the school-room one morning, bidding her come to the parlor to meet her father. The fair face flushed and the brow darkened with trouble. It was not the usual time for her father's annual visit. Did it mean that he was going to take her away from the school? Her young heart beat to the old tune of the friendly clock at home as she went to answer the summons: "Poor-child! Poor-child! Poor-child! Poor-child!"

But in the square, plain parlor, with its hair-cloth furniture, its gray paper window-shades, and its neutral-tinted ingrain carpet, there sat two men with Friend Ruth, instead of one.

Her father looked older than ever before. His hair was silvering about the edges, though he was still what would have been called a young man. The stranger was younger, yet with an old look about his eyes, as if they had been living longer than the rest of his face.

Dawn paused in the doorway and looked from one to the other. She had put up her hand as she reached the door, and drawn from her head the net which held her beautiful curls in leash. They fell about her lovely face in the fashion of the day. They were grown long and thick, but still kept their baby softness and fineness of texture. She made a charming picture standing thus with the door-latch in her hand, hesitating almost shyly, though she was not unduly shy. Even in her Quaker garb, with the sheer folds of the snowy kerchief about her neck, she looked an unusually beautiful girl. The young stranger saw and took notice as he rose to receive the impersonal introduction that her father gave.

The girl looked at them both gravely, with an alert watchfulness. Of the stare of open admiration with which the stranger regarded her, she seemed not even to be aware, though Friend Ruth noticed it with disapproval.

Dawn took the chair to which Friend Ruth motioned her, at some distance from the young man, and sat demurely waiting, her eyes wide with apprehension. Her father asked about her conduct and standing in the school, but no flush of embarrassment came to the face of the watching girl, though Friend Ruth gave unwonted praise of the past year's work. At another time it would have astonished and pleased her, but now she felt it was a mere preliminary to the real object of her father's visit.

As soon as there came a break in the conversation, the stranger took a part, admiring the location of the school, and saying he would be glad if he might look about the place, as he had a friend who wished to send his daughter away to school somewhere, and it would be a pleasure to be able to speak in detail of this delightful spot. Was there a view of the Hudson from this point? Indeed! Perhaps the young lady would be so kind as to show it to him?

Friend Ruth hesitated, but the father waved a command to his daughter. Frowning, she arose to obey. She felt the whole thing was a subterfuge to get her from the room while the real object of her father's unexpected visit was divulged.

She led the way through the wide hall, out to the pillared veranda, and down the sloping lawn to the bluff which overlooked the river, where plied a steamer on its silver course. Apathetically she pointed out the places of interest. She scarcely heard her companion's eager attempts at conversation. He noted the absent look in her dark eyes.

"You do not like it here?" he asked, letting his tone become gentle, in coaxing confidence.

"Oh, yes," she answered quickly, with a flit of trouble across her face. "At least, I think I do. I do not care to go away."

"Not to your beautiful home?" he asked insinuatingly. "And your mother?" he added, his eyes narrowing to observe her expression more closely.

"She is not my mother," answered the girl coldly, and became at once reserved, as if she were sorry for having spoken so plainly.

"Oh, I beg your pardon! I did not know," murmured the stranger, making mental note of her change of expression.

Suddenly her eyes flashed wide upon him, and she

dashed a question out with a way that compelled an answer:

"Has my father come to take me home, do you know?"

"Oh, no, not at all," answered the young man suavely. He was delighted to have found this key to her thoughts. It led just where he desired. "We are merely taking a business trip together, and your father stopped off to see how things were going with you. I am sure I am delighted that he did, for it has given me great pleasure to meet you."

"Why?" asked the girl, lifting relieved eyes to his face in mild astonishment.

He gave a half-embarrassed laugh at this frank way of meeting him.

"Now, surely, you do not need to ask me that," he said, looking down at her meaningly, his eyes gazing into the innocent ones in open and intimate admiration. "You must know how beautiful you are!"

With a startled expression, she searched his face, and then, not finding it pleasant, turned away with a look resembling her father in its sternness.

"I don't think that is a nice way for a man to talk to a girl," she said in a displeased tone. "I am too big to be spoken to in that way. I am past sixteen, and shall be done school next year."

He dropped the offending manner at once, and begged her pardon, pleading that her father had talked of her as a child. He asked also that she would let him be her friend, for he felt that they would be congenial, and all the more that she was growing into womanhood.

Her gravity did not relax, however, and her eyes searched his face suspiciously.

"I think we would better go into the house," she said soberly. "Friend Ruth will not like my staying out so long, and I must see my father again."

"But will you be my friend?" he insisted, as they turned their steps toward the house.

"How could we be friends? You are not in the school, and I never go away. Besides, I don't see what would be the use."

"Don't you like me at all?" he asked, putting on the tone which had turned many a girl's head.

"Why, I don't know you even a little bit. How could I like you? Besides, why should I?" answered Dawn frankly.

"You are deliciously plain-spoken."

She caught her lip between her teeth in a vexed way. Why would he persist in talking to her as if she were a child?

"There, now I have vexed you again," he said, pretending to be much dismayed, "but indeed you misunderstand me. I do not look upon you as a child at all. Many a girl is married at your age, and you will soon be a lovely woman. I want you for my friend. Are you not willing?"

"I don't know," said the girl bluntly, looking troubled. "I should have to think about it, and I don't see why I should. I shall be here a whole year yet, and I shall never see you. I wish I could stay here always," she ended passionately. "I never want to go home."

"Perhaps you will not need to go there," he said insinuatingly, wondering how it was she was so different from other girls. She did not seem to understand coquetry. Her eyes met his now in mild question.

"You may marry and have a home of your own," he answered her unspoken question. A startled expression came into her eyes.

"Oh, no," she said quickly; "I don't think that will ever happen. I don't want that to happen;" and she drew away from him as if the thought frightened her. "Married people are not happy."

"Nonsense!" said the young man gayly. He had planted the seed in what looked like fallow ground, and perhaps one day it would blossom for him. "There are plenty of happy married people. I've a good old father and mother who just worship each other. They've been happy as clams all their lives, and I know a great many more."

"My father and mother were not happy," said Dawn gravely. "Friend Ruth and Friend Isaac do not seem to be very happy either, though of course this isn't a real

home. But they are never cross," she added in conscien-
tious explanation.

"If you were married, you could have a real home
of your own, and have things just as you wanted them,"
the young man remarked cunningly.

"That would be nice," said the girl thoughtfully. "I
should like that part, but I think I would like it better
without being married. There are father and Friend Ruth
looking for us. Let us hurry."

"But you have not told me whether you will let me
be your friend," he said, detaining her under a great elm
tree, and looking off toward the river, as if he were still
watching the steamer. "If you will let me be your friend,
I will get permission to come and see you now and then,
and I will bring you a box of sweets. You will like that,
won't you? All girls are fond of sweets."

"I don't know," answered Dawn slowly, looking at
him with troubled eyes, and wondering why it was that
his eyes reminded her of a fish.

"The other girls would like the sweets," he suggested.

"Could I give them away?" she asked with a flash
of interest.

"You may do anything you like with them," he responded eagerly. "So it is all settled, then, and I may
be your friend?"

"I don't know," said Dawn again. "I suppose it will
have to be as father and Friend Ruth say."

"No need to consult them in the matter. Leave that
to me. All I want is your consent. Remember I am going
to visit you next month and bring you something nice."

But by this time the others had reached them.

"Charming view, Mr. Van Rensselaer. I had no idea
you could see New York so plainly from this point," said
the young man.

Dawn stepped over and stood beside Friend Ruth,
looking thoughtfully down the river. She would like the
box of confections well enough, for not many sweets
were allowed at the school and they could have a treat
down in the woods, beside the brook. But somehow she
had a vague uneasiness about this friendship. She did not
like the stranger's face.

Her father and the other man went away after the noonday meal. The stranger's name, she learned, was Harrington Winthrop, and that he was interested in a business enterprise with her father. The matter passed entirely from her mind, only, after that, when she sat alone to brood over her life, a new dream took the place of the old. Always there was a lovely home all her own, with comfortable chairs and plenty of books, and thin, sprigged china, such as had been her mother's. In this home she was sole mistress. Day by day she dreamed out the pretty rooms, and dwelt in them, and even occasionally let her imagination people them. The image of her beautiful mother hovered about that home and stayed, but there came into it no one to annoy or disturb.

When the two men settled themselves in the stage that night, the younger began to talk:

"Do you know you have a very beautiful daughter, Mr. Van Rensselaer?"

The father started from the reverie into which he had fallen. The look of the moonlight was reminding him of a night over sixteen years ago, when he and Mary had taken this same stage trip. Strange he could not get away from the thought of it. Ah, yes! it had been the look of his daughter that had brought back Mary's face, for the girl was grown to be the image of her mother, save for a certain sad flitting of severity. In the moonlight outside the coach he seemed to see again the sweet face in the coffin, and he compared it with the warm living face of the girl whom he had been to see that day. He knew that between his daughter and him was an impenetrable barrier that could never be removed, and the thought of it pierced his soul as it never had before. A great yearning and pity for his motherless, fatherless girl had come into his cold, empty heart as he had watched her move silently about. But ever present was the thought that he had no right—no right in her either, no matter how much he might try. No one would have suspected him of such feelings. He hid them deep under his grim and brilliant exterior, sternly self-contained in any situation. But now, in the half-darkness, a new thought came into his mind, and he started and gave his attention to the words of his companion.

"Is she your only child?"

The question made him start again. There was a long pause, so long that Harrington Winthrop thought he had not been heard; then a husky voice answered out of the shadows of the coach:

"No, there was another—a little boy. He died soon after his mother."

Outside in the moonlight, the vision of a ruddy-haired boy rode in a wreath of mist. The words were the man's acknowledgment to the two who ever attended him now through life. He did not wish to give his confidence to this business companion.

"Ah! Then this beautiful young woman will likely be sole heir to the Van Rensselaer estate," said the young man to himself, rejoicing inwardly at the ease with which he was obtaining information.

There was silence in the coach while Winthrop pondered the great discovery he had made, and how he should act upon it.

But the elder man was lost in gloomy thoughts. He had a vague feeling that Mary, out there in the moonlight with her bright-haired boy, would hold him to account for the little girl she had loved and lost in life. A sudden glimpse into the future had been given him, partly by the young man's words, partly by the beauty of Dawn herself. She was blossoming into womanhood, and with that change would come new perplexities. She could not stay always at the school. Where in the world was there a place for his child? More and more he saw that the woman whom in the fierceness of his wrath he had selected to take the place of mother to the girl was both unable and unwilling to do so. He shrank from the time when his daughter would have to come home. As he thought of it, it seemed an impossible situation to have her there; it would be almost like having Mary in the flesh to live with them, with reproachful eyes ever upon their smallest acts. At that moment it came to him that he was enduring the torments of a lost soul, his conscience having sat in judgment and condemned him.

The stage-coach rumbled on, stopping now and again through the night for a change of horses, and the two who sat within its gloomy depths said little to each other, yet slept not, for one was musing on the evil of the past and its results, while the other was plotting evil for the future.

## CHAPTER III

HARRINGTON WINTHROP kept his promise about the sweets. Five times during the winter that followed his first visit with Mr. Van Rensselaer, he invented some excuse to visit Dawn.

The first time he came, he found her in the maple grove behind the pasture, with a group of other girls, all decked in autumn leaves and playing out some story that Dawn had read.

He persuaded her to walk a little way into the woods with him; and when he came to take his leave asked for a kiss, but Dawn sprang away from him in sudden panic:

"No," she said sharply; "I have never kissed anybody but my mother." Then, fearing she had been impolite in view of his gift, she added:

"We don't kiss people here at this school. It isn't the custom."

And she knew so little of the customs of the world that the incident passed without further apprehension on her part, or understanding of the young man's meaning.

"That's all right, my dear," he said pleasantly. "But don't forget about the house. I'm going to tell you all about it next time I come. You still want a home of your very own, don't you?"

"Why, of course," said Dawn; "but I can't see how you can know anything about it, or care. What have you to do with it?" And then with sudden alarm, "Has my father been talking to you about any such thing?"

"No, indeed! Your father does not even know I am

interested in you. I care for my own sake. Didn't I tell you that I liked you the minute I saw you? And I'm just as interested in this future home of yours as you are."

"I'm sure I can't see why," said Dawn, perplexed, yet trying to be polite.

"Suppose you think about it hard, dear, and see if you can find out why I care. Just think it all over, everything I have said, and then if you are still in doubt go and look in the looking-glass and keep on thinking, and I'm sure you'll find out by the time I come back. I'm coming soon again, and I want you to be watching for me every day. I'll bring you something nice next time, besides another box of sweets."

Dawn tried to smile, but felt uncomfortable. She murmured her thanks again, and turned uneasily toward the woods and her companions, and he deemed it prudent to leave her without further ado.

Back in the woods, the girls were making merry with her confections, and had nothing but praise for the handsome stranger who had brought them; but all through the eager questions and merry jibes Dawn was silent and thoughtful.

"Where are your thoughts, Dawn?" said Desire Hathaway. "Has the stranger stolen them away to pay for his goodies?"

"She looks as if he had asked her to marry him, and she didn't know whether to say yes or to wait for somebody else," laughed Matilda Hale, a new-comer among them, and older than the rest.

"I guess he kissed her good-by," chimed in silly Polly Phelps, who aspired to be Matilda's shadow. "I peeked through the bushes and saw him bending over her."

Amid the thoughtless laugh that rose, Dawn stood defiant, the crimson leaping into her cheeks, the steel into her eyes. For an instant she looked as if she would turn upon the offending Matilda and tear her to pieces. Then a sudden revelation came to her: this, *this* was what the handsome stranger had meant!

Instantly the light of anger died out of her face, and a gentle dignity took its place. Her little clenched

hands relaxed, the tenseness of the graceful body soft-
ened, and she turned toward the offender with a haughty
condescension:

"Matilda, we don't talk in that way here," she said,
and the laughter died out of the faces of her companions
and left instead amazement and admiration. They had
seen Dawn angry before, and had not expected the affair
to end so amicably. They felt it showed a marvellous
self-control, and left her mistress of the situation. Matilda
bit her lip in a vexed way and tossed her head. She felt
she had lost prestige by the little incident, and Dawn was
still the recognized leader of the school. It was not a
pleasant thought to the older girl.

Dawn turned and walked slowly away from them all,
out of the woods, down through the meadow, where
grazed her quiet friends, the sheep. She still carried her
gentle dignity, and none of the girls spoke until she was
out of sight behind the group of chestnuts at the corner
of the meadow.

Then Desire Hathaway voiced the general feeling:

"Isn't she just like a queen?"

"Oh, if you want to look at it that way!" sneered
Matilda, with another toss of her head. "There are a
good many kinds of queens, you know. I must say, I
thought she looked like a pretty wicked one for a minute
or two. She would have enjoyed tearing my eyes out if
she had dared."

"Dared!" cried Desire. "You don't know her. She
will dare anything that she thinks is worth while. I thought
it was just splendid, the way she controlled herself."

"Oh, well, just as you think, of course," shrugged
Matilda. "Come on, Polly; let's go finish our sewing."

Dawn stumbled on blindly in the pasture, trying to
take in the appalling thought that *perhaps* the young
man wanted to marry her!

Tears of indignation welled into her eyes, but she
brushed them angrily aside. Why was life so dreadful, she
wondered. Why did men exist to break women's hearts?
—for she never doubted that the married state was one of
heart-break. Such had been the lesson burned deep into
her soul by suffering. A home of her own had been a

sweet thought, but the serpent had entered her Eden, and she cared no more to stay there.

The next time Winthrop came it was openly, with a message from her father. All through the interview, which lasted for an hour, and was prolonged over the noonday meal, Dawn sat stiffly on the other side of Friend Ruth, watching the fishy eyes of the stranger and listening to his fulsome flatteries of the place, her small hands folded decorously, but her young heart beating painfully under the sheer folds of the 'kerchief.

On his fourth visit he bore a private letter from her father to Friend Ruth, and wore an air of assurance which made the girl's heart sink with nameless foreboding. Not even the praises of the girls for her handsome lover, their open envy of her future lot, or their merry taunts, could rouse her from a gravity which had begun to settle upon her.

This time Friend Ruth seemed to look upon the visitor in a different light. Not only was Dawn allowed to talk with him alone, but she was sent out with him for a walk in the woods.

Reluctantly she obeyed, frightened, she knew not why.

Harrington Winthrop had a winning way with him, and he was determined to win this proud, beautiful girl. Also, he was wise in the ways of the world, he did not force any undue attention upon her, but confined his conversation to telling her about the beautiful home he had seen. Rightly guessing that there was still much of the child about her, he went on to picture the house in detail, not hesitating to embellish it at will where his memory failed.

There was a garden with a fountain, and there should be flowers, all in profusion. There were clipped hedges, gravel paths, an arbor in a shady place, where she might bring her book or sewing, and where the sunshine would peer through the branches just enough to scatter gold about the leafy way.

In spite of her prejudices, she was interested. She could not help it. The longing for a real home of her own was great.

Then came the most difficult part of his task, which was to reconcile her to himself.

Skilfully he led the conversation about till he himself was the subject—his life since he had become a man and gone out into the world. Pathetically he talked of his own loneliness, until he touched the maternal chord in her nature and made her feel sorry for him. He opened up for her gaze depths of sympathy, tenderness, and pathos, which were purely imaginary and wholly impossible to his own nature. He launched into details of his own feelings which were the inspiration of the moment, because he saw they touched her. He told her how he had often been lonely almost to desperation, and how he had many and many a time pictured a home of his own, with a lovely wife at its head. The girl winced at the name "wife," but he went steadily on trying to take the strangeness out of the word, trying to touch her heart and fire her tenderness; for he rightly read the possibilities of love in the beautiful face, and it put him on his mettle to make it bloom for him.

He succeeded so far as to make her conscience sharply reprove her for the dislike she had for him. Of course if he had been lonely, too, and had had a care for her loneliness, it was a different matter. Perhaps, after all, they had something on common, and he would not be such a dreadful addition to the home she had longed for. At least, she had no right to shut him out of a dream that he held in common with her, and she tried to put aside her own feelings and look at him fairly.

So they walked the deeper into the woods, and while she did not say much in reply to his eloquent words, she did not seem actively opposed. He let his voice grow more and more tender, though he did not trouble her with words of love. He let a care for her become apparent: as they walked over the rough growth in the woods, he held the branches aside for her, and helped her over a log, and once across the stones of a little brook, touching her hand and arm deferentially. It did not appeal to Dawn in the way he hoped that it would, nor awaken any tenderness for him, but she let him lead her along a path which, had she been alone, she would have cleared at a bound, and counted an easy thing.

When he parted from her that evening to take the night boat, he gave her shrinking fingers a slight pressure in token of the understanding between them, and Dawn understood it was the sealing of a kind of unspoken contract.

After that Dawn was not surprised to receive a letter from her father in which he spoke of the young man's desire to make her his wife, and formally gave his consent. It never seemed to occur to him that the girl might have any question about the matter. A dull kind of rebellion rose in her breast and smouldered there as she read her father's letter; yet she accepted his arrangements for her life, because it seemed the only way out from a home that could never be a happy one for her; and because it offered a spot that might be called her own, and a possible opportunity to live out some of her childish dreams.

When Harrington Winthrop came again, she no longer yielded to her inward shrinking from him, but took him as she took hard tasks that she did not like but that were inevitable; and he, finding her unresisting, was careful not to do anything to mar the pleasant understanding between them. Meantime, he congratulated himself constantly upon the ease with which he had possessed himself of a promised wife whose private fortune would be no small one.

## CHAPTER IV

DAWN settled into a gravity that was premature. She counted every day of her precious school year, as if it had been a priceless treasure that was slipping from her.

There were times when she roused to her old self again, and plunged madly into fun, leading her companions into wild amusements that they would never have originated by themselves. Then again she would sober down, and they could get her to say very little. It began to be whispered about that she was to be married when she had finished school, and the girls all looked at her with a kind of envying awe.

Thus the winter passed and the spring came on, the spring that was to be her last at school. The first few days of warm weather she spent exploring old haunts, watching for the spring blossoms, and reverently touching the green moss, hunting anemones, hepaticas, and violets.

Then, as if she could stand her own thoughts no longer, she suddenly proposed the acting of another play. It was the first since that time in the autumn when Harrington Winthrop broke in upon them, and they had never been able to induce her to finish it. Now she selected another one that seemed to her to have the very heart of spring and life bound up in it. She got it out of an old book which had been her mother's—"Tales of William Shakespeare," by name. It was not used as a text-book in the excellent school of Friend Ruth and Friend Isaac, and the child had always kept it safely hidden.

The play she had selected had many elves and sprites of the air in it. Dawn drilled her willing subjects, and rehearsed them, until at last she felt they were ready for the final presentation.

The scene of the play was to be on the sloping hillside just above the meadow, where the maples on the hill were flanked by a thicket of elderberry bushes that did double duty of background, and screen for the dressing-rooms.

The audience of girls was seated in breathless silence, augmented by a group of kindly cows and stupid sheep, who stood in patient rows and waited mildly for any tender bites or chance blossoms of cowslips the girls might put between the bars of the fence. Now and then, as the play went on, they lifted calm eyes of bewilderment over the turbulent scenes in the mimic play-house, or out of their placid world of monotonous duty, wondered whatever the children could be at now.

It chanced that day that Harrington Winthrop was passing, and, most unexpectedly, he had with him his younger brother, who was on his way back to Harvard

College, after a brief visit home to see his mother, who had been ill.

Charles Winthrop had met his elder brother in the coach, and had boyishly insisted on accompanying him when he stopped on what he professed was a friendly errand at this school. Charles had long been separated from his brother, and wanted to talk over old days and ask many questions, for Harrington had been away from home most of the time for nearly ten years and had travelled in the West and the South a great deal, which seemed a charmed country to the younger man.

Now Harrington had not been anxious for company on this visit, but he could not well shake his brother off without arousing suspicions, therefore as they neared the school he told him that he was about to visit the girl whom he expected in a few months to make his wife.

Charles in his hearty boyish way congratulated him and expressed a desire to see the girl who was his brother's choice.

They were told at the house that Dawn was out with the other girls in the meadows, and so went in search of her. They arrived on the scene just as the closing act was about to begin.

The little company of players stood out bravely in costumes designed entirely by Dawn. The outfit of the school was far too sombre to play any part in the gaiety of the occasion. An occasional patchwork quilt had been pressed into service, and one or two gray or scarlet blankets, but most of the players were dressed in white literally covered with flowers or green leaves.

The two young men skirted the foot of the hill and came upon the scene just when Dawn, as queen of the air, attended by her sprites and nymphs, came into view with a gentle, gliding run learned surely from the birds, for nowhere else could such grace be found. She was clad in white drapery of homespun linen, one of her own mother's finest sheets. It was drawn about her slender form, over her shoulders, in a fashion all her own, though graceful as any Greek goddess. Her white throat and round white arms were bare, the long, dark curls had been set free, and about her brow was a wreath of exquisite crab-apple blossoms, whose delicate tinting matched the rose of her cheeks. About her throat, arms, wrists, and ankles—for her feet were bare—were close-fitting chains of the same blossoms. Here and there the white drapery of her garment, which fell half way from the knee to the ankle, was fastened with a spray of blossoms. It was a daring costume for a Quaker-reared maiden to don, and she knew it, but she expected no eyes to look upon her save her companions and the friendly cattle. She stood poised on the green slope, holding in her hands and high above her head a soft scarf of white—an old curtain which she had saved from the rag-bag and wet and stretched in the sun till it was soft and pliable. She had mended it, and fastened the darns with blossoms, and edged it also with blossoms plucked close from the stem and sewed down in a fine flat border.

Behind her came her maidens, their garments sewed over with maple leaves, tender and green and fluttering. They were crowned and wreathed also with maple leaves, and made a beautiful setting for Dawn's delicate beauty.

Then down the hillside they came, the maidens with festoons of leaves fastened together by their stems, which they held aloft as their leader held her scarf. They sang a strange, sweet song that had in it the wildness of the thrush's song, the sweetness of the robin's.

It was Dawn who had composed the melody, and taught it to them. She had learned it from the birds, and interpreted old Shakespeare's words. They sang it as the zephyrs sing.

The little audience sat with bated breath; the old cows chewed their cud thoughtfully, one with soft eyes heaved a long, clover-scented sigh, marvelling on the ways of the world. The two strangers stood entranced and astonished; but the heart of one of them thrilled with a strange new joy.

Charles Winthrop saw only the beautiful face of Dawn Van Rensselaer. All the rest were but a setting for her. He seemed to know instantly as he looked that there was no other girl in the world like this. He knew not who she might be, but he looked at her as if his spirit were calling to hers across the meadow-land that sepa-rated them. Then suddenly, half poised as she was, in the very midst of her song, Dawn became aware of his presence and stopped. She met his gaze, and, without her own volition, it seemed, her eyes were shining and smiling to meet his smile. It was just a fleeting instant that they gazed thus, and then the joy went out of the girl's face, and a frightened look took its place. She had seen the other man standing beside him, and he was frowning.

Harrington Winthrop had caught the look on his brother's face, and its answer in the face of the girl upon whom he had set his seal of possession, and an unreasoning anger had taken possession of him. This girl had looked at Charles as Harrington had never been able to make her look at him, not even since she had in a tacit way consented to marry him.

"This is foolish child's play!" he said in a vexed tone to his brother. "Let us go back to the house and wait until she has returned."

"Oh, no, let us stay!" said Charles. "This is beautiful! Exquisite! At least, if you must go, let me stay. I wish to see the finish."

"I wish you to go," said Harrington, and there was something in his brother's voice that reminded Charles of the days when he used to be ordered back from following on a fishing or swimming expedition. He looked at his brother's angry face, and then back to the beautiful girl on the hillside. But the light had gone out of her eyes. The song had died on her lips. There was no sparkling smile now. Instead, there was an angry, steel-like flash in the eyes. She held the fluttering scarf in front of her now, in long loose folds covering her feet and ankles, and as the two men turned and gazed at her her head went up proudly, even as the queen of the air might have raised her head. One hand went up in quick command, pointing straight at the two young men, and in quite the phrase of the play she had been acting she spoke:

"Hence, strange spirits!" she cried. "Hence! Begone! Ye have no right amongst us, being unbidden. Go, I tell ye! Go, or I, the queen of the air, will bring evil upon ye! Go, ye have angered me!"

Dawn had made Shakespeare so much her constant companion that the language came easily to her. She

picked up phrases here and there and strung them together without hesitation. Her anger helped her on, and her
splendid command of herself had a strange effect upon
her audience.

The other girls listened in open-mouthed wonder
that Dawn should dare to speak before these strangers
and not be covered with confusion. Almost they thought
it was part of the play. But the two to whom she spoke
turned and obeyed her command, the one because he
was angry and wished to get his brother away, the other
because there had been a certain appeal in her lovely eyes
which had reached his soul and made him bow in reverence to her command. Then all at once, as he turned
away, he knew that she was the girl whom his brother
intended to make his wife, and a great sadness and sense
of a loss came over him.

There was mutiny in her eyes as Dawn came back
to the house a little later, and greeted her lover with a
haughty manner. He had managed it that Charles should
sit alone in the gray parlor and wait while he met the
girl out in the entrance to the orchard and walked away
with her to a sheltered place overlooking the river. There
was no hint of the queen of the air in her demure dress,
the well-sheathed curls, the small prunella slippers that
peered from under the deep hem of her gray gown, but
her bearing was queenly as she waited for him to speak.
He saw that he was treading on dangerous ground.

"Do you really like such childish play?" he asked a
trifle contemptuously.

"You had no right to come there!" she flashed. "If
you did not like it, you should have gone away."

He was disconcerted. He did not wish to anger her,
for he had come for another purpose.

"Well, never mind. If you enjoyed yourself, I suppose it does not matter whether I liked it or not. Let us
talk of something else. Your play-days are almost over.
You will soon begin to live real life."

She looked at him and felt that she came near to
hating him. A sudden, unspeakable terror seized her.
She let him talk on about the house they were to have,
and tried to remember that he was lonesome and wanted
a home as badly as she did, but somehow she felt noth-

ing but fear and dislike. So, though she walked by his side, she heard little of what he said, only saying when he asked if she wished this or that: "I suppose so. I suppose it will be as you like."

As they came back to the house again, she asked him suddenly:

"Who was the young man with you?"

The frown came into his face again.

"Why do you ask?" he asked sharply.

"He did not feel the way you did about us out there on the hill."

"How do you know?" He watched her keenly, but her face told him nothing.

"I saw it in his eyes," she said quietly, and without more words went into the house and up to her room.

Dawn stood at the little window of her room and watched the two men go down the path from the door. Through the small panes her eyes followed them until they were out of sight, and her heart swelled with thoughts strange and new and fearful. How could she go and live with this man who had frowned at her innocent happiness? Would he not be worse than the woman who had taken her dear mother's place? And how could he be so cruel as to look at her in that way? It was the look she remembered on her father's face the day he sent her mother away. It was the cruelty of men. Perhaps they could not help it. Perhaps God made them so. But that other one had been different. He had understood and smiled. Her heart leaped out toward him as she remembered his look.

Was it because he was young, she wondered, that he had understood? He had seemed far younger than his companion, yet there had been something fine and manly in his face, in the broadness of his shoulders, and the set of his head, as he walked down the path, away from the house. Perhaps when he was older he would grow that way too, and not understand any more.

She sighed and dropped her face against the glass, and, now that they were out of sight, the haughty look melted into tears.

# CHAPTER V

THE day that Dawn left school to go back to her home was one long agony to her.

All the other girls were happy in the thought of home-going, some of them looking forward to returning for another year, others to entering into a bright girlhood filled with gaieties. But to Dawn it meant going into the gray of a looming fate where never again would she be happy, never again free.

Ever since the day of the play when she had seen her future husband frown, she had looked forward to her marriage with terror.

He had not come after that, but instead wrote her long letters full of plans about the house, *their* house, that they were to occupy *together*. The letters impressed that thought most deeply and made the whole hateful to her. It grew to seem that it was *his* house, and she would be his prisoner in it. Yet somehow he had succeeded in impressing her with the feeling that she was pledged to him in sacred honor, and that it would be a dreadful thing to break a tie like that. This was made stronger by her father's letters, which now grew more frequent, as if he sought to atone to his motherless child for the wrong he had done her.

Just the day before her home-going there came one of these letters, in which he told her that everything had been prepared for her marriage to take place within a week after her arrival. He told her of the trousseau which his wife had prepared for her, which was as elaborate and complete as such an outfit could be for one of her station in life. He also spoke about the dignity of her origin, and with unwonted elaboration commended her judgment in selecting so old and so fine a family as that of the house of Winthrop with which to ally herself. He added that it would have pleased her mother's

family, and that Mr. Winthrop was one of his oldest
and most valued friends.

Somehow that letter seemed to Dawn to put the seal
of finality upon her fate. There was no turning back now.
Just as her father used to compel her to go upstairs alone
when he discovered that she was afraid of the dark, so
she felt that if he once discovered her dislike for her future husband he would but hasten the marriage, and be
in league with her husband against her always.

When the time came to leave the school, she clung
with such fervor about the neck of the impassive Friend
Ruth that the astonished lady almost lost her breath, and
a strange wild thrill went through her unmotherly bosom,
as of something that might have been and was lost.
She looked earnestly down into the beautiful face of the
girl who had so often defied her rules, and saw an appeal
in those lovely eyes to which she would most certainly
have responded had she understood, for she was a good
woman and always sought to do her best.

But the boat left at once, and clinging arms had
perforce to be removed. Once on the deck with the others,
Dawn looked back at Friend Ruth as impassively as
always, though the usually calm face of the woman
searched her out with troubled glance, still wondering
what had come over her wild young pupil. Somehow, as
she watched the steamer plough away until Dawn was
a mere blur with the others, Friend Ruth could not help
being glad that the beautiful dark curls had never been
cut.

The day was perfect, and the scenery along the Pali-
sades had never looked more beautiful, yet Dawn saw
nothing of it. She sat by the rail looking gloomily down
into the water, and a curious fancy seized her that she
would like to float out there on the water forever and
get away from life. Then she began to consider the possibility of running away.

It was not the first time this thought had entered
her mind. The week before she left the school, she had
thought of it seriously, and even planned the route, but
always at night there had come that fearful dream of her
future husband following her, and bringing her home to
a lifelong punishment.

She had almost got her courage up to the point of deciding to disappear in the crowd at Albany, and so elude the people with whom she was expected to journey to her home, when, to her dismay, she looked down at the landing-place where they were stopping, a few miles below Albany, and saw her father coming on board the boat. He had not expected to be able to meet her and had written that she was to come with acquaintances of his. Her heart stood still in panic, and for a moment she looked wildly at the rail of the steamer, as if she might climb over and escape. Then in a moment her father had seen her and stood beside her. He stooped and kissed her forehead coldly, almost shyly. This startled her, too, for he had not kissed her since the days before her mother was sent away, and a strange, sharp pain went through her heart, a pang of things that might have been. She looked up in wonder. She did not know how like her dead mother she had grown.

But the stern face was cold as ever, and his voice conveyed no smallest part of the emotion he felt at sight of her lovely face.

He talked to her gravely of her school life, and then he went on to speak of the Winthrop family, and to tell her in detail bits of its history calculated to make her understand its importance.

Dawn listened with growing alarm at the thought of all that would be expected of her. Yet not a breath of her trouble did she allow her father to see. It might have made a difference if she could have known how her father's heart was aching with the anguish of his great mistake, and perhaps if the father could have known the breaking of the young heart it might have melted the coldness of his reserve and brought some sympathy to the surface. But they could not see, and the agony went on.

Dawn walked sadly, reluctantly, into the unloved, unloving home. As the days dragged by, she grew to have a hunted look, and the rose flush on her sweet round cheek faded to a marble white, while under her eyes were dark circles.

Her father saw the look, but knew not what it meant. Yet it pierced his soul, for it was the same look that her mother had worn in her coffin, and he was the readier to have the marriage hastened, both for her sake and his own, for he realized she was not happy here in the home where there was so much to remind her of what had passed. He felt she never would forgive him, and that her only hope was to be happily married. Winthrop had so represented her feelings to him that he had taken it for granted she was only too eager to go to a home of her own.

The house had been bought—at least, the father supposed so—not knowing that but a small payment had been made, with a promise to pay the balance soon after the marriage. The young man had laid his plans nicely, and meant to profess that some investment of his had failed, making it impossible for him to make the final payments, and that he had disliked to postpone the marriage or to tell of his predicament, feeling sure that he would have the money by the time the payment was due. Naturally, his wife's fortune would suffice to pay for the house, which of course she would not let go then. If the house was not exactly what he had described to the little school-girl, certainly it was large enough and showy enough to make up for the lack of some of the things which had seemed important to her; and he had taken care that it should be so far from the home of her father that the latter could keep no eye on his son-in-law's business affairs. If all went well, he intended to have his wife's fortune in his own hands before their first year of married life should have passed. After that it would not matter to him whether the girl was pleased with her home or not. She could no longer help herself.

But of all this the father suspected nothing.

Dawn took no interest in her clothes. The stepmother was chagrined that after all her efforts Dawn was not pleased.

"I should think you might show a little gratitude, after all the trouble I've taken," Mrs. Van Rensselaer snapped angrily.

Dawn turned wide eyes of astonishment upon her.

"For what?" she asked. "I didn't want the things. I supposed you did it to please father."

"Didn't want them!" exclaimed her step-mother.

"And how would you expect to get married without them?"

"I don't want to be married!" said Dawn desperately, and then closed her lips tightly, with a frightened look toward the door. She had not meant to let any one know that. The words had come of themselves out of her weary heart.

"Well, upon my word! You're the queerest girl! Any other girl in the world would be in high feather over your chances; but you always were the stubbornest, most contrary creature that ever drew breath. Whatever did you say you'd get married for if you didn't want to?"

"I don't think I ever did," said the girl sadly. "It just came in spite of me."

"That's all foolishness. Don't talk such things to me. No girl has to be married unless she chooses, and I'll warrant you had your hand in it from the start. Besides, it's too late to talk of such things now. It wouldn't be honorable to draw back now, after he's got the house bought and all."

"I know it," said Dawn miserably, and stood looking out the window blindly, swallowing hard to keep back the tears. She felt that she must have reached the limit of her endurance when she would let her step-mother see her state of mind.

Mrs. Van Rensselaer eyed her keenly, suspiciously. At last she ventured another question.

"Have you got any other beau in your head, Jemima?" she said. "Because if you have, you'd better put him out pretty suddenly. If your father should find it out, he would—I don't know what he would do. He would certainly punish you well, big girl as you are. Is that what's the matter? Answer me! Have you got another beau?"

Dawn looked up with great angry, flashing eyes, horror changing into contempt.

"I have never even thought of such a dreadful thing!" she said, with a withering look, and swept haughtily from the room. But on the way upstairs the color crept slowly into her cheeks, and her eyes drooped half-ashamed. Was there? Yes, there was some one else enshrined within her heart, some one whose face had smiled in sympathy just once, and toward whom she felt as she had never felt to any human being save her mother. Of course he was nothing to her but the vision of a moment, and never, never, could he be called by the hateful word her stepmother had used, that detestable word "beau." It seemed to the poor, tried child as if she could almost kill any one who used that word.

After that, Dawn endured her misery in secret, speaking not at all, unless spoken to. The older woman looked at her curiously, almost nervously, sometimes, as if the girl were half uncanny. She was glad in her heart that the day of the wedding was close at hand, for if she knew anything about signs, that girl was on the verge of throwing over a fine marriage, and then they would have her on their hands for years, perhaps. Mrs. Van Rensselaer had suffered not a little for her share in the tragedy of these lives with which she had bound up her own, and was not willing to endure more. She shut her thin lips and determined to watch the girl carefully and prevent if possible any slip between cup and lip.

Meantime, with ever-growing dread, Dawn counted the hours, and watched sleepless through the long nights, now calling on her dead mother for help, now praying to be saved in some way from the nameless fear which, try as she would, she could not shake off. The family relatives on both sides were gathering and starting, some on long journeys, to attend the wedding.

## CHAPTER VI

CHARLES WINTHROP had written his family that matters which he wished to complete would detain him at the college for a few weeks, and begged his father to make his excuses at the wedding. He had an instinctive feeling that Harrington would not care, as well as an inexplicable aversion to being a witness at the wedding ceremony of his elder brother and the girl who had burst upon his vision that afternoon and seemed to open a new world to him.

He had long ago put by the strange, sweet sense of having discovered in her a familiar friend—one who fitted into his longings and his ideals as though he had always been waiting for her. He called the thought a foolish sentimentality, and, in view of the relation in which she was soon to be placed to him, he tried to be as matter-of-fact as possible with regard to her. He sent several pleasant brotherly messages—which never reached her—through the medium of Harrington. He tried to accept the thought of a new sister as a delightful thing, and always he regarded her beauty and grace with the utmost reverence. The father, while feeling that Charles's absence was almost a discourtesy to his brother, nevertheless gave reluctant consent.

Then, a few days before the wedding, there came over Charles an overwhelming feeling that he must go. All his former arguments in favor of remaining away seemed as water. He felt as if the eyes and the smile of the girl he had seen upon the hillside called him imperatively. Try as he would to tell himself that with his present feelings it was foolish, even dangerous, for him to go near her, and that his brother was already a little jealous owing to the look that had passed between them, it made no difference; he felt that he must go, and go he did. Without waiting to do more than throw a few necessities into a valise, he took the first stage-coach that started from Boston. All through the long journey his heart beat wildly with the thought that he was to meet her. He was ashamed of the feeling. Yet in vain he told himself that it was wrong; that he ought to go back. Once he flung himself out of the coach at a station where they were taking on fresh horses, determined to return to Boston, and then madly climbed up to the seat with the driver just as the coach started again. After that he grimly faced the matter, asking himself if it were not better to go on after all, meet his new sister-in-law on a common, every-day basis, and get this nonsense out of his head forever. Then he tried to sleep and forget, but her face and her smile haunted him, and there seemed to be an appeal in her eyes that called him to her aid.

When he presented himself at his father's door in the early morning of the day before the wedding, his face was gray with combat, yet in his eyes was the light of a noble resolve. In spite of all his reasoning, he could not help the feeling that he had come because he was needed, but he was here, and there was a duty connected with it which he felt strong to do. It was therefore not a surprise to him when his father met him with eager welcome and a grave face.

"My son, you have come just when I needed you most," he said as he drew the young man inside the library door. And then Charles noticed that his father seemed suddenly aged and heavy with sorrow. He knew it was nothing connected with the immediate family of the household, for they had all welcomed him with eager clamor and delight.

"Sit down, Charles."

His father was fastening the door against intrusion, and the young man's heart stood still with apprehension.

Mr. Winthrop turned and looked in his son's face with feverishly bright eyes that showed their lack of sleep. Then he seated himself in the arm-chair before the desk, drawing Charles's chair close, that he might speak in lowered tones.

"Something terrible has occurred, Charles. Your mother does not know yet. The blow has fallen so suddenly that I find myself unable to believe it is true. I am dazed. I can scarcely think. Charles, your only brother, my son——" The old man paused, and with a sudden contraction of his heart Charles noticed that there were tears coursing down his father's wrinkled cheeks. The voice quavered and went on:

"Our first-born has been guilty of a great wrong. It is best to face the truth, my boy. Harrington has committed a crime. I don't see how it can be thought otherwise by any honest person. I am trying to look at the facts, but even as I speak the words I cannot realize that they are true of one of our family."

Charles waited, his eyes fixed upon the old man's

face, and a great indignation growing within him toward the brother who could dare bring dishonor upon such a father!

Mr. Winthrop bowed his head upon his hand for a moment, as though he could not bear to reveal the whole truth. Then he roused himself as one who has need of haste.

"Charles, your brother already has a wife and two little children, yet he was proposing to wed another woman. He has dared to court and win an innocent young girl, and to hoodwink her honorable father. And the worst of it is that he meant to carry it out and marry her! Oh the shame of it! We are disgraced, Charles! We are all disgraced!" With a low groan the father buried his face in his hands and bowed himself upon the desk.

The heart of the young man grew hot. A great desire for vengeance was surging over him. He arose excitedly from his chair.

"Harrington has done this, father!"

The words burst from his lips more like a judgment pronounced than like a question or a statement of fact. It was as if the acknowledgment of his brother's sin were a kind of climax in his thought of that brother, whom he had been all these years attempting to idealize, as a boy so often idealizes an elder brother. The words bore with them, too, the recognition of all the pain and disappointment and perplexity of many things throughout the years. Charles's finer nature suddenly revolted in disgust from all that he saw his brother to be.

He stood splendidly indignant, above the bowed head of his father, a picture of fine, strong manhood, ready to avenge the rights of insulted womanhood. There before him arose a vision obscuring the walls of the book-lined library—the vision of a girl, fresh, fair, lovely, with eyes alight, cheeks aglow, floating hair, and fluttering white drapery, garlanded in pink and white blossoms that filled the air with the breath of a spring morning. It blazed upon him with clearness and beauty, and veiled by no hindering sense of wrong. With a great heart throb of joy, he recognized that she no longer belonged to his brother.

The thought had scarcely thrilled his senses before

he was ashamed of it. How could he think of joy or anything else in the midst of the shame and trouble that had fallen upon them all? And most of all upon the beautiful girl, who would bear the heaviest burden.

True, there was another side to the matter, a side in which she might be thankful that Harrington's true character had been discovered before things had gone further; but there was mortification, and disgrace inevitable. Then, it was to be presumed that she had loved Harrington, or why should she be about to marry him? Poor child! His heart stood still in pity as he realized what the sin of his brother would mean to her.

These thoughts went swiftly through his mind as he stood beside his father. It seemed to him that in the instant of the elder man's silence he reviewed the whole catastrophe in its various phases and lived through years of experience and knowledge. Then his father's trembling voice took up the story again:

"Yes, Harrington did that!" They were Charles's own words, but somehow, on his father's tongue, they spoke a new pathos, and again the young man saw another side to the whole terrible matter. Harrington was the oldest son, adored of his mother. Though he had been gone from home for years, he had yet remained her idol until it had seemed his every virtue had grown to perfection, while all his faults were utterly forgotten. During his visits, which had been few and far between, the whole family had put itself out of its routine, and hung upon his wishes. His stories had been listened to with the deference due to one older and wiser than any of them could ever hope to be. His wishes had been law, his opinions gospel truth. Charles recalled how his mother had always called together the entire family to listen to the reading of one of Harrington's rare epistles, demanding a solemnity and attention second only to that required at family worship. These letters always ended with a description of some new enterprise in which he was deeply involved, and which required large sums of money. His father and mother had always managed to send him something to "help out" at such times, and made no secret of it, rather rejoicing that they were able to do so.

Charles knew that his father owned large and valuable tracts of land, and was well off; yet it had not always been convenient to send Harrington large sums of money, and often the family luxuries and pleasures had been somewhat curtailed in consequence. All such sacrifices had been cheerfuly made for the family idol, by himself as well as by his three sisters, his maiden aunt, and his father and mother.

At this critical moment it occurred to Charles to wonder if his father had ever received any interest from these many sums of money which he from time to time had put into Harrington's business schemes.

Then his father's voice drowned all other thoughts:

"I do not know how to tell your poor mother!" The trembling tones were almost unrecognizable to the son. "She ought to know at once. We must plan what to do. The Van Rensselaers must be told."

He bowed his head with another groan.

The son sat down and endeavored to get a better grasp of the situation.

"Since when have you known this, Father?" he asked keenly.

"Last night. Mother had gone to bed, and I did not disturb her. I felt I must think it all out—what to do— before I told them; but I cannot see my way any clearer. It is a most infamous thing to have happened in a respectable family. Charles, I'm sorry to have to say it, but I'm afraid your brother is a—a—a—*scoundrel!*"

The old gentleman's face was red and excited as he brought forth the awful utterance. It was the thought which had been growing in his mind all through the long night watch, but he had not been willing to acknowledge it. He arose now and began to pace the room.

"He certainly is, if this is true, Father," said the son, frowning. "But are you quite sure it is not some miserable blackmailing scheme? Such stories are often trumped up at the last minute to get money out of respectable people. I've heard of it in Boston. It is rare, of course, but it could happen. I cannot think Harrington would do such an awful thing."

"Son, it is all too true," said the old man sadly. "Do you remember William McCord? You know he was my trusted farm-hand for years, and I have kept in touch with him by letter ever since he went out West to take up a claim on gold land. Well, it was he that brought me the terrible news. He came last evening, after mother and the girls had gone upstairs. He did not want to see them and have them question him till he had told me all. He brought letters and proofs from Harrington's wife and the minister who married them, and, moreover, he was an eye-witness to the fact that Harrington lived in the West with his wife and two children. You yourself know that William McCord could not tell a lie."

"No," assented Charles; "never."

"Harrington's wife is a good, respectable woman, though not very well educated. She is the daughter of a Virginia man who went out there to hunt for gold. He died a couple of years ago, and now the daughter and her children have no one to look after them. It seems Harrington has neglected them for the past three years, only coming home once in six months, and giving them very little money. He has told them a story of hard luck.

"The wife is desperate now. She has been ill, and needs many things for herself and the children. At last she learned of Harrington's intended marriage through William, whose sister had written him the home news.

"She sold what few possessions she had and brought the proceeds to William, begging him to come on here and find out if the story was true. William refused to take her money, but started at once, at his own expense, and came straight to me with the story. Just think of it, Charles! Our grandchildren actually cold and hungry and almost naked—our own flesh and blood! Your nephew and niece, Charles."

The younger man frowned. He had very little sympathy at present to expend upon any possible nephews and nieces. He was thinking of a lovely girl with eyes like stars. What were cold and hunger compared to her plight?

"Where is my brother?" The boy looked older than he had ever seemed to his father as he asked the question.

"I do not know. He has always told us to write to an address in New York, but often he has not answered our letters for weeks. I am afraid there is still more to be

told than we know. McCord tells me he was under some
sort of a cloud financially out there—some trouble about
shares in a gold mine. I'm afraid he has been speculating.
He has borrowed a great deal of money from me at one
time and another, but he has always told me that he was
doing nicely and that some day I should have a handsome
return for all I had put in. But if that is the case, why
should he have dared to involve a sweet and innocent
young girl in it all? Why should he dare do so dreadful
a thing!—unless he is under the impression that his first
wife is dead. I cannot think that my boy would do this
thing!"

The father's head dropped upon his breast, but the
brother stood erect with flashing eyes.

"I see it all clearly, Father. He is marrying this girl
for her money. He needs money for some of his schemes,
and he is afraid to ask you for any more, lest you suspect
something. He told me once that she was very rich. I
think you are right: my brother is a scoundrel!"

The father groaned aloud.

"But, Father, what are you going to do about it?
Have you sent word to Mr. Van Rensselaer? The wedding
is set for to-morrow morning. There will be scarcely time
to stop the guests from coming."

Outside the window, wheels could be heard on the
gravel, as the old coachman drove the family carriage up
to the front steps. Pompey, the stable boy, followed, driving the mare in the carryall.

Almost simultaneously came the hurry of ladies'
feet down the staircase, and the swish of silken skirts.
Betty and Cordelia and Madeline rushed through the hall
and climbed into the carryall, with soft excitement and
gentle laughter. This wedding journey was a great event,
and they had talked of nothing else for weeks.

"Come, Charles. Come, Father, aren't you ready?"
called Betty. "It is high time we started. Mother is all
dressed, and Aunt Martha is just tying her bonnet.
Charles, Mother wants you to ride in the carriage with
her this morning; but you are to change off with us by-
and-by, so we'll all have a good look at you."

The father caught his breath and looked helplessly

at his son. "I did not realize it was getting so late," he murmured. "Of course the journey must be stopped."

"Of course, Father," agreed Charles decidedly. "Go quickly and tell Mother all about it. I will tell the girls and Aunt Martha," he added.

With a look as though he were going to his death, the older man hurried up the stairs to his wife, and Charles went out to the piazza. The two servants stood grinning happily, feeling the overflow of the festive occasion. Charles could not reveal his secret there.

"Come into the house, a minute, girls. I've something to tell you."

"Indeed, no, Charles!" said Cordelia emphatically. "I will not climb out over the wheels again. I nearly ruined my pelisse getting in. It is very dusty. And I have covered myself all nicely for the journey. Won't it keep?"

"Cordelia, you must come," said the young man imperiously, and stalked into the house, uncertain whether they would follow him.

In a moment Betty appeared roguishly in the parlor door, whither Charles had gone.

"They won't come, Charles," she said. "It's no use. If you had news of an earthquake or a new railroad, they wouldn't stir. Nothing weighs against one's wedding garments, and Cordelia has taken special pains."

But Charles did not respond to Betty's nonsense in his usual merry way.

"Betty, listen," he said gravely. "An awful thing has happened."

"Is Harrington dead?" asked Betty, with wide, frightened eyes and blanched face.

"No, but he might better be, Betty. He has a wife and two little children out West, and he has deserted them to marry again."

Betty did not scream nor exclaim, "How dreadful!" Instead, she sat down quickly in the first chair at hand.

After an instant's silence, she said in her matter-of-fact way:

"Then there won't be any wedding, of course! And what will that poor girl do? Has anybody thought about her? Somehow, I'm not surprised. I've always secretly thought Harrington was selfish. It's like him never to think how he would make other people suffer. His letters always put Father and Mother in hot water. Have they told her yet, Charles? Oh, I wish I could go and help comfort her! I can't think of anything more mortifying for her."

"Betty, it is good that she will be saved from anything worse. It is good to have it found out beforehand."

"Oh, yes, of course; but she won't think of that. With all the wedding guests coming, how can she have time to be thankful that she is saved from marrying a selfish, bad man? Charles, it is a shame! Somebody ought to be at hand to step in and take Harrington's place. If I were a man, I'd throw myself at her feet and offer to marry her. Say, Charles, why don't you do it yourself?" declared Betty romantically.

The heart of the young man leaped up with a great bound, and a flood of color went over his face and neck. But the parlor was darkened, and, moreover, the girls in the carryall were diligently calling; so Betty vanished to impart the news, and Charles was alone for the moment, with a new thought, which almost took his breath from him.

Then down the oaken staircase, with soft, lady-like, but decided rustle, came Madam Winthrop.

Behind her, nervous, protesting, came her husband's anxious footsteps.

"But, Mother, really, it won't do. We couldn't go, you know, under the circumstances."

"Don't say another word, Mr. Winthrop," Charles heard his mother's most majestic voice. "I intend to go, and there is no need of further talk. Depend upon it, Harrington will be able fully to explain all this impossible story when he arrives, and it is not for his family to lose faith in him."

"But, Mother, you don't understand," protested her husband, still hastening after her and putting out a detaining hand.

"Indeed, I do understand," said the woman's voice coldly. "I understand that my boy is being persecuted. It is you, apparently, who do not understand. I am his mother, and I intend to stand by him, and not let a breath of this wretched scandal touch him. The wedding will go on as planned, of course, and what would the world think if his family were not present? How could you possibly explain your absence except by bringing out these most unfatherly suspicions? No, Mr. Winthrop, there is all the more need of haste, that we may forestall any of these wicked rumors. Let us start at once."

"But, Janet——"

"No! You needn't 'But Janet' me. I don't wish to hear another word. I'm going, no matter what you say, and so are Martha and the girls. You can stay at home if you like, I suppose. You are a man, and, of course, will do as you please. I will explain your absence the best way I can. But I'm going! Come, Martha; we will get into the back seat!"

Charles stepped out of the darkened parlor and intercepted his mother.

"Mother, really, you're making a mistake. You have not stopped to think what you are going into. It won't do for you and the girls to go. I will go with father——"

But the imperious lady shook her son's hand from her arm as though it had been a viper.

"Charles, you forget yourself!" she said. "It is not for you to tell your mother she is making a mistake. You must not think that because you have been to college you can therefore teach your mother how to conduct her affairs. Stand out of my way, and then follow me to the carriage. You are displeasing me greatly. It would have been better for you to remain in Boston than to come here to talk to your mother in this way."

The majestic lady marched on her way to the carriage, followed by her frightened sister-in-law, who scuttled after her tearfully, not knowing which to dread the most, her sister-in-law's tyranny, the wrath of her brother, or the scorn of her nephew. The habit of her life had been always to follow the stronger nature. In this case it was Madam Winthrop.

Father and son stood looking on helplessly. Then the father called:

"Well, Janet, if you must go, leave the girls at home with Martha."

The aunt drew back timidly from the carriage-step she was approaching.

"Get in at once, Martha!" commanded Madam Winthrop, already established in the back seat of the coach. "We have no time to waste. Girls, you may drive on ahead until we reach the cross-roads. Elizabeth, your conduct is unseemly for such a joyous occasion. What will the neighbors think to see your flushed, excited face? Wipe your eyes and pull down your veil. Drive on, Cordelia, and see that Elizabeth's conduct is more decorous."

She waved the carryall on, and Cordelia and Madeleine, awed and half-frightened, obeyed, while excitable Betty strove to put by the signs of her perturbation until she was out of her mother's sight. In brief whispers she had succeeded in conveying to her sisters a slight knowledge of what had occurred.

The old coachman and the stable boy stood wondering by and marvelled that the wedding had gone to Madam's head. They had seen her in these imperious moods, but had not thought this an occasion for one. Someone must have displeased her very much, for her to get in a towering rage on the day before her eldest son's wedding.

"Now Mr. Winthrop, we are ready, if you and Charles will take your seats."

Father and son looked at each other in dismay.

"I guess there's nothing for it but to get in, Father. Perhaps you can bring her to her senses on the way, and I can drive back with her, or they can stop at an inn, while we go on. It really won't do to delay, for we have a duty to the Van Rensselaers."

"You are right, Charles. We must go. Perhaps, as you say, we can persuade Mother on the way. I am dubious, however. She is very set in her way."

"Mr. Winthrop, you will need only to get your hat," called his wife from the coach. "I have had your portmanteau and Charles's fastened on behind. Your things are all here. Your hat is lying on the hall table."

With a sigh of submission, the strong man obediently got his hat and took his place on the front seat of the coach, while Charles indignantly swung himself up beside his father. Then the family started for the wedding that was not to be.

# CHAPTER VII

THE long journey was anything but what it had promised to be when it was anticipated. The carryall containing the three girls headed the procession. They were talking in subdued and frightened tones, Madeleine and Cordelia endeavoring to find out from Betty more than the child really knew. When she could not satisfy their curiosity and anxiety with facts, she supplied them with running comments on human nature and her elder brother in particular. Now and again they pulled her up sharply with: "Betty, be still!" or "I am ashamed of you Elizabeth. You jump to conclusions. I am sure there must be some explanation. Charles was very wrong to tell you until he had made sure about it. You see Mother does not believe the story, or she would never go."

"Mother wouldn't believe Harrington had done wrong if she saw him do it," declared Betty irreverently.

"Now, Betty! How you talk! One would think you didn't love Harrington."

"Well, I don't very much, and that's a fact," shrugged Betty. "Charles is worth two of him. Harrington always hushes me up when he comes home, and talks as if I were a baby yet. Besides, he is selfish. Look how he wouldn't take me to Harriet Howegate's corn-husking when he was home the last time just because he was too lazy to change his clothes! I don't see why I should love him if I don't, just because he happens to belong to the same family. I'm sure he can't love us much, or he wouldn't have gone off so long ago and stayed away from us so much."

"Why, Betty!" said Madeleine, shocked. "He had to go and earn his living and make a man's way in the world."

"No, he didn't. He could have stayed at home and gone into business with Father, as Father wanted him to. I haven't a bit of patience with Harrington."

"I'm sure, Betty, that's a very shocking way to talk

51

about your own brother, and Mother would highly disap-
prove!" said Madeleine.

"If I were you, I should keep still, Betty," advised
Cordelia.

Betty pouted, and a solemn silence settled upon the
three as the old gray horse plodded sleepily over the road.

The occupants of the coach were by no means at
ease. Aunt Martha sat shrivelled in the back seat, with
the ready tears coursing silently down her cheeks. She had
heard enough of what her brother had told his wife, to
be filled with gloomy apprehensions. Aunt Martha was
always sure of the worst.

Madam Winthrop sat severely silent, with her delicate, cameo features held high. Her keen blue eyes never
wavered, nor did her firm, thin lips quiver. Apparently,
she had not one misgiving, and her only regret seemed
to be that the rest of the family had taken leave of their
senses. She looked straight in front of her, ignoring the
sad gray head of her husband, and the yellow curls of the
strong young son with whom she was offended. They
would all see their mistake soon enough, and meantime
she was giving them a bit of a lesson not to doubt the
idol of her heart. To do her justice, she firmly believed
she was right, and was amazed that her husband had taken
the attitude he had. Of course Harrington would not do
such a dreadful thing. Such things did not happen in real
life. It was out of the question. She dismissed the subject
with that, and fell to going over her own arrangements
and the wardrobe of the family, with satisfaction.

The sound of the horses' hoofs on the old corduroy
road, and the husky crickets by the wayside, beat a funeral dirge for the heart of the Father in the front seat.
His countenance was heavy, and now and again he
brought forth an audible sigh.

The lugubrious attitude of her family annoyed Madam Winthrop. She turned to her sister-in-law sharply.

"For pity's sake, Martha, do stop snivelling! One
would think you were going to a funeral instead of to a
wedding. I must say I don't think you honor your nephew
very much, showing such distrust in him. Do wipe your
eyes and sit up. If you go on this way, you won't be able
to come to the ceremony to-morrow morning, and you

know how that will annoy Harrington. I must say, Mr. Winthrop, you are acting in a very strange manner, for the father of such a son."

She always called him Mr. Winthrop when he had offended her. At other times it was "Father."

Her husband turned in the seat and faced her solemnly.

"Janet," he said sadly, "it's no use for you to try to blind yourself to the truth. You'll only have it harder to bear in the end. You might as well understand the awful truth that our boy Harrington has committed a great sin, and we ought to be thankful that it was discovered before any more harm was done. You don't seem to see what a task we've got before us to tell that father and his innocent young daughter that the man in whom they trusted, our son, has played them false."

"Now, Mr. Winthrop, I don't want to hear another word of such talk. You must be beside yourself!" Madam Winthrop half arose in her seat and cried out shrilly: "Stop it, I say! Don't you dare say such words in my presence again! If you do, I shall get right out of this carriage and walk! *Walk,* I tell you! And what will the servants think of you then? You will find out your mistake in due time, of course, and be ashamed of yourself. Until then I must ask you not to speak to me on the subject. No. Charles, don't you dare to interfere between me and your Father again. I have had enough of your disrespect for one day. Just keep absolutely quiet until you can speak in a proper way. I simply will not stand such talk."

She sat up with dignity, and spoke to them both as if they were naughty children. Her husband looked into her eyes sadly for a moment, and then turned deliberately back to his horses. He knew by former experience that it was well nigh impossible to convince his wife of anything against her will. Well, she would have to go on and take the consequences of her stubbornness. There was no other way. And perhaps it was as well, for, with her excitable nature, there was no telling what state it might throw her into, once she realized the truth about her idolized son. She might lose consciousness and have to be carried back, and so perhaps delay them. His first duty now was to tell the sad truth to his old friend Van Rensselaer and his poor daughter. Every step that the horses took made him shrink more and more from the task before him. It seemed that his shame and disgrace were being burnt into his soul with a red hot iron. He kept thinking how he should tell his story to his host when he reached his journey's end, and the horses' hoofs beat out the dirge of a funeral; while keeping pace behind, with decorous bearing, rode the two old servants, pondering what had cast a shadow over the gay party they had hoped to escort.

As the young man in the front seat of the coach sat and frowned at the shining chestnut backs of the horses, he was conning over and over a thought that his sister had put into his heart, and each time it ran like sweet fire along his veins, until it began to seem a possibility, and fairly took his breath away.

The day was wonderful. The air was fine and rare, the sky clear, with not a fleck of cloud to mar the blue— a blue that fairly called attention to itself as being bluer than ever before. But not one of all that little company of wedding-goers saw it.

The foliage everywhere was washed fresh for the occasion by a shower that had passed in the night. Diamonds strung themselves from grass-blade to grass-blade, and begemmed even the mullein stalks. Late dandelions flared and gleamed, shy sweet-brier smiled here and there by the roadside in delicate pink cups, inviting the bees. The birds in the trees were singing everywhere, and the sweet winds lifted branches and played a subdued accompaniment. To the soul of the young man, their music came in happy harmonies, and, while he was not conscious of it, little by little they began to play him a kind of wedding march, the joyous melody of his thoughts, now glad, now fearful, yet ever growing sweeter and more sure of the victorious climax.

He grew presently unconscious of the inharmony behind him: of Aunt Martha and her efforts not to "sniff"; of his mother's disapproval; and of his father's heavy heart. He thought only of the girl whom he had seen upon the hillside, and the smile her eyes had given him as they met his. Every time he thought upon it now his heart-beats quickened. All the pent-up flood of emotion that she had set going that spring afternoon upon the Hudson hillside, and that he had fought bravely all these weeks, and thought he had conquered, came now upon him with the power of stored-up energy and swept over his being in a flood-tide of gladness.

In vain he shamed himself for such unseemly joy when his only brother was in disgrace. In vain he told himself that the girl-bride would be plunged into grief when her bridegroom turned out to be no bridegroom at all. Still his heart would catch the faint melody of the wedding-march those birds and winds and branches were breathing, and would go singing along with a new gladness.

The morning was a silent one for the whole party. Even the coachman checked Pompey's levity when a robin chased a chipmunk across a distant path, and the old darkey snapped him up sharply when he ventured a question or a wonder about "Marsa" and "Missus."

But while each held to his own thoughts, and the horses sped willingly over the miles, in the heart of the young man in the front seat was growing a steady purpose.

About noon they stopped at an inn to dine, and give the horses a brief respite.

Madam Winthrop would not lie down, as they urged her, nor would she permit her husband or her son to talk with her concerning the forbidden theme. She kept the three girls with her also, that nothing might be said to them to prejudice them against their brother.

Aunt Martha, however, unable to bear up longer under the scornful scrutiny of her sister-in-law, was glad to take refuge on the high four-poster bed that the landlady put at her service, and weep a few consoling tears into the homespun linen pillow-slip. Aunt Martha was by no means sure that all was well with the boy whom she adored, though she acknowledged to herself that he had his weaknesses. Had she not seen those very weaknesses from babyhood upward, and helped many times to hide them from his blind mother and adoring sisters? Her fearful soul accepted the possibility of his sin, yet loved him in spite of it all. She resented the thought that public opinion would be against Harrington if he had done this

thing, and, could she have had her way, would have had
public opinion changed to suit his special need. She felt
in her secret soul that prodigies like Harrington should not
be expected to follow the laws like ordinary mortals.

Madam Winthrop sat bolt upright in a wooden chair,
and eyed her three daughters suspiciously. Now and then
she made a remark about their conduct at the wedding,
and they acquiesced meekly. They had learned never to
dispute with their mother when she was in her present
mood.

Charles and his father wandered by common consent
into the woods near-by. It was the son who spoke first.

"Father, I've been thinking all the morning about
what you said of her—Miss Van Rensselaer." He spoke
the name shyly, reverently, and his heart throbbed painfully. He felt himself very young and presumptuous. The
bright color glowed in his face. "It will be terrible for
her." He breathed the words as if they hurt him.

"Yes," assented the father; "I cannot get her out of
my mind, the poor innocent child! Think of Betty,
Charles. Suppose it was Betty."

The young man frowned.

"Father, did you ever see her?"

"No," said the older man, wonder at his son's ve-
hemence. "Did you?"

"Yes, I saw her once, when I met Harrington on my
way to Boston. I stopped off with him at the school
where she was being educated, and we saw her. She is
beautiful, Father, beautiful, and very young. She looked
as if she could not stand a thing like this, as if it might
crush her. Don't you think we ought to do something for
her, to make it easier? Isn't it our place? I mean—say, Father, in the Bible, you know, when the older brother died,
or failed in any way, the younger brother had to take
up the obligation. Do you understand what I mean, Father? Do you think I could? I mean, do you think she
would let me? It wouldn't be so public and mortifying,
you know, and I think girls care a great deal about that.
Betty would, I'm sure."

The father looked up in astonishment.

"What do you mean, Charles? Do you mean you
would marry her?"

"Why, yes, Father, that's what I meant. What do you think of it?"

The boy in him came to the front for an instant and looked out of his eyes, though he shrank from the blunt way the older man had of stating facts.

His father eyed him keenly.

"But you're only a boy, Charles, and you're not through college yet. How could you marry?"

"I'm past twenty-one," boasted the boy, and vanished into the man. A graver look came out upon his face.

"I could leave college, if it were necessary, or I could go on and finish. I could work part of the time and take care of her." The last words he breathed gently, reverently, like a benediction.

The father stopped in the wooded path and grasped his son's hand.

"Boy, you've got good stuff in you! I'm proud of you," he said, lifting his head triumphantly. "If only your brother had been like that!" Then he bowed his head in bitter thought.

But the young man's thoughts were not on Harrington now. He grasped his father's hand, and waited impatiently for further words from him.

"Well, Father?"

The old man lifted his head.

"But, Boy, you do not know her. You have seen her only once. You can't spoil your own life that way."

A flood of color went over the younger face, and into his eyes came a depth of earnestness that showed his father that the man had awakened in his son. He was no longer a boy.

"Father, I do not need to know her. I love her already. I have loved her ever since I saw her. That was why I did not want to come to the wedding. I felt that I could not bear it."

The kindly older gaze searched the fine young face tenderly, but the lover's eyes looked back at him and wavered not.

"Is it so, Son?"—the words were grave. "Then God pity you—and bless you," he added, with an upward look. "I am afraid there is no easy way ahead of you. Yet I am proud to call you my son."

After this they walked on silently through the woods, over a pathway of flecked gold, where the sunlight sifted through the leafy branches. No sound came to interrupt the silence beyond the whisking of a squirrel or the flirt of a bird's wings in the branches.

The dinner-bell pealed forth from the inn, and they turned quietly to retrace their steps. They were almost in sight of the house before either spoke. Then the father said:

"Son, she does not know you. Have you any idea how she will take all this?"

"None at all, Father." It was spoken humbly.

"What is your idea? Have you made any plans?"

"Not yet—only, that I shall tell her at once, if I may, and let her decide. If she is willing, the wedding may go on as planned."

A light came into the older man's face, though he looked troubled.

"Well said, Charles! Perhaps you may succeed. But I fear, I fear. Nevertheless, your noble action helps me to hold up my head and look her father in the eye. If I have one son who is a scoundrel, at least I have one who is not, and who is willing to face his brother's obligations."

They went in then and sat down to a dinner of which both were able to partake more enjoyably than either had supposed possible.

"Charles, isn't there going to be an awful time when we get there?" whispered Betty, as they passed out to the carriages.

"I hope not, Betty," said Charles, with a solemn light in his eyes that made the girl wonder.

Charles took his seat beside his father with hopefulness, and all that long afternoon the music of nature rang on; but now to both men the dirge was almost lost in the swelling and sounding of the wedding march.

## CHAPTER VIII

ALL the afternoon, Madam Winthrop had steadily refused to converse about her oldest son. The party were nearing the edge of the town where the Van Rensselaers lived.

Twice Charles had endeavored to bring his mother's mind to the subject, and once his father had said: "Now, Mother, it is absolutely necessary that you put aside your attitude and let me tell you all about this matter." But to all advances she was adamant.

"I shall never allow you to say such wicked things about my son," declared the old lady, rising from her seat and attempting to get out of the coach. They were compelled to give it up and trust to developments.

The stars were coming out when they entered the village streets. The father called to his daughters to wait a moment, and he stopped the coach horses. Turning around in his seat, he faced his wife.

"Janet," said he, and his voice was firm as when he was a young man, "it is best that the family stop at the inn while Charles and I go on to the house and make the family acquainted with the truth. I wish you and Martha and the girls to stop here and wait until our return."

The old lady looked ahead impatiently, as if she did not see her husband.

"I shall do nothing of the kind, Mr. Winthrop," she said. "You may as well save time by driving on."

The anger was rising in the old gentleman's face. He had been defied for years and had borne it with fortitude and a measure of amusement. He had always felt that he could assert himself when he chose. But now he had chosen, and apparently he had been mistaken all these years. His wife would not obey. It was mortifying, and especially before his son and his sister. He turned sharply to Martha, sitting frightened and meek in the dark corner of the coach.

"Martha, get out," he commanded in a tone she had never disobeyed.

Martha proceeded to obey hastily.

"Don't you do any such foolish thing, Martha Winthrop. You stay right where you are. I won't have any scenes," said Madam Winthrop.

Martha paused and put her mitted hand on her heart.

"Martha, this is my carriage, and you are my sister, and I tell you to get out."

Martha had not heard that voice from her brother's lips for forty years. She got out.

"Pompey, Caesar"—to the two negroes who drove up at that moment—"see that the ladies are cared for in the inn until our return. Attend to the other carriage, and tell the young ladies it is my wish that they remain in the inn parlor until I come back."

With grave dignity, the master of the situation guided his horse past the carryall and down the dim evening street. Madam Winthrop sat amazed, with two red spots on her cheeks.

"It seems to me, Mr. Winthrop," she said coldly, when they had gone some distance, "that you are carrying things with a pretty high hand. If I had known that such traits would ever develop in you, I am sure I should never have left the shelter of my father's house."

Her husband made no reply.

As the coach drew up before the fine old house, Mr. Van Rensselaer came out to greet the arrivals. Madam Winthrop sat up with grave dignity, and allowed him to hand her down and escort her into the house.

Mrs. Van Rensselaer met her with nervous ceremony in the wide hall and took her into the stately parlor. Once there, the lady looked about her as if in search of some one, scarcely noticing her hostess.

"Where is my son?" she asked. "I supposed he would be here. Will you tell Harrington that his mother wishes to see him at once? It is most important."

"You son has not yet arrived," said the other woman, watching her jealously. "We do not expect him until the morning train."

She mentioned the train with an air of pride, for the new railroad was a matter of vast importance to the little city. A few miles of railroad was a wonderful distinction in a land where railroads had just begun to be. But the guest had no recognition for such things.

"Not here yet? I supposed of course he would have arrived. Then, if it is convenient, I will go directly to my room, as I am very much worn-out. No, thank you. I could not eat a mouthful to-night. You may send me a cup of tea if you please."

Dawn had fled in a panic far into the depths of the garden. Crouched behind the tall, clipped hedges, her heart beating wildly, she listened, while frightened tears stood in her eyes. If she had dared, if she had known where to go, she would have fled out into the dark, unknown world at that moment, so did her heart revolt at the thought of her marriage. She listened. The night was very sweet with roses and honeysuckles and faint waft of mignonette all about her, mingled with the breath of heliotrope. But only the night sounds came to her—the plaintive cricket monotonously playing his part in the symphony of the evening; the tree-toads shrilly piping here and there, with the bass of a frog in the mill-pond just below the hill; the screech-owl coming in with his obligato; the murmur of the brook in the ravine not far away; and the sighing of the night-wind over all.

A sudden hush seemed to have come over the house, with only the faint echo of voices. Oh, if there were but a place in the world where she might slip away and never be found! It would be terrible to leave them that way, with the wedding all prepared, but she would not care what she did if only she might get away from it all.

The coach had been sent to the stables, and the gentlemen were closeted with Mr. Van Rensselaer in his library, the room made memorable to Dawn by so many sorrowful scenes. It was right and fitting that the revelation should be made within the sombre walls where had been enacted so many tragedies connected with the little girl.

What passed within that door no one knew exactly, save the three who took part in the low-voiced conversation. The lady of the house sat in gloomy mortification within her stately parlor, reviewing with vexed mind the recent interview between herself and the mother of the bridegroom. Mrs. Van Rensselaer decided that the other woman was a most unpleasant person, with whom she wished to have as little to do as possible in future. It was well that she and her step-daughter had little in common, if this was the kind of family she was marrying into.

The low tones in the library went on. The lady of the house did not like the idea of being shut out.

What could they be talking about? How very strange! Had something happened to the bridegroom? They looked so solemn when they came in. Mrs. Van Rensselaer caught her breath at the thought. It would be nothing short of a catastrophe to have the girl-bride on her hands, if the wedding were to be delayed for any reason. The child was almost beside herself now with excitement and nervousness. It was positively uncanny to have her around. She was making herself sick, one could see that at a glance, even if one didn't love her very much. Of course she would settle down and be all right after she was married. Girls always did. This girl was particularly headstrong, and it was as well that her prospective husband was older than herself, and would be able to control her wild fancies and put her through wise discipline. Mrs. Van Rensselaer was one of those who think all women save themselves need discipline.

While she meditated, Dawn flitted in at the front door noiselessly and stole up the stair like a wraith, her white dress flashing by the parlor before her step-mother could sense what it was.

The woman started angrily. It was one of the things about the girl that vexed her, this stealing softly by and giving no warning that she was near. Her step-mother named it "slyness."

In a moment more the library door opened and her name was called.

She went into the hall with an attitude that said plainly she felt insulted by the way things were going.

"Where is Jemima?" asked her husband, and she saw by his face that something unusual had happened. His look was that he had worn the day he came home from seeing his dead wife. Jemima indeed! Why did he not consult her first? She bustled up to the door.

"Jemima has gone to her room," she said decidedly. "By this time she has retired. It would be better not to disturb her. She has been very nervous and excited all day."

To the two guests inside the library, the protest sounded like loving solicitation. Perhaps the woman meant it should. She had been wont to show her interest thus before Dawn's father, and seldom let him know her true feeling toward the girl.

Mr. Van Rensselaer's severe brow did not relax. He was used to having life thicken around him in hard experiences, both for himself and for those who were dependent upon him.

"It will be necessary for her to know to-night, I think, Maria," he said. "Sit down and I will give you the facts. It may be best for you to tell her, after all."

With the injured importance of one who feels she should have been told at the first, Mrs. Van Rensselaer sat down upon the extreme edge of a stiff chair, grudgingly, not to seem too eager to be told.

"Maria, Mr. Winthrop has kindly come to inform us of a most unfortunate state of things relating to the young man who was to have married Jemima to-morrow morning."

Mrs. Van Rensselear held her breath, and her face actually blanched with the vision of the future. "Was to have married!" Then something had occurred to stop it. Her premonitions had been correct. Well, she would do something to get that whimsical minx out of her house, any way. Her husband needn't think she was to live her lifetime out in the same house with that girl. She set her lips together hard in a thin line of defence.

"I realize that the whole thing is painful in the extreme to my friend, Mr. Winthrop, so it is not necessary for us to discuss the matter at length. It is sufficient for you and my daughter to know that it has been discovered by Mr. Winthrop that his son Harrington is already married to a woman who is still living, and who is the mother of his two children. The situation is most embarrassing on both sides, and it will be necessary for my daughter to understand it at once."

There was a quick, eager movement of the young man on the other side of the big desk, but no one noticed him.

Mrs. Van Rensselaer was perhaps the only one in the room whose heart was not wrung with the anguish of the moment.

"A most unpleasant state of things, Mr. Winthrop," she said sharply, turning to the elder guest.

The old man bowed his head in assent, too overcome to reply.

"But one for which Mr. Winthrop and his family are in no wise to blame, of course," said Mr. Van Rensselaer quickly.

"I suppose not," said his wife dryly, in a tone which implied that there was more than one way of looking at the matter.

"The first thing is to tell Jemima," said her father.

"I'm sure I don't in the least see why," responded his wife. "The first thing is to plan what is to be done. Jemima is far better off asleep until we arrange it all. She will make a fuss, of course. Girls always make a fuss, whatever happens."

Charles eyed the woman indignantly, the color rising in his face.

"But, Mr. Van Rensselaer, I——" he began eagerly.

"Yes, certainly, Mr. Winthrop; I am coming to that. There is another matter, Maria, that slightly changes the affair. This young man, Mr. Charles Winthrop, has most thoughtfully offered a suggestion which may help us out of the dilemma in which we are all placed."

Mrs. Van Rensselaer turned toward him sharply, and saw that he was good to look upon.

"Well?" she said dryly, as her husband hesitated.

"If Miss Van Rensselaer is willing," put in Charles shyly, with wistful eyes and a smile that would have melted any but a woman with a heart made of pig iron.

Mrs. Van Rensselaer pursed her lips at the "Miss" applied to Jemima, and thought in her heart she would see that "Miss Van Rensselaer" was willing for anything that would help them out of this most embarrassing situation.

"Mr. Winthrop has offered his hand to my daughter," went on the father, dropping his eyes and getting out the sentence stiffly. It was all painful to him. Somehow, in the last few minutes, it had come to him that she who had been Mary Montgomery would think he had bungled her daughter's life most terribly. He was shaken with the thought. It had been a relief to think that the girl was to be happily married. But now!

"He proposes to marry her himself, to-morrow morning, at the hour appointed for the other marriage," went on Mr. Van Rensselaer.

"With her consent, of course," put in Charles.

"Very commendable, I'm sure," commented Mrs. Van Rensselaer, while she did some rapid thinking.

Here was her chance. The girl must marry this young man, whether she would or no. All those relatives who were coming to-morrow should not have a chance to scoff at her proud arrangements. The step-mother desired that they should all see how well she had done for the girl who was not her own. Besides, he was a goodly youth, full as handsome as the other man, and of the same family. What was there to object to? The girl might even be pleased, though there was no forecasting that. Such a queer girl would probably do the opposite from what was expected of her. The matter with her was that she was too young to know what she did want, and in the present circumstances it was best for her that some one else should decide her fate. She—Mrs. Van Rensselaer—would decide it. She would take matters into her own hands and see that all went the way it should go. Meantime, she picked at a bit of thread on her immaculate gown, and, to make time for thought, murmured again:

"Most commendable, I'm sure."

Charles's face lighted with hope. He was ready to fall upon the cold-looking lady's neck and embrace her, if that would hasten matters. He thought she looked more pleasing than when he had first seen her.

"I think, Mr. Van Rensselaer, you would do well to leave this matter in my hands now. As you say, it is a very delicate situation, and one that must be handled most carefully. I will go to Jemima at once and talk with her. I must break the news gently——"

"Of course, of course—the poor lamb!" murmured the kind old father of the reprobate bridegroom.

"She is very nervous and quite unstrung with the day's preparation," went on the step-mother, the more to work her will upon the feelings of those present.

"Of course, of course—poor child! Don't distress her any more than is necessary, I beg. It is dreadful for her, dreadful!"

."But it isn't quite as if she had never seen me," put in Charles wistfully. "Tell her I have loved her from the very first sight I had of her——"

The woman turned the chilly search-light of her eyes upon the young man's ardent face, and a sense of foreboding passed over him. Poor soul, she was only wondering what it must be like to have some one talk in that way about one. Still, she was keen to see an advantage, and knew it would help her in the task she had set herself to get rid of her step-daughter.

"Whatever you think best, Maria," assented Dawn's father wearily. He was glad, after all, not to have to tell the girl. He had come to fear her eyes, which were like her mother's, and her temper, which was his own.

"Of course, of course," said old Mr. Winthrop.

Dawn's father bowed once more his assent. In his heart he heard again the words: "You have no right. You have no right!" Would the sin of his youth never be expiated by sorrow?

Mrs. Van Rensselaer arose.

"I will go up and talk with her," she said coolly, as though it were quite an ordinary matter under discussion.

"You will ask her to come down and let me talk to her?" asked Charles, following her into the hall. "I think perhaps I can make her see it better than any one else."

The woman looked him over, frowning. This ardent youth was going to be hard to control. She must be wary or he would upset all her plans, as well as his own.

"I will see what is best," she answered coldly. "Remember she has retired, and this will be a great shock to her. It would be better for you to give her a little time to recover and to think it over. Leave it to me. I will do my best for you."

She tried to smile, but conveyed rather an expression of arrogance than of anything else.

"Of course." The young man drew back thoughtfully. "Do not hurry her."

She passed up the stairs, and Charles wandered out the front door and into the moonlit garden. He stood and listened to the harmony of sound and looked up reverently toward a chamber window where glimmered a candlelight. He wondered if even now she was listening to his message, and his heart was lifted high with hope.

## CHAPTER IX

WHEN Mrs. Rensselaer came down stairs a half-hour later she found Charles in the parlor anxiously awaiting her coming. Her face was bland and encouraging. She tried to smile, though smiles were foreign to her nature.

"Well," she said, seating herself and signing to the young man to take a chair opposite her, "she is naturally very much shocked."

"Of course she would be," said Charles, somewhat sadly, and waited.

"I think, as I said, it will take her a few hours to become adjusted to the new state of things, and it would not be well for you to see her to-night. There will be plenty of time in the morning. The hour was set late, so that all the relatives could arrive, you know. She will undoubtedly accept your proposal, but you must give her a little time."

"You think she will?" asked the young man, brightening. "Oh, that is good! Certainly I can wait until morning. Poor little girl, it must be very hard for her!"

A hard glitter in his hostess's eye did not encourage conversation along these lines, and he soon excused himself to go and meet his father, who had gone to the inn to see that the rest of the family were comfortable for the night.

The household settled to quiet at last, but it was like the sullen silence before a storm.

A heavy burden had fallen upon Mr. Van Rensselaer. He seemed to be arraigned before his first wife's searching eyes, for the trouble that had befallen their child. He could not get away from the vision of her dead face.

His wife spent the night in feverish planning for the morning, a fiendish determination in her heart to be rid of her step-daughter, no matter to what she had to resort in order to compass it.

Mr. Winthrop had leisure now to think upon his oldest son, and the sin which he had been about to commit, and tears trickled down his cheeks as he watched through the long hours of the night. His wife vouchsafed him no word or look. To all appearances, she was asleep, but no one ever knew what struggles were going on within her soul. Perhaps she was holding herself in abeyance for the coming of the beloved son who would explain all.

In the spacious chamber assigned to him, Charles spent much of the night in a vision with a white-robed girl upon a hillside, and his waking visions and those sleeping were so blended that he was scarce aware when starlight merged into morning, and he heard the birds twitter in the branches near his window.

Of all that household, only Dawn slept. Her heart, bowed with its burden of apprehension, had reached the limit of endurance, and the long lashes lay still upon the white cheeks, while her soul ceased from its troubling for a little while.

She awoke with a start of painful realization, while yet the first crimson streak of morning lay in the east. Its rosy light reminded her of the day, and what it was to mean for her. With a sound that was like both a sob and a prayer, she rose quickly, and, slipping on the little white gown she had worn the evening before, nor stopping to do more than brush out the mass of curls, she hastened stealthily down the stairs and, taking care to close the door behind her that her escape should not be noticed, went out into the garden. She would slip back quietly, before the guests were astir, she told herself. She wanted one more hour to herself in the dewy garden, before life shut her in forever from freedom and her girlhood.

Five minutes later, her step-mother, in dressing-gown and slippers, crossed the hall hastily and pushed open the girl's door. She had fallen asleep toward morning, and had slept later than she had intended. But she had her plans carefully laid, and determined to settle the girl's part before any one was up.

At that same instant, Charles, whose heart was alive for the possibilities of the new day, stepped out on the balcony in front of his window, and with easy agility swung himself over the railing and dropped to the terrace beneath. He was too impatient to sleep longer, and felt that somehow he would be nearer his heart's desire if he got out into the dewy morning world.

He walked slowly down the carefully tended paths, into the garden, stopping to notice a bird's note here, the glint of dew-drops over the lawn, the newly opened flowers in the beds of poppies, bachelor buttons, foxglove, asters, and sweet-peas. A great thorny branch that must have evaded the gardener's careful training reached out as if to catch his attention, and there upon its tip was a spray of delicate buds, just half blown, exquisite as an angel's wings, and with the warm glow of the sunrise in the sheathlike, curling petals. Were they white or pink or yellow? A warm white, living and tender, like a maiden's cheek. He reached for the spray and cut it off, feeling sure he could make his peace with the mistress of the house when he confessed his theft. He stood a moment looking at the beautiful roses, one almost full blown, the other two curling apart, like a baby trying to waken. He drank in their fragrance in a long, deep breath, and then, thinking his fanciful thoughts of the girl to whom he had given his heart so freely before he yet knew her, he walked slowly on to the little arbor hid among the yew trees.

Mrs. Van Rensselaer stood in the doorway of Dawn's room, aghast, scarcely able to believe her eyes. Yes, the girl was gone. Where? was her instant thought. Perhaps she had fled, and would make them more trouble. A great fear clutched at the woman's heart lest she had made a

terrible mistake by not talking the matter over with her
step-daughter the night before, and making her understand what she was to do. Now, perhaps, it would be
found out by them all, and by her husband in particular,
that she had not yet told the girl anything. Mrs. Van
Rensselaer. had a decided fear of her husband. Their wills
had never really clashed so far, but for some years she
had had a feeling that if they ever did, he would be
terrible. She shrank back with a wild beating of her heart,
and looked about the shadowy hall as if she expected to
find the girl lurking there. Then her stern common-sense
came to the surface, and she went boldly into the room
and made a systematic search. It did not take but a minute to make sure that Dawn was not there, and that
wherever she was she had taken nothing with her, save
the clothes she had worn the evening before. It suddenly occurred to the step-mother that she ought to have
gone into the room before retiring last night and made
sure that her charge was there; but so sure had she been
that she had heard Dawn come in, it had not occurred to
her to do it. Besides, where could the girl go? She was
very likely maundering about that dull old garden she
had haunted ever since her return from school.

With that, Mrs. Van Rensselaer looked out of the
window, just in time to catch sight of her young guest
cutting the roses. With keen apprehension, she saw what
might be about to happen, and knew that instant action
was the only thing that could prevent a catastrophe.

Regardless of dressing-gown and slippers, and of the
night-cap which concealed her scant twist of hair, she
descended the stairs, strode out the front door and down
the garden path, coming in sight of the young man just as
he turned the corner of the yew hedge into the walk that
led into the green arbor.

Charles stopped suddenly, for there sat Dawn in her
little white gown, with her head bowed upon her arms, on
the rustic table, and her wealth of dark curls covering
her. Her young frame shook with sobbing, yet so quietly
did she weep that he had not heard her.

Her ear, alert with apprehension, caught the sound
of his foot upon the gravel, and she raised her head as
suddenly as he had stopped.

She looked at him with frightened eyes, out of which the tears had fled down her white cheeks. The face was full of anguish, yet sweet and pitiful withal, framed in its ripple of dark hair.

One instant she looked at him as if he were a vision from whence she could not tell, then that great light grew in her eyes, as he had seen it on the hillside, and before he knew what he was doing he had smiled. Then the light in her eyes grew into an answering smile and lit up her whole beautiful, sorrowful face. It was like a rainbow in the pale dawn of the morning, that smile, with the teardrops still upon her lashes.

"Jemima, what on earth!" broke in the harsh voice of her step-mother. "You certainly do take the craziest notions! You out here in that rig at this time in the morning! I guess you didn't count on company rising early, too. And your hair not combed either! I certainly am mortified. Run in quick and get tidied up. There's plenty to do this morning, without mooning in the garden. You'll excuse her"——to the guest. "She had no idea any one else would be out here so early."

The smile had gone from the girl's face, and instead the fright had come back at sound of her tormentor's jangling voice. She looked down at her little rumpled frock, put back her hair with trembling hand, and a flood of sweet, shamed color came into the white face, just as the sun burst up behind the hedge and touched the green with rosy morning brightness.

Without a word in reply, she turned to go, but her eyes met those of Charles with a pleading that went to his heart, and his eyes answered unspeakable things, of which neither knew the meaning, though each felt the strange joy they brought.

As he stood back to let her pass, he held out to her the spray of lovely rosebuds, and without a word she took them and went swiftly on into the house. Not a word had passed between them, yet each felt that something wonderful had happened.

Dawn looked neither to right nor to left, fearing lest she should see some one less welcome, and so she fled to her room, with the sound of her step-mother's clanging voice, uttering some commonplaces about the morning and the garden, floating to her in indistinct waves.

"You will let me see her now just as soon as she is ready to come down?" Charles asked eagerly at the door.

"I will talk with her at once, and let you know what she says," answered the vexed lady evasively. She was all out of breath and flurried with the anxiety lest she had been too late. It had been a narrow escape. She did not like to begin an important day like this with being flustered. Besides, she had become conscious of her night-cap, the ugly lines of her dessing-gown, the flop-flop of her slippers. A long wisp of hair had escaped from her cap and was tickling her nose, as she ascended the stairs with as much dignity as the circumstances and her slippers allowed, in full sight of the ardent lover.

"Well, Jemima Van Rensselaer, I hope you're satisfied!" she flared out, as soon as she was inside the girl's door. "What on earth took you out in the wet at this unearthly hour? And on your wedding day, too! I should think you'd be ashamed! I declare I shall be glad to my soul when this day's over and I can wash my hands of the responsibility of you. If your father knew the freaks and fancies and the queer actions of you I'm not sure what he wouldn't do to you! Now, look here! Sit down. I want to talk to you."

But Dawn had flung herself upon her bed in a paroxysm of tears, and was smothering her wild sobs in the pillow. She did not hear a word.

Nor could threats nor protests, nor even a thorough shaking, bring her out of it until the tears had wept themselves out. But finally she lay quiet and white upon the bed, and even the hard-hearted woman who did not love her was stirred to a sort of pity for the abject woe that was upon her face.

"Say, look here, Jemima"—even the hated name brought forth no sign from the girl—"now put away all this foolishness. Girls always feel kind of queer at getting married and making a change in life. I did, myself."

Dawn wondered indifferently if her step-mother had ever been a girl. She certainly had not been one when she married Dawn's father.

"You'll feel all right once you get in your own home and have things the way you want them around you."

Dawn shuddered. She would have *him* around her.

"Now, do get up and wash your face. A bride oughtn't to look as if she was just getting over the measles. Besides, you'll be wanted pretty soon to go downstairs——"

"Oh!" Dawn involuntarily put her hand over her heart. "Must I go down and see all those dreadful people? Couldn't I just stay here till—till—till it's time?"

Now, this was exactly what Mrs. Van Rensselaer wanted her to say, and, moreover, had been counting upon. If Dawn had assented to going down, her step-mother would have found some excuse for keeping her upstairs. But she did not wish the girl to know it, so she assumed a look of mild disapproval.

"It's very queer for you not to want to meet your mother-in-law and father-in-law, and all your new sisters——"

Dawn shuddered more violently, and clasped her hands quickly over her eyes, as if to shut out the unpleasant vision of her new kindred.

"Oh, no, no, please!" she besought, looking up at her step-mother with more earnest pleading than she had ever shown her before.

"Well"—grimly—"I suppose it can be managed, but you'll want to have a talk with him that's so soon to be your husband——"

"Oh, no, no!" cried Dawn wildly. "I do not want to see him. I cannot talk with him now. I could never, never, go through that awful ceremony afterward if I were to see him now. I should run away or something I'm sure I should. I don't want to see anybody until I have to."

"He'll think it very strange. I don't see how I can explain it. He's very anxious to talk to you. He sent you a message last night, but you were asleep."

So that was what the knock had meant! Dawn was glad she had not answered it.

"Oh, please, please," she said, clasping her hands in the attitude of pleading, "couldn't you just explain to him that I'm a very silly girl, but I should like just these last few minutes to myself. Tell him that if he has any message, please to tell it to you, and to let me be by myself now. Tell him he doesn't know how a girl feels when she is going to stop being a girl. Tell him, please, that if he has any sympathy for me at all, he won't ask to see me now. It is only a little while, and I want it to myself."

Her great pleading eyes met Mrs. Van Rensselaer's cold gaze, and her whole slender figure took an attitude of intense wistfulness. The elder woman, cold and unloving as she was, could not but acknowledge that the girl was very beautiful. Her heart might have been touched more had it not been for the gnawing thought that this child's mother had been the canker-worm which had blighted the step-mother's whole life.

She turned grimly from the girl, well content that her plans were coming out as she desired, yet not entirely comfortable in mind or conscience. Almost she determined to risk telling the girl everything, yet dared not, lest she utterly refuse to be married even at this late hour.

"Well, I suppose you must have your own way. You always have," she said grimly.

Dawn wondered when.

"I'll do my best to explain your state of mind," continued Mrs. Van Rensselaer, "though I'm sure I don't know how he'll take it. It's my opinion he isn't going to have a bed of roses through life, being a husband to you, any way, and I suppose he may as well begin to learn."

With which unsympathetic remark, she went heavily out of the girl's room, and into her own, where she speedily got herself into her wedding garments. A red spot burned in either sallow cheek, but her mouth wore the line of victory. So far she had carried out her schemes well.

## CHAPTER X

AT breakfast time, as the other guests were coming downstairs, Mrs. Van Rensselaer beckoned Charles inside the dining-room door, and gave him his message in a low tone.

"It will be all right, Mr. Winthrop. Your offer will be accepted gratefully, but she asks you to be kind enough to leave her to herself until the time for the ceremony. She is so much shaken by this whole thing that she is afraid to talk about it, lest it will unnerve her. She says she does not need to talk it over, that you are very kind, and if you have any message, you can send it by me after breakfast."

"Thank you, thank you!" said Charles, his face bright with the joy of knowing that his strange suit had been successful. He was disappointed, of course, not to see the girl at once, but it would not be long before she was his wife, and he could talk with her as much as he pleased. After all, there was something wonderful in her trusting him enough to marry him, when she had seen him but twice. Had she, perhaps, had the same feeling about him that he had about her? Had that been the explanation of the light in her eyes?

These thoughts played a happy trill in his heart as he greeted his father and mother and seated himself at the table. All through the meal, he was planning the message he would send to his beloved.

When her step-mother had left the room, Dawn had fastened the door securely against all intrusion. she was determined to have to herself what little time was left.

On the couch under her window was spread the beautiful frock which her step-mother had prepared for her to wear. It was of white satin, rich and elaborate, and encrusted with much beautiful lace, which had been in her father's family for years, and was yellow with age. It

was traditional that all the brides of the house had worn
these rare laces. Dawn hated the frock and the lace. She
would much rather have worn a simple muslin of her own
mother, but as the marriage was not to her taste, why
should her dress be, either? What mattered it? Let them
all have their way with her.

Mrs. Van Rensselaer had taken much pride in preparing the beautiful garments, but Dawn knew why. She
knew that it was for others to look upon, so that they
would praise the step-mother for having been so good
to the child who had been thrust upon her care under
circumstances which, to put it mildly, were unpleasant. It
spoke of no loving kindness toward her.

And so Dawn did not go over to the couch, as many
another girl might have done, to examine again the filmy
hand-embroidered garments, the silk stockings, and the
dainty satin slippers, sewed over with seed-pearls that
were also an heirloom in the family. They meant to her
nothing but signs of her coming bondage.

Instead, she went to the little three-legged mahogany
stand, where she had placed in a tall pitcher her spray
of rosebuds. She bent over to take in their delicate fragrance, and the eyes of him who had given them to her
seemed to be looking into her soul again, as twice they had
looked before.

It was a strange thing—and she thought of it afterward many times—that she did not yet know who he was,
and had never stopped to question. It had not even occurred to her to wonder if he were a relative or only a
friend, or how he came to be in her home. She accepted
him as she would have accepted a respite in some quiet
place for her fevered spirit, or the visit of an angel with a
message of strength from heaven. She had a vague feeling
that if he had come before things might have been different.

She knelt beside the stand and let her hot cheek rest
against a cool bud; she touched her lips to another, and
then laid the roses on her eyelids. It seemed almost like
a pitying human hand upon her spirit, and comforted her
tired heart. She felt that she was growing old, very, very
old, in these last few hours, to meet the requirements of
her wedding day, and the touch of the buds seemed to

steady and help her, as her mother's hand and lips might have done.

By and by she would have to get up and put on those fine garments lying over there in the morning sunlight, and go downstairs, for them all to stare at her misery; but now she would forget it all for a little while, and just think of her new-found friend, who had looked at her with such a wonderful smile—a smile in which there seemed no place for fault-finding or sternness or grim solemnity—the things which had seemed to make up the main part of her girlhood life.

Meantime, Mr. Winthrop and his host had gone to meet the train, upon which the expectant bridegroom would arrive.

As they neared the tavern that served as a station for the new railroad, they saw an old man, a woman, and two little children sitting upon a settle on the front stoop. The man arose and came a step or two toward them, and Mr. Winthrop saw that it was William McCord.

He seemed embarrassed and he spoke apologetically:

"Mr. Winthrop, sir, I don't jest know what you'll think about me bein' here—I don't, and I'm sorry's I can be about it; but, you see, I knowed Harrington pretty well. I knowed he might find a way to smooth it all over and pull the wool over your eyes, and I'd passed my word I'd come here with her and stop the marriage, if so be it turned out you couldn't or wouldn't feel called upon to do so. I didn't count on your comin' down to the train. You see, we ben watchin' every train sence yesterday, to make sure he didn't get away to the house without our seein' him. That poor girl there ain't et scarce a mouthful sence she started from home—only just a drop o' coffee now an' then—and she ain't slep' neither. She's jest keepin' alive to hunt him up and try to persuade him to come home to her an' the children. You see, I had to let her come. I couldn't say no. She was up here day 'fore yesterday, when I come to see you. She didn't want I should tell you, because she ain't got the clo'es and fixin's she'd like to hev you see her in, but she was determined to come——"

He paused and looked back toward the bench where the woman and the children sat.

Mr. Winthrop's face had taken on a look of distress as he recognized William McCord. He turned to his companion and explained in a low tone, "This is the man who brought me the evidence."

Mr. Van Rensselaer regarded the man with keen eyes, and decided at once that any word from a man with such a face was as good as an affidavit.

When William looked toward the woman her worn face flamed crimson, then turned deadly white again. She must have been unusually pretty not so very many years ago, but sorrow, toil and poverty had left their ineradicable marks upon her face and stripped her of all claim to beauty now. Her dress was plain, and as neat as could be expected under the circumstances. Her roughened hair showed an attempt to put it into order, and her eyes looked as though she had not slept for many nights. In spite of her shrinking, there was a dignity about her. The bony hand that held the youngest child wore a wedding ring, now much too large for the finger.

The oldest child, a girl apparently of five, had yellow hair and rather bold blue eyes that reminded Mr. Winthrop startlingly of his eldest son's when he was a small boy. The youngest, a sallow, sickly boy, looked like his mother.

The kindly face of Mr. Winthrop was overspread with trouble, but he grasped the humbler man's hand warmly:

"That's all right, William," he said heartily. "I suppose she felt she must come, and there's no harm done. Only, for our friend Mr. Van Rensselaer's sake, keep the matter as quiet as possible."

"Certainly, certainly, Mr. Winthrop, and thank you, sir," said the old man gratefully.

Then he looked questioningly toward the woman, and took a step in her direction.

"Alberty, this here is his father," said William McCord and withdrew hastily.

Mr. Van Rensselaer at once engaged him in earnest conversation, giving the other man opportunity to talk with his unknown daughter-in-law without being observed.

The woman looked up abashed into the kindly eyes

bent upon her. Yet she felt the right was on her side, and she had no need to quail before any one.

"It has given me great sorrow, madam, to learn of my son's behavior," he began. "It is particularly distressing to us because he is our first born, and deeply loved by us." He paused, overcome by his emotion, and the dry-eyed woman, who looked as if she had long ago shed all the tears she had to shed, glanced up wonderingly and said in a voice that betrayed her lack of culture:

"Yes, that's one trouble with him: folks always like him too well. He thinks he can do anything he wants, and it won't make no diff'runce. But he can't go no further with me. I've jest made up my mind to take a stand, even ef I have to go to that rich girl and show her them children."

The father in him almost shuddered at the vernacular. Of what could Harrington have been thinking when he married this woman—Harrington, who had been brought up amid the refinements of life, and been almost too sensitive to unpleasant things? It was the old story of a pretty face, and a boy far from home and acquaintances, with no one to advise, and no danger of being found out.

"I used to like him a lot myself," went on the tired voice, "an' I might even yet ef he'd behave himself and stay home, an' pervide good fer us like he used to." There was a pleasant drawl to her tone, like a weary child's. The father's heart was touched.

"Has my son sent you money during his absences?" The question had to be asked, but it cut the old gentleman to the heart to speak the words.

She turned dull eyes on him.

"Never a cent! He always said he was havin' a hard time to get money enough to keep goin', business was so bad, but I took notice he was dressed up good and smart every time he come home, which wa'n't often." She sighed as if it did not matter much.

"I could stand it all," she began again in her monotonous tone, "but I can't stand him gettin' married again. It ain't right, and it ain't the law, an' I knew ef I didn't stop it, nobody would, so I come on."

"That was right," sighed the old gentleman, fumbling in his pocket, "perfectly right. Here, I want you to take this with you."

He handed her a roll of bills, but she drew back, a red spot coming in either sallow cheek.

"I ain't an object of charity, thank you. I put a mortgage on pap's shack to git the money to come out here, but when I get back I've got plenty of work, an' I can pay it off in a year or so."

"This is not charity," said the disconcerted old gentleman. "This belongs to you. I often lend Harrington money, and sometimes give him some, and this was to be given to him. I think it is safer with you. He can work for his own after this, and I will see that all I should have given him comes to your hands. I have your address. Take it for the children. I guess I have a right to give something to my own grandchildren," he said with a great stretch of his pride, looking down at the two forlorn little specimens of childhood hiding, half frightened, behind their mother's skirts.

The woman melted at once, the first warm tinge of life springing into her eyes at the mention of her children as his relatives.

"Oh, if you put it that way, I'll take it o' course. It ain't no fault of theirs that their father don't do right by me, and they do need a sight of things I can't manage to get anyhow. Last winter Harry was sick for four months —he's named after his pa, Harry is." She pushed his hair fondly out of his eyes, and, moistening her fingers at her lips, rubbed vigorously at a black streak on Harry's nose, at which he as vigorously protested.

But the train was near at hand. Even then the distant rumble of its wheels could be heard.

Mr. Van Rensselaer and William McCord drew near, the latter with an attitude of deferential expectancy.

"Mr. Winthrop," said his host, "would it not be well to let your son's wife meet him first?"

The old father bowed. He saw at once the wisdom of this.

"I'd like ye to stand where ye could get a glimpse o' his face when he first catches sight o' his wife. It will be a better proof that I've told ye the truth than all the words I've said to ye," whispered William.

"I have never doubted your word, William," said the father sadly.

With much shouting and blowing of the trumpet, the morning train lumbered in, and the passengers began rapidly to emerge. There were loud talk, and tooting of the horn, and a clatter of machinery, as the fireman jumped down and attended to some detail of the engine's mechanism. Some said he did this to show off before the gaping crowd, who had not yet grown used to the fact that a machine could draw a number of loaded carriages through the country, without the aid of horses.

The two old gentlemen had rapidly withdrawn into a secluded place, by a wide-spreading apple-tree.

## CHAPTER XI

ONE of the first to get out of the carriages was Harrington Winthrop. A high stock held his chin well tilted in the air, his gray trousers were immaculate, and his coat fitted about his slender waist as trimly as any lady's. He wore a high gray beaver hat and carried a shiny new portmanteau. Altogether, he looked quite a dandy, and the eyes of his waiting wife filled with a light of pride even while her heart quaked.

Only an instant she paused to watch him. He was making straight for the Van Rensselaer carriage, which stood not far away, and which he supposed had been sent to bring him to the house. He walked with an importance and pride that any one might see. He did not take note of any one on the platform, though he was conscious that many were watching him.

Then, suddenly, the woman with the two little children clinging to her skirts, stepped in his way. The little girl looked up into his face with bold blue eyes, and cried out: "It's my pa! It's my pa! Oh, doesn't he look pretty?"

The two men standing close together under the appletree were near enough to hear the child's cry, and many bystanders turned and looked at the fine gentleman beset by the poor-looking woman and children.

Harrington Winthrop turned his elegant self about with a start and found himself face to face with the worn shadow of the woman who for a time had been his plaything, and whom he had tossed aside as easily and as carelessly as if she had been a doll.

The start, the pallor, the quick, furtive side-glance, all told their tale to the watchers, without other need of words. Then anger surged into young Winthrop's face, and he cried out:

"Stand back, you vagabonds! What have I to do with you? Get out of my way, woman! There is a carriage waiting for me."

But the woman stood her ground, with grim determination, great red waves of restrained anger marking her face and forehead, as if he had struck her with his words. She looked up at him. She had planned it all for so many hours, and now she was calm in this terrible crisis. It would not do to make a public disturbance. Neither for his sake nor for her own, did she wish to have people see or hear, if it could be avoided, so she had schooled herself to be self-controlled.

"Harrington," she said, speaking low and rapidly, "I'm your wife, and you know it. I've come to keep you from an awful sin, and I will do it. You can't forgit me an' the children, and marry a rich girl. It would be wicked. But I've fixed it so you can't do it, any way. If you'll come off quiet with me now, I won't say a word to disgrace you here where I s'pose folks knows you; but if you try to git away from me, I'll tell the whole world who I be, an' prove it too!"

Now, if the young man had known that there were those watching who knew his story he would have been more careful, but his casual glance about the platform had given him no hint of any but the villagers, few of whom he knew even slightly. Yet his wife's face and voice were such that he thought it the part of wisdom to temporize; so he dropped his angry manner and spoke in a low tone. But it happened that the two witnesses under the appletree had also, by common consent, moved toward him.

With William McCord in their rear, they came and stood quite close to Harrington, and though he did not see them, every word that he spoke was audible.

"Look here, Alberta, what in the name of common sense are you doing up here? Isn't it hard enough for me to have to work and scrape and do all in my power to get my business going again, so that I can come home to you and the children and keep you in the way you ought to be kept, without having you come traipsing around here in such clothes as that? Don't you know you'd ruin my business if anybody thought you belonged to me? Everybody thinks I'm a successful business man, and they must think so or I'm lost and shall never come back to you. Here, take this money. A man just paid me a bill that he has been owing me for two years, and I needed the money to help me in a new deal, but as you are here you'll have to have it to get home with. Now, run along back, and take good care of the children till I come home a rich man. Then we'll live like folks. And what is all this nonsense you are talking about my marrying a rich girl? How ever could you get such an idea? Why, I couldn't marry anybody as long as you are my wife. You must have heard some foolish gossip. Take it quick and run along, or people will be looking and talking, and I shall be ruined."

The thin hand of the wife went out to the money he offered her, but instead of taking it, she struck it into the air, and it fell scattering in every direction. Suddenly the young man became aware of the nearness of others, and, looking up, he saw in quick succession his father, Mr. Van Rensselaer, and William McCord!

He knew at once that they had heard every word he had spoken to his wife, even before their condemning eyes had searched his soul. The presence of William McCord made it plain to him that they had known the story before his arrival, and he realized instantly that he had given the final testimony against himself.

It was too late to turn back and deny knowledge of the woman. There stood his father's former farm manager, who had lived in the Western town where Harrington had married his wife. That McCord would ever come East again and bring back tales against him had not occurred to the careless young scapegrace. McCord was a quiet, silent man, who went about his own business, and seldom, if ever, wrote letters. Young Winthrop had never given an uneasy thought to him, but now he stood and looked at him in growing dismay.

Turning, Harrington met his father's passionate, loving reproach, his wife's bitter hopelessness, and the scorn of the man he had hoped soon to call his father-in-law.

The voice of Mr. Winthrop broke out in bitterness: "Oh, my son, my son!" and the father's kind face was turned away. He was weeping.

This kind of reproach had ever angered Harrington Winthrop beyond all endurance. It seethed over his frightened, fretted spirit now like acid in a wound. The voice of the trainman cried out, "All aboard!" the trumpet sounded, and the wheels moved. The fireman jumped on board. Then Harrington Winthrop grasped his portmanteau, pushed aside his frightened children, who were eagerly gathering up the scattered money, and sprang into a vacant carriage. His game was up and he knew it.

With a wild cry, the wife caught up her little boy, and, dragging her little girl, rushed after him. A couple of men standing by pushed her up into the carriage with her husband, which happened to be occupied by no one else. Before he had time to turn about and notice what had happened, the train was going rapidly on its way, and the reunited family had ample opportunity to discuss their situation. Harrington Winthrop had completed the last link in the chain of evidence against him: he had fled.

Mr. Van Rensselaer stood looking after the vanishing train with satisfaction. He had watched the changing expressions on the face of the young man who had expected to become the husband of his only daughter: the cruelty, the craven fear, the hate, and the utter selfishness of the man! Suppose his daughter had stood where that poor wife had stood, and begged of him to come home to her and care for her! What an escape!

The daughter who had been the object of so little of his thought or care had suddenly become dear to him. Mary's daughter, the child of his real love! He saw how utterly selfish and unfatherly had been his whole action with regard to her; how almost criminal in his self-absorption. There had come, too, a revelation from the sight of that poor, hollow-eyed, deserted wife, a revelation of what his treatment of his own wife, Mary, had been. He was stung with a remorse such as he had not known before.

As William McCord watched the departing train, he might have been said fairly to glow with contentment over the ways things had come out. Not that he felt that matters would be materially improved for the poor broken-hearted woman who was making her last frantic effort to get back what she had lost. But he was justified, fully justified, in the eyes of his benefactor. He could now with a clear conscience take his way back to his claim in western Mississippi, and feel that he had done his duty.

As for Mr. Winthrop, he was filled with horror. His son's face had been a revelation to him. Until now it had been impossible for him to conceive that Harrington had done this wrong. Underneath all his conviction of the truth of William McCord's story, there had still been a lingering hope that in some way the beloved son would explain things satisfactorily.

Mr. Winthrop now realized that he had never really known his boy at all. The old father gazed after the train in the dim distance, saw it round a curve and vanish from his sight, then turned and walked with bowed head away from them all. He felt that such sorrow was too heavy for him.

## CHAPTER XII

Dawn was already dressed for the wedding.

Her step-mother surveyed her with a kind of grim pride. The shimmering satin fitted the slim, girlish form to perfection, and the yellow lace set off the pink and cream complexion. It was a beautiful frock, and all who saw it would be sure to say so.

There had been some contention about the arrangement of the girl's hair. Dawn wanted to be married with her curls down her back, as she had always worn them, but her step-mother was firm. That could not be. If her hair had been only long enough to reach to her shoulders, it would not have seemed so absurd, for many young women wore their short ringlets all about the neck. But Dawn's hair fell far below her waist in rich, abundant curls. It was out of the question for her to be married looking so like a child.

The argument had waxed hot, and at one point Dawn had declared that she would not be married at all unless she could wear her hair as she had always worn it. Finally her step-mother threatened to go for the girl's father to settle the dispute. Dawn's face was white, and she turned away to hide her emotion. Then in a strange, hard voice she said:

"I will put it up if it must be."

After all, what did that or anything else matter? Certainly not enough to invoke her father's wrath upon her at this most trying moment of her life.

She drew the mass of beautiful curls up on her head, fastening them with a large tortoise-shell comb which had been her mother's and was treasured by the young girl. The ends of the curls fell in a little shower over the back of the comb, making a lovely effect. The step-mother thought it far too careless and mussy-looking, and frowned at the sweet, artistic head, but Dawn gave it a pat here and there and would have no more to say about it. With her own hands, she arranged the filmy veil. She would not have her step-mother's assistance. Mrs. Van Rensselaer stood by, watching the quick, assured way in which the young bride draped the delicate fabric. The elder woman was half jealous of the girl's deftness.

"Put on your gloves, and you'll do very nicely, though I must say I'd rather see your hair smooth for once. But the veil hides the frowsiness. Now, is there anything you'd like to know about what you've got to do?"

Dawn looked at her step-mother in horror.

"I haven't got to do anything, have I?" There was genuine distress in her voice. She had been so absorbed in the great thought of the result of this act that the ceremony itself, about which so many girls worry, had not entered into her mind in the least.

"Well," said Mrs. Van Rensselaer—there was satisfaction in her voice, for Dawn was unconsciously making it easier for her than she had dared to hope—"there isn't much, of course. Nothing but to keep your eyes down and walk in and say yes. It's all very simple. The main thing is never to look up. It is counted very bad manners to look up. A bride who raises her eyes during the ceremony, or before, is called very bold and—and immodest!"

The step-mother's voice sounded queer to herself, and she picked at an invisible thread on her sleeve. This was the first out-and-out bald lie she had ever told in her life, though she had made many a misleading statement; but that, of course, to a woman with a conscience, was a very different thing. This woman thought she had a conscience, and she was excusing her present action on the ground of necessity, and the circumstances. "She's getting a far better husband every way, anyhow, and it isn't as if she was much attached to the other man. One can see she was afraid of him. I'm really doing her a service, and she'll thank me when she finds it out." This was what she told her conscience now, and went on with her advice to Dawn.

"You want to walk downstairs very slowly, with your eyes on the hem of your frock. You mustn't look up for anything."

"I'm sure I don't know what I should want to look up for," said Dawn coldly. "I'd much rather look down. I'm glad it's quite polite to do so."

"That's right," commended her step-mother, with unusual alacrity. "And it won't do a bit of harm to keep it up some afterward too, at least, till you get out to the dining-room, and then you can look into your plate a good deal. People will only think you are shy and modest, and say nice things about you for it."

"I don't care what people think," observed the girl. "Is that all?"

"Oh, there'll be things he'll ask you—the minister,

you know. The regular service. He'll say a lot of things, and then ask you, 'Do you thus promise?' And then you say, 'Yes,' or you can just nod your head."

"But suppose I don't like to promise those things? Won't he marry me?" The girl asked the question sharply, as if she saw a possibility of escape somewhere; but the older woman was so relieved that her task had been performed that she took little notice of the question.

"Oh, yes," she answered carelessly, thinking the girl was anxious about saying her part at the right time. "If you don't get it in, he'll go right on, any way, and it'll soon be over. You know Doctor Parker is very deaf, and he wouldn't know whether you said yes or no. Now, if there isn't anything else, I'll go down, for I hear more carriages coming, and I'll be needed. You're sure you don't want to see *him* before the ceremony."

"No," said Dawn, turning away from her with a quick gasp of her breath. Oh, if she need never see him, how happy she would be!

"Well, then, I'll go down. You be all ready when I call you to come. Now, mind you don't once raise your eyes until the ceremony is over and you are out in the dining-room. Above all things, don't look up at your husband even then. Nobody should see you look at each other. It makes them think you are foolish and silly."

"I shall certainly not look at him," said Dawn with white lips.

Then the step-mother went out of the room.

Dawn fastened the door and went quickly over to the stand, where the roses had been unnoticed by Mrs. Van Rensselaer. Had she seen them, it would have been like her to throw them out of the window, lest the water should upset on the white satin frock.

The girl bent over and breathed in their fragrance again, and then, carefully drying the stem on a towel, she slipped them up under her veil and fastened them upon her breast with a little pearl pin that had belonged to her mother. She went to her glass and viewed the effect through her veil, with a white, wan smile at the buds nestling among the beautiful lace. She would have one thing as she wanted it, any way: if she must be married, she would wear the flowers that had been given to her with a smile by somebody that understood. This was the last time she would have the right to wear another man's flowers. After to-day she would belong to her husband, but until she did she would wear the only flowers that had ever meant anything to her.

Then she closed her eyes and tried to get her spirit calmed, but she felt like one of those old queens in a tower that they used to study about at school: who was soon to go out and have her head cut off with the guillotine.

A few minutes later Mr. Winthrop again ascended the stairs to his wife's room.

"They want you to come down, Janet," he said gently. "Martha and the girls have come, and they are all waiting for you."

"I shall not come down until I have had a talk with my son Harrington," said that lady decidedly.

"Are you not coming down to the ceremony?" asked her husband. It went very hard with him to deceive the wife of his youth, but there seemed no other way to deal with her in the present situation.

"The ceremony?" She arose with alacrity. "What do you mean? Has Harrington come, and has he explained everything? It has turned out just as I supposed it would."

She stopped in front of the glass and smoothed her hair. She had arrayed herself in her best immediately after breakfast.

"I should think it was time an apology was due from you, Mr. Winthrop." Madam Winthrop stood haughtily in the middle of the room, aware that her small figure was elegant, and feeling that she had entire command of the situation. There was a becoming triumph in the brightness of her eyes and the set of her cameo lips.

"The wedding is to be at once," said her husband gravely, motioning her to precede him.

"What was Harrington's explanation?" she whispered, eager as any girl, now that she thought she had come off triumphant.

"There is no time to talk about it now," said her husband, again motioning her down the stairs.

She had a mind to make another stand before his grave authority, but in reality she was too much relieved from the awful strain she had been under during the past twenty-four hours for her to care to hold out against him longer. She went quietly down the stairs and took the place Mrs. Van Rensselaer most ungraciously assigned her. There was in that lady's eye something unquelled which gave the bridegroom's mother some uneasiness and took her mind from the ceremony, so that she failed to notice as the little procession passed by her almost immediately, that Harrington was not a part of it, and that her youngest son occupied the place of the bridegroom.

It was not until the clear voice rang out in the words, "I do," that something in the boyish accents made her look up and stretch her neck to see her son. How strange that Harrington's voice should sound so exactly like Charles's! But some one was standing so that the bridegroom's face could not be seen by her.

The little bride, with downcast eyes and palpitating heart, stood demurely by his side, her cold hands trembling within the gloves her step-mother had brought from New York for the occasion. One lay upon a fine black coat-sleeve that had put itself within reaching distance. She had not put the glove there herself. 'A hand, a strong, warm hand, had taken it and put it there, a hand that against her will had sent a strange thrill through her, and left her faint and frightened. That had been at the foot of the stairs, and she had walked with it thus down the room. She had not looked up to see to whom that sleeve belonged. She believed she knew, and it sent no pleasant thought to her heart. Yet she had to acknowledge that the arm had steadied her and kept her from stumbling, and had guided her safely into the vacant spot in front of the minister.

Dawn did not look beyond the hem of her garments, but kept her long lashes drooping on her crimson cheeks, a lovely but frightened bride. She felt keenly the moment the service began, and knew that she was surrendering forever her liberty and girlhood. Good-by to everything that she had ever counted happy in this life. No house, no pretty dishes, no handsome furniture, could ever make up for that now, and her heart cried out in anguish that she had not vetoed the idea when it was first proposed to her, before it had gone so far that retraction was dishonorable.

When the vows were read, and she heard their terrible binding import, she longed to cry out her horror in a great, echoing, *"No!"* that should have no doubt in any mind, and would even penetrate to the good minister's deaf ears. But her tongue was tied by fear of her father and his friends, and she dared not lift her voice. Yet she would not speak to make promises her heart could not echo, and so she stood silent, with no nod of her head, no breath of a "yes." The minister, after waiting an instant for the desired assent, passed monotonously and solemnly on to the end, and pronounced those two, who knew each of the other as little almost as it was possible for two human beings to know, man and wife.

During the prayer that followed, Dawn had hard work to keep back the tears that were struggling to creep out and cool her flushed cheeks; but the breath of the roses at her breast seemed to steal up and comfort her, and once, just before the end, a strong hand, warm and gentle, was placed over her gloved one for just an instant, with a pressure that seemed to promise help. Yet because she thought it was an unloved hand, it only made her heart beat the more wildly, and she was glad when the prayer was ended and the hand was taken away.

They came crowding about her after it was over, in the order of their rank, stiffly at first and with great formality. The bride still kept her eyes drooped, barely glancing up at those who took her hand or kissed her and never once lifting her eyes to the man who stood by her side. It was the first and only mandate of her step-mother's that she obeyed to the letter and to the end.

Mrs. Van Rensselaer gave her a cold kiss, and whispered that she was doing very well; and her father gave her the second kiss she could remember from him since he had sent her own mother away, and said in a low tone: "Poor child! I hope you will be happy now!"

She puzzled over that sentence long. Why had he called her "poor child," and yet seemed so sure by his tone that she had attained a height upon which happiness was assured? It touched her more than anything else that he had ever said to her.

Mr. Winthrop bowed low over Dawn's hand and told her he was glad to have another dear daughter, and Madam Winthrop, coming up from the side away from the bridegroom, graciously kissed her and called her a sweet child. Then she turned to meet her son, and stopped aghast, saying, "Charles! Where is Harrington?"

Now, Dawn might have heard the disturbance and been much enlightened, and all Mrs. Van Rensselaer's fine plans might have been exposed, if it had not been that Madeleine and Cordelia stepped up to their new sister-in-law close behind their mother, while Betty had rushed in and smothered her with kisses, whispering: "Oh, you darling sister! How I am going to enjoy you!" The three girls stood gushing and fluttering over the young bride, so that she did not hear what went on.

For, as it happened, Charles bent low over his mother, so that the stream of relatives should not hear, and said in a quiet voice:

"Mother dear, congratulate me instead of Harrington. It is I who have been married. Harrington has just gone away on the train with his wife and children. Don't feel sorry, little Mother. You would not let us tell you. Be careful, Mother; people are looking, watching you. Mother!"

But Madam Winthrop said not a word. Instead, her pretty cameo face went white as death, and she slipped quietly down at the feet of her husband and son in a blessed unconsciousness. For the sake of herself and all concerned, it was the best thing she could have done. What might have happened had she kept her senses, it is not pleasant to contemplate, for she was a person of strong will and a fiery temper, although cultured and beloved beyond most women of her day.

They said that the room was close, and she had fainted. They made way for her and brought fans and ice water, but her husband and her son quietly carried her from the room, and when Betty suddenly realized that something was going on, and turned around, they told her that her mother had fainted. Someone—an angular old maid, with a sarcastic twirl to her mouth and an unpleasant way of always saying the wrong thing at the right time—told Dawn she hoped it wasn't a bad omen that her husband had had to leave her side just when the ceremony was over. This was the first intimation that the young bride had had that her husband was gone. She cast a sidewise glance and discovered that there were ladies all around her. She raised her eyes again, just a little higher, and swept a wider circle, and finally cast a guarded glance about the entire room, but could not see the dreaded face. Then she drew a sigh of relief at this small respite. She heard some one say that he had gone to help his father take his mother upstairs. Dawn had a wild impulse to fly away where he could not find her when he returned, but knew she could not.

She would gladly have gone upstairs to wait on the sick mother, if only he were not there also.

People kept coming around to congratulate her, and saying how sad it was that Madam Winthrop's strength had given way at just that moment. Betty stayed close by, and Dawn dared to look at the other girl's sweet dimpled face, all pink and white, with heavenly blue eyes and golden hair. They reminded the bride of him whom she had seen in the garden that morning. It was a pleasant thought, and Dawn continued to watch Betty, when she was sure her step-mother was not looking at her.

By and by Mrs. Van Rensselaer passed behind her and whispered "They are coming downstairs now. Mrs. Winthrop is better. We will go out to the dining-room, and you must cut the wedding cake, you know. You are doing very well, only remember what I said: not to look around too much. A shy bride is the very best kind of bride."

A cold trembling came over the young wife. He was coming back, and a chill seemed to have crept into the sunny day. She hastily dropped her eyes, with the strange determination not to look upon her husband until absolutely compelled to do so. There seemed somehow a fascination to her keeping this up as long as possible.

When Charles came down and hastened to her side, she was talking earnestly with his Aunt Martha, who was telling a pretty little incident of Charles's babyhood. Dawn had not the faintest conception of who Charles was, but she nodded and smiled, and Aunt Martha thought her a sweet child, and took her immediately into her gentle heart. She was somewhat aghast at the manner in which events had marched into the family history that day, but she thought it not polite to mention it to Dawn.

A distant relative of Mr. Van Rensselaer came up just then and murmured is a disagreeable whisper:

"Your husband is a sight younger than I expected, Jemima! I had been led to expect he was quite a settled man, a good ten or fifteen years older'n you, but he's real handsome. You mustn't get proud, child."

Dawn started back as if she had been stung, and became aware at once of a black-coated figure standing close by her side.

She was grateful to the people who kept talking to her and to him, so that there would be no chance of his speaking to her, or of her having to answer him now. She felt it would be more than she could do, and look at him now she would not, not till she absolute must. It would unnerve her to look him the face and know that she was his wife, and that he had a right over her from hence= forth. Then, all at once, she heard his voice, and it was not Harrington's at all. A quick glance assured her it was her friend of the roses. Perhaps, then, Harrington was still upstairs with his mother. She drew a breath of relief.

A few mouthfuls of the wedding breakfast she managed to swallow, and she pushed a knife through the great white-coated fruit-cake, black with spice and all things good, which had been made when Mrs. Van Renssalaer first heard of the possibility of this marriage, and kept in ripening ever since. Dawn's step-mother was a fine housekeeper, and knew how to be ready for emergencies.

It was over at last, and Mrs. Van Rensselaer came to say that it was time for her to go upstairs and change her frock for the journey. Dawn had never before followed her step-mother with so much willingness as now. Her feet fairly kissed the oaken stairs as she mounted; but she had gone up only three steps when some one came quickly up and, standing by the stairs, touched her on the shoulder, saying in a voice that sent a thrill of joy through her:

"We're to go in the train; did you know it?"

Forgetting her vows and her step-mother's warnings, she looked down and saw that it was the young man of the garden again. Her face lit with a beautiful smile, and some people down in the hall, who were watching them, said one to another: "See how much they love each other, the dear children!" and turned away with a regretful smile and a sigh toward their own lost youth.

"Oh!" breathed Dawn. "I did not know it, but"— she paused—"I'm so glad you are going, too!"

In saying this, she had no thought of disloyalty to the man she thought she had married. It was merely the involuntary expression of her frightened heart that suddenly saw a rift in the dark cloud.

"Oh, so am I" he smiled. "And I'm glad you wore my roses next your heart. Put them on again when you come down, won't you?"

"I will," she promised, and let her eyes dwell on him for an instant; then fled up the stairs as her step-mother called in a voice intended to be a whisper:

"Jemima, do, for pity's sake, hurry! You will be late for the train, and then there'll be a great to-do."

Mrs. Van Rensselaer was in hot water lest the girl should learn the true state of affairs before she got away from the house. It had given the step-mother no small fright to see Charles talking with the girl over the railing. She looked at Dawn keenly, but there actually was some look of interest in the girl's eyes. Mrs. Van Rensselaer drew a sigh of relief as she hurried about to help the young wife with dressing.

## CHAPER XIII

THERE were no pleasant memories about the room Dawn occupied for her to look about upon for the last time, and bid good-by. Long ago Mrs. Van Rensselaer had cleared away every trace of her predecessor, by remodelling all the rooms, and taking for her own the large, sunny one which had been occupied by the child. If there had been memories left after the overhauling, they would have been made hateful by the new occupant. Dawn had been away from home so long that during this brief stay she had been given a guest-room, and now she turned from it without a glance, if anything, to get away from the place that had witnessed her deepest grief.

She would have liked to run down into the old garden and get one more glimpse of her woods, the ravine, the old mill, and the moss-covered dam, with the babbling brook in the distance, but that of course would be thought unpardonable; so she walked quietly downstairs, turning over in her mind the comfort it was that during the journey she was not to be entirely alone with the man she had married. She did not know where she was going. She had not cared to inquire which of several houses he had told her about had finally been purchased. She was going with him as any thoughtless child might have gone.

If only the step-mother had let what conscience she had guide her, and had told the girl the truth, many things might have been different. If allowed to hear the earnest profession of love from Charles Winthrop's lips, Dawn would undoubtedly have gone to him gladly, out of the shadow of horror that seemed about to engulf her. A sweet memory of her wedding morning would have been saved to her, and she would have been spared much pain. The step-mother might have kept her contented conscience, too, to the end of her days, and not been tormented with the thought that she had veered from the righteous path.

But Dawn did not know, and went down the stairs with a heavy heart, looking for only a brief alleviation of her trouble. She determined that she would not look at her husband, if possible, until this stranger was gone.

The little bustle of departure was over at last. They put her into the carriage, and still Harrington Winthrop had not appeared. She began to feel her heart beating wildly at the thought that he would soon be coming to sit beside her. Some one standing on the piazza asked where Mr. Winthrop had gone, and some one else said that his mother had sent for him, that she was conscious again and had wished to see him before he left. Dawn thought they were speaking of Harrington. She wished his mother

would keep him a long time, and then it occurred to her
that the train would go, and the young man with it
probably, and she would be left, after all, to take the
journey alone with her husband. Of course it would have
to be alone with him sooner or later, for the rest of her
life, but oh, how she dreaded it!

Then, to her inexpressible relief, Charles came rushing down the stairs, and some one called out a question
about his father:

"Is not Mr. Winthrop going to be able to get away
just to the station?"

Dawn again thought they were speaking of Harrington.

"Yes," said Charles; "he will be down in a moment.
He told me to drive on, and he would come in our carriage, which is here, you know."

With that, he jumped into the seat beside Dawn,
the servant fastened the carriage door, and the horses
started on their way down the curving carriage drive and
out through the great gate, with its two white balls on the
tops of the white pillars.

Dawn could scarcely believe it true that she was
going to the station without Harrington. His mother must
be very ill indeed, poor lady! Was it wrong to be glad,
she wondered, because it gave her another reprieve, brief
though it might be?

She had tucked the spray of roses into the bosom of
her travelling frock—a dark green silk, plaided with bars
of black, and a little black silk mantilla, which made
her feel quite grown-up, and which, Mrs. Van Rensselaer
had been assured by the New York merchants, was the
very latest thing for brides. A great, wide poke-bonnet of
white chip, trimmed with dark green ribbons and a
modest plume to match, framed her sweet face, and
helped to hide its shyness as she sat trembling happy at
her escape. Her hands, in pretty gray kid gloves, lay
meekly folded in her lap. Nothing about her demure
manner told of the tumult of emotions in her heart.

Beside her sat a friend—she knew that by the light
in his eyes. Before her was a brief ride to the inn where
the train stopped. It would last but a few minutes, and
during that time she would like to say something, to have

him say something, anything, just to feel the pleasant comradeship which she had seen in his eyes, that she might remember him always, her one friend. But her tongue was tied, and her eyes could not raise themselves to look upon his face any more than if he had been the dreaded husband.

Charles was kept busy for a minute or two, bowing to the guests who had lined themselves up along the driveway to see the couple depart. Dawn glanced shyly at them from her lowered lids, and smiled now and then as she recognized a relative or the kindly face of an old servant. Then the carriage passed out into the street, while her companion sat back very close to her, as if she needed him, and, reaching over, took one of her little cold hands in his strong, warm one. It brought comfort and a thrill of joy. Dawn did not stop to question if he had a right, or if she were doing wrong to allow such familiarity in a stranger, with her, a married woman, and belonging to another man. Such questions had not been brought up for her consideration, though she had a few fixed little principles of her own, sweet and fine and natural. But now she thought only on her great need, and how this strong hand met it. She longed to turn and fling her tired head upon his big, high shoulder and weep out her sorrow.

She did not do so, of course, but sat quietly with her hand enfolded in his for a moment, and dared to lift her sweet eyes to his. Then, without any warning, the tears, which had been repressed so long she had forgotten any danger from them, sprang into her eyes.

He thought her heart was tender with memories of the home she was leaving, and perhaps, he thought jealously, she was sighing for her false fiancé; but with a lover's true impulse, and in spite of the village street through which they were passing—although it happily chanced that this was a quiet part—he bent and kissed her.

An old lady out among her flowers in the front yard saw them, and nodded to herself: "Bless their dear hearts! May they always be so happy!" and brushed away a tear as she thought of a grave upon a hillside, and a day far agone when her own hopes were put beneath the ground.

It was a very short drive. Almost immediately after they had passed the old lady's house, they turned a corner which brought them into the liveliest part of the town, where people were stretching their necks to watch them, and all was stir and bustle. Only a few rods away stood the inn, with the railroad tracks gleaming in the distance. People were already gathering to watching for the incoming train; and some few to go a journey, though there were not so many travellers in those days.

With his kiss upon her lips and a tumult of strange joy in her heart, Dawn was handed from the carriage to the platform. Then her heat stood still with fear again, as she remembered who was to come in the other carriage, soon after them.

A part of the company had started on foot for the station, among them Betty Winthrop, and they now came trooping up around the bride and groom, with laughing talk of slippers and rice which they had reserved for the novelty of throwing at a train instead of a carriage.

Dawn was surrounded and taken possession of. She had no further opportunity to wonder, or to think, or to fear. But over her there hovered a sense of calamity, for with that kiss had come a consciousness that she was not being loyal to her own ideals of what a wife should be, and it troubled her more than had all her fears. Nevertheless, it had been sweet, and she kept trying to cast it aside with the thought that it was over forever now and she would have no further cause to err in this way again. Perhaps the kiss was sent to comfort her on the dreary way she had yet to go.

The other carriage drove up at last. It had been a long time coming, for Madam Winthrop had returned to consciousness only to fall from one fit of weeping into another, and then to blame the unfortunate girl, whom she called "that little scheming hussy," declaring that "she wasn't satisfied with leading astray a man of integrity like Harrington, but when she found it was impossible to make him swerve from his duty she had worked upon Charles's tender heart and made him marry her out of pity."

She was scarcely to blame, poor lady, for her nerves had been on a continual strain for many hours, and

when one took into account her extraordinary love for the
son who had left her when but a boy, and who faults she
had entirely overlooked, it was not strange. But it was
hard on her son Charles, and on her devoted husband,
whose love for her was deep, yet whose desire to make
everybody else happy and comfortable was also great.
It had been a trial to him, indeed, that she should behave
in this unseemly way in the house of his friend. He had
found it useless to talk with her or to try to pacify her, so
at last he left her with his sister until she should grow
calm, and hastened in the carriage to see the bridal couple
off. It had been arranged that Charles should bring his
young wife home for the present until further arrangements for their new life could be made.

Dawn's heart bounded with excitement when she
saw that no one was sitting in the carriage but the elder
Mr. Winthrop. She did not know whether to be glad or
sorry. If he did not come in time for the train, perhaps
her new friend would go on without them, and yet, after
what had happened, perhaps it was right that he should.
But her heart sank at the thought, and involuntarily she
left her eyes to drink in the strong, handsome outlines of
his face.

Charles Winthrop turned instantly and met the gaze
of his wife with a look of such deep love, reverence,
and tender care that it sent the color rushing to her
cheeks, and the blood bounding through her heart. It
seemed almost as if she were again on the point of tears,
so many emotions had followed one another through her
weary soul that morning; but just then there came a distant rumble, and they said the train was coming. Everybody rushed at Dawn at once and kissed her. Betty fairly
smothered her, saying "Oh, you dear, dear, *dear!* I shall
have you to-night at home!"

Then they hurried her to a seat in the railway carriage, and Charles sat down beside her. Nobody seemed
to think it strange that he had done so, and nobody said it
was too bad her husband was detained. They did not
even seem to be looking for him, and wondering why he
was not there. Dawn was bewildered and fairly held her
breath, wondering if it could be possible that she was to
start off on her wedding journey without the bridegroom.

Though she had not been to many weddings, she knew
enough to feel that her situation was a strange one. The
only explanation she could think of was that his mother
had been so ill that he had to remain with her for a time,
and would come later and explain. But even then it made
her heart sink to think that he should have cared so little
for her embarrassment that he had sent her no word. It
augured ill for the future. Nevertheless, she was conscious
of a great relief that he had not come, and a great comfort
in the presence of this other man.

There was a good deal of fun and confusion when at
last the train started, with a showering of rice and old
slippers, and a stretching of necks from the other carriages
to see what it was all about. But they were soon under
way, and Dawn sat back with intense delight to enjoy
the new sensation of a railway ride, without the expected
attendant inconvenience of an unloved husband. It was
perhaps not ideal, but she could not help it, and when
one's heart has been breaking slowly for weeks and rapidly for the last few hours, it is but nature to let it throb on
naturally for a few minutes if it will. How could she help
being happy? The sky was blue, blue; the bits of water
they glimpsed far away, the winding ribbon of the river
in the distance, were blue also. The trees seemed fairly to
spread themselves in the summer sunshine, and the whole
world looked washed anew for happiness, basking in the
sunlight of heaven. The birds that flew away at sound of
the strange creature that went rumbling through the
country, the sleepy cows that gazed deligently upon the
hillsides, the dull sheep that raised unwondering eyes and
bleating voice at the moving monster, all seemed new
creations to the girl. She cried out with delight at everything, and Charles entered into her joy.

It was not Charles's first ride upon a train, therefore
when she asked some question about their wonderful
mode of travel he fell to explaining it all carefully to her,
with a learned manner that fascinated her, and before
she knew it she was watching his face and his eyes, and
her heart was glowing with the thought of him. Then he
suddenly caught her hand that lay in her lap, and, taking
its forefinger between his own thumb and finger, her hand
enclosed in his, he made it point to a tiny white house

nestled upon a hillside far away, with a glimpse of water in the distance and a shelter of feathery trees all about.

"There! See there!" he cried. "Do you see that house up there? How would you like it if you and I lived there?"

Instantly that little house seemed to Dawn a very heaven of peace, to which she would gladly fly from the grander house that she thought awaited her at the end of her journey. She caught her breath and pressed her free hand hard upon her frightened, happy heart, and cried, "Oh! Oh!" so wistfully that he stooped and kissed her once, and then again, and whispered, "Darling! My darling!"

They were alone in their carriage, you remember, and as the train was not then going round a curve, but was sleepily jogging through a lovely wooded place, no one in any of the other carriages could see.

Dawn felt the thrill of his touch go through her again, and then her conscience roused, and she drew herself away, quite shyly, and not at all as if she were angry. Her cheeks were crimson under her drooping lashes.

Her lover watched her adoringly. He was shy himself, and felt that maybe he had gone too far in a public place like a railway carriage; but she had been so charming, and was she not his?

Then her trembling lips brought out a question which shot a pang of jealous pain through his heart.

"Won't you tell me—please—where is—m'—where is——" She hesitated painfully, wishing he would understand and finish the sentence for her; but he only looked down anxiously, trying to understand what she wanted.

"Won't you please tell me where—Mr. Winthrop is?"

He understood at once that she did not mean his father, but his scoundrel brother. His face shadowed with a frown. Was she, then, thinking only of him who had tried to cover her with shame and disgrace? And would it always be so, that she would hark away from his love to that which had gone before? He sighed impatiently, but tried to answer her gently, a strange pity in his voice:

"I thought they had told you. It was strange they did

not. He took the train at once. He found it was necessary, you understand."

"Oh!" There was immense relief in Dawn's exclamation, and the color came back to her cheeks, which had grown pale with apprehension when she asked the question.

"Then he will not come on this train at all?" she asked, and a light broke into her eyes.

"You poor child!" said he gently. "Were you afraid of that?" He laid his hand over hers comfortingly.

"I have been so tired and so frightened," murmured Dawn; and now she had to let the tears come rolling down her cheeks, though she tried hard enough to keep them back. But somehow she felt he would understand it all, and she lay back and let him wipe them away with his large, cool handkerchief that smelled of rose-leaves; and between the tears he laid a kiss now and then that seemed like healing ointment to her sore heart, so she no more tried to contend with her conscience as to what was right for married women to do in such circumstances. She only knew she had found some one who acted toward her as she remembered her dear mother doing. The kisses seemed such as an angel's might be, if an angel stooped to kiss. So she ceased trying to understand, and just took the comfort of it. Perhaps it had been sent to her to help her in her time of need. Remember, she was very young, and had been facing a great terror.

They presently trundled out of the woods into a little village, and the comforting had to cease. Dawn sat up with rosy cheeks and bright eyes, the tears all gone, and looked about her with interest. They talked in low tones of the people they saw come and go on the platform, and laughed at a couple of geese who were squawking and gabbling at the train for coming so close to their nice mud-puddle by the track, putting in a natural protest against the march of civilization.

But an old lady with many bandboxes and a carpetbag was put into their coach just before the train started on its way again, and there could be no more quiet confidences. Dawn had thought she would presently ask a few more questions about her husband, and why he had

found it necessary to take another train. Most of all, she
wanted to know when and where she was to meet him.
But now there was no more opportunity to ask questions.

At Albany, they waited for the stage-coach, and
walked about exploring the city, more absorbed in their
own pleasant converse than in sight-seeing, however.

"Do you know, they have never told me your name.
I heard it first in the ceremony this morning," said
Charles, with a smile. "It is strange, isn't it? But we have
had so little time, and before that I was away, and they
always wrote of you as 'Miss Van Rensselaer.' I never
asked your name because I liked to think of you as I saw
you first, all spring blossoms, like some spirit of the air,
and I thought a name might destroy the vision."

The pink came softly into the girl's cheek at his
earnest words, and it filled her heart with a glow of
pleasure like to nothing she had ever felt before.

"They wouldn't have told you my real name if you
had asked," said she, showing her dimples in a smile
answering to his. "I was christened Jemima, but my mother, my own dear mother, who died a good many years
ago, told me my name was Dawn, and she always called
me that. She wouldn't consent to my being named Jemima
until she found out that the meaning of it was 'Dawn of
the Morning,' and she always called me that. I always
made everybody at school call me so too. They did not
know the other name at school. I love the name because
my mother loved it, and said it meant something sweet
and dear to her."

She looked up, and the eyes she met were full of
sweet understanding.

"Dawn! What a beautiful name! How glad I am it is
that! It just fits you as I saw you first. You might have
been personifying Dawn. You shall be the Dawn of my
morning always."

They were in sight of the stage-coach now, and as
they saw that the driver was preparing to start, they had
to hurry to it, so they had no further opportunity to talk;
but each had been given a vision into the heart of the
other.

Dawn was still ignorant of where she was going, and
as she sat in the coach and saw others climbing in to fill

the seats, she suddenly realized that there would be no more opportunity now for the questions she should have asked while they were walking. But she had hesitated to spoil their pleasant walk, and had dismissed her fears and troubles, entering into the spirit that Charles had seemed to manifest.

As he sat close beside her through the long miles, his arm rested against hers, and now and again came a gentle pressure, as if he would let her know he was there. Then the remembrance of his lips upon hers swelled over her in a mingling of remorse and joy, and her heart cried out to itself, "Oh, I love him! I love him! What shall I do? If I only were not married, perhaps I might have him for a friend. I never had a real friend. But now, I suppose, I can never see him any more."

By and by, when they stopped to change horses, Charles found seats for them on the top of the coach with the driver. It was lovely up there, with a wide view of the beautiful country through which they were riding, and no one to bother them; for the old coach driver was not of a garrulous disposition, as most of those worthies were, and they had their talk to themselves. Still, he was there, and Dawn dared venture no more confidential questions.

The day drew to a close, and they came to the last change of horses before reaching the home of the Winthrops.

## CHAPTER XIV

"We are almost home," said Charles joyously. He felt that it was a very happy moment.

"Oh, are we going to your home?" she asked, catching her breath and wondering what that meant.

"Why, yes, didn't you know? I supposed Mrs. Van Rensselaer would tell you all the plans. She said you did not wish to come down to talk them over beforehand."

"I know," said Dawn, a shadow creeping over the happy face. "I could not." She looked at him with appealing eyes, as if she knew he would understand.

"I understood," he answered her. "You had been through too heavy a strain, a shock——" He paused.

She looked puzzled, and wondered how he knew that her marriage was a shock to her. Was it because his eyes understood her from the first? Was it a kind of spirit understanding spirit? Dawn was not a philosopher, but something like this flashed through her thoughts.

"But she told me nothing. Indeed, I did not ask. Perhaps it was my fault," she added.

"Certainly not," said Charles vehemently. "It was her business to tell you the plans. I expressly asked her to do so after we had them all arranged. I asked her to see if they had your approval. I should not have made any arrangements without it."

"Oh!" Dawn had never had her approval of anything asked in her life. She could scarcely understand why it should be done. It was very nice, but how and why did this delightful person seem to have had the arranging of her plans? It was all a mystery, but she could not ask about it now before the coach driver. Perhaps the future would unravel the mystery.

"Just how much did she tell you, any way?" asked Charles, lowering his voice as much as possible, to make it confidential without actually putting it beyond the hearing of the driver.

Dawn considered.

"Why, I don't really think she told me anything," she said at last, half apologetically, "except how to behave during the ceremony. I think it was my fault, I really do. She said I ought to go down and talk it over, but I said I didn't need to go, that I wanted to be by myself at the last. I suppose she thought I didn't care about the arrangements. I never thought I had anything to do with them, any way. I thought that was all fixed, like everything else."

There was a sad little droop to the corners of her red lips, which gave Charles's heart an unhappy twinge. The driver turned a suspicious eye toward them, and they sat silent for a while, Charles thinking it over, and being

somehow depressed that she should feel so about their
marriage. To her, of course, it must be somewhat of a
forced thing, but to him it had been all joy until now
when he was suddenly brought face to face with the
situation as he thought he saw it.

Dawn was going over sadly all their bright beautiful
day together, and thinking, wondering, how near it was
to the end, and whether she would ever see this dear
companion again. She treasured every moment of his
company, even when they were silent together; every
glance, every syllable, yes, every kiss and gentle touch of
his hand; even while she dimly perceived (and chided
herself) that this was not the right attitude for a bride of
a few hours to have toward a man who was not her husband. But to her it was like stolen sunshine to a lifetime
prisoner. She felt she must take it, as it would never pass
her way again. All the same, her conscience was beginning
to trouble her, for she was naturally a right-minded girl,
and, in spite of the fact that her ideals of married life
were not as some girls', she had her own ideas of what
should be. She turned toward him suddenly:

"I want to tell you how much I thank you for this
beautiful day," she said, her heart in her eyes. "It is the
best day I ever had—I mean our part of it. I was afraid I
might not have another chance to tell you."

The dusk was growing deeper now, and dim lights
ahead showed that a town was not far away. Charles
reached out his hand and took hers gently in his own,
hiding them both under his coat on the seat between
them. The driver was looking the other way, hunting for
his big tin horn, wherewith to announce his approach
somewhere, and had not seen.

"Dear! You dear!" Charles murmured softly in her
ear. "But there'll be plenty of chances to tell me everything soon now."

"Oh, will there?" she said joyfully. "I was afraid
there wouldn't be."

"Did you think we were going to spend our days in
a coach?" he laughed.

Dawn's hand trembled in the big, comforting grasp,
and longed to settle down and take strength from it; but
she knew she ought to put a stop to this, and she sat

shrinking and pondering how to draw away her hand without offending her kind friend, who, in spite of his frank, true eyes, seemed not to have a thought but that the course he was pursuing was perfectly right and proper. It all puzzled her, more and more as she felt the approach of the moment when she must meet her unwelcome bridegroom.

A long blast on the driver's horn sent a startled shock through her slender frame, and instantly Charles's grasp on the little, timid hand tightened, as if he would enfold her in his greater strength and soothe her fears. She was glad it was dark, for she was sure there were tears in her eyes; yet she dared not lift her other hand to wipe them away, lest he see her.

With a swirl and a lurch the coach turned in at an open gateway and drove furiously up to a wide farmhouse on a hill behind a circle of elm trees. The driver jumped down and began to unfasten a trunk from behind. Dawn could not see whether it was her own or not, but she took heart from the fact that Charles sat still and steadily held her hand, and that other people were climbing out of the coach below, and talking to a man and woman who came out of the big hall door in a stream of light to greet them. This was not her new home yet, then. There were still a few moments more of grace before her doom should fall. Now she must know. It was her only chance. In a moment more the driver would be back beside them, and perhaps the next stop would end their ride.

She leaned over close to Charles and whispered in his ear: "Tell me quick before the driver comes back: will *he* be there?" The tears were trembling on her lashes. She was glad she was not on the side of the coach next to the house.

"Will who be there, dear?" murmured Charles, marvelling at the sweetness of having her so close to him.

"Oh, don't you know?" she said desperately, as if it hurt her to speak the name. "Why—my—Mr. Winthrop —Mr. Harrington Winthrop."

It was a pitiful attempt to put into the name the dignity that her position as wife demanded. She was scarcely more than a little girl, and her situation was terrible to her.

Charles started and looked down at her. Was she still wanting to see the man who had sought to do her so terrible an injury, or was she dreading to see him? He looked at her and saw fear written in her eyes, and his heart was touched. However she might have felt toward Harrington before, of course now she dreaded having to meet him after what he had done. But whatever had put into her head the idea that he would be there? How strange of Mrs. Van Rensselaer not to have told her that Harrington had gone away on the train with his wife!

"No, he will not be there!" he said almost harshly. "I doubt if he is ever there again."

There was something in his tone that Dawn could not understand, but she must find out quickly what it all meant, though she was trembling now from head to foot, and scarcely knew what question to ask next. It was all so strange and mixed up.

"Then, where—where will I have to meet him?" she asked, grasping his arm with her free hand and watching his face as if her very life depended upon the answer.

Charles looked down at her, his whole soul in his eyes.

"Never, dear, never. I will guard you from that, at least."

"Oh, why!" cried Dawn, more than ever bewildered by his words. "Why—but, how can you? Hasn't he the right? Wasn't I married to him this morning? Nobody can keep us apart now, can they? The minister said, 'Till death do you part!'" A long, slow shudder passed over her as she spoke, and though her words were low, lest some one hear, her tone was like the cry of one who had given up for lost.

Forgetting the people who were clattering joyous welcomes below, Charles put his arm close about her, as if he were shielding her from a present terrible danger. He looked into her face and spoke in low, firm tones:

"I don't just seem to understand you, dear, but you mustn't be so frightened. There isn't anything in the world to be afraid of. I will try to make everything just as you want it——"

"But how can you?" Dawn's breath came in short sobs. She was almost at the limit of her self-control. "Will he let you? Will it be right?"

"Dear, listen! I don't know what you mean by some of the things you have said. I'm afraid all the trouble has upset you. Perhaps you have a fever——"

"No! No!" said Dawn, almost impatiently, for she saw that the driver had landed the trunk on the piazza and was preparing to come back to the coach, and that some of the passengers were climbing in again. There would be but a moment more.

"It is I that do not understand," she added, and her voice was very steady. She felt as if she must make her meaning plain now. "I was married to him this morning, and now he is gone away somewhere, and you say I need never see him again. He went away just after the ceremony. They said his mother fainted and he took her away. I have not seen him since. What does it all mean? I do not understand. It is like some awful dream."

Charles's heart sank in horror as he listened to her words. Had she lost her mind, or, more awful yet, had she in some mysterious way been married to him without knowing it? The latter seemed almost incredible, yet if it were true, what sorrow might it not mean to them both! Poor child! He must be very gentle with her, whatever were the case. And meantime the driver's foot was upon the wheel.

Charles leaned over as if to tuck the linen robe about her to protect her from the dust, and whispered:

"You were not married to him at all. Don't you remember?"

"Do you mean I was not married, then? But I heard the minister say the words, 'I pronounce you husband and wife, and what God hath joined——' " Dawn shuddered again. "I heard it. I didn't look up, but I heard it. You needn't be afraid to tell me the truth. I will not cry or anything."

The driver plumped down on the seat with a loud laugh at some joke the old farmer was getting off, and vowed he would be late if they kept him any longer, that he must go around by Applebee's and Deacon Forsythe's yet, and it was almost dark. Then with another hearty laugh he chirruped to his horses, and they strained and started, and with a lurch and a swirl of the coach they were flying down the stony road to the gate again, and there was no more opportunity to talk unheard.

Dawn braced herself to endure the awful uncertainty that her question had put into tangible form, and Charles, as he took hold of the little trembling hand once more with a reassuring pressure, sought in his mind for something to say which should calm her fears and at the same time not enlighten the driver as to their subject of conversation.

"Don't worry," he said in a tone that tried to be light and gay. "I'll explain it all as soon as we get home. Meantime, do you want to be told where we are?" and he launched into a voluble description of the people who dwelt along the road.

Dawn understood, and kept silent except for a monosyllable now and then, to keep up appearances before the driver, and presently the coach halted again before the gate of another farm-house, where the gleaming candles from the many-paned windows testified to the comfort of the inhabitants. To their relief, the driver jumped down again to deliver a big package, and they had another moment to talk.

"Wasn't I married at all, then? Tell me quick, please," she pleaded, the minute the driver had left them.

"Yes, but not to Harrington," he said gravely. He had not yet decided how he ought to tell her or whether he had not better wait until they were at home, lest it make her ill. It seemed so strange for her to talk in this way. He paused an instant, and looked keenly into her face, but the light from the coach lantern did not shine in the right way for him to see her clearly, and it was dark now. He did not see the wave of relief that swept over her anxious face.

"Oh!" she gasped, as if a great burden had suddenly been lifted from her and she could breathe the free air again. "Oh!" And for a minute she could think of nothing else save that she was free from the man she had come to dread almost more than death. How it came about, or what else might have happened, must stand in abeyance until she could take in this great, soul-reviving truth. She was not married to Harrington Winthrop!

Charles waited an instant, and then, seeing that the driver would soon be back, and that Dawn was not going to ask a question to help him on, he spoke again.

"Don't you remember, Dawn"—his voice lingered over the name, the first time he had used it, and it went through her heart with a wonderful thrill—"don't you remember that you and I were married this morning?"

"Oh, was it you?"

Dawn's face shone up at him out of the darkness, but he dared not interpret the look. The driver suddenly jumped up on the seat and started the horses on again, but Dawn clasped her hands close about his arm and clung to him in the darkness, her whole soul surging with gladness.

He held her arm close to him within his own, but his heart was beating anxiously to know what effect this would have upon her, and whether she remembered now. At last she ventured the question—for how could the driver attach any significance to such simple words:

"Are you sure?"

"Sure!" he answered gravely, and added as if he could not keep the words back: "Are you glad or sorry?"

"Oh, glad, glad!" instantly came the words, and then they said no more, but let the joy and the wonder of it sweep over them. They were both very young and very happy just then, and what are hows and whys to such as they?

The lights of the village grew closer, and beamed past them, and in a moment more, with a rattle and flourish, they drew up before the old Winthrop house, a beautiful colonial structure, with lights in all the windows and a festive air about it that made all the passengers in the coach look out and wonder. A shout of laughter, and "Here they come!" was heard from the house, and Betty, in white, with blue ribbons all in a flutter, came flying down the path of light from the open door to greet them.

"I'll explain it all when we get by ourselves, dear," whispered Charles, leaning over her again, as if to see if she was leaving any baggage behind. "Don't worry. Just be happy."

"Oh, I will!" laughed Dawn joyously. "But how did it ever come to be true?" And then as she got down from the coach she was instantly smothered in Betty's open arms.

## CHAPTER XV

"Do they all know and understand?" whispered Dawn to Charles, as they turned to walk up to the house, Betty fluttering ahead carrying Dawn's hand-bag and silk cape.

"Yes, they all know and understand, dear. It is all right," said Charles reassuringly.

Old Mr. Winthrop stooped and kissed her as she came up the steps, and said, "Welcome home, daughter!" Cordelia and Madeleine, too, made her warmly welcome. Just behind them stood Aunt Martha, with arms spread wide to receive her in a motherly embrace.

"Mother is lying down, resting now," explained Betty, "and sent word she would see you after supper."

They bore Dawn off to the second story, where Betty took entire possession of her and showed her the rooms they had hastily prepared; for of course Harrington had not intended bringing his prospective bride home, and Betty and her sisters had had much ado to put things in bridal array after their own arrival home from the wedding.

"We'll get some of these pictures and things out of your way to-morrow, so you will have room for your own things, but we hadn't much time to-night, you know. We got home only two hours ahead of you, if we did come by a shorter cut. Horses cannot travel as fast as railroad trains, I guess," chattered Betty. "Do you think you will be comfortable to-night? Or, I could take some more things out, if you want to unpack your own," she added anxiously.

Dawn looked around on the exquisitely appointed rooms. The great bedroom, with high-canopied bed; curtains and valance of blue-flowered chintz to match the window draperies; the wall-paper of dreamy landscapes, with hazy blue skies, and rivers winding like blue ribbons among sunny hills; the fine old mahogany furniture; the little glow of fire in the open fireplace, with the great, stuffed, chintz-covered chair drawn up before it—all seemed like heaven to her.

Through the open door one entered a hastily improvised private sitting-room. The girls had had the furniture taken from the connecting bedroom, and in its place had put a desk, reading-table, chairs, and bookcase of mahogany. Candles burned brightly everywhere in silver candlesticks, with tall glass candle-shades over them. Some books and papers were scattered on the table, and a comfortable chair stood ready for some one to occupy. The rooms could not have been more home-like. And all this was for her and—him! She caught her breath with the happiness of it, and a pink tinge stole into her cheeks.

"Do you think you can be happy here?" Betty asked anxiously.

"Oh, happier than I ever was in my life!" cried Dawn. "Only, it seems too beautiful to be true. It seems as if I was dreaming;" and in a pretty little way she had when she was surprised and pleased, she clasped her hands over her heart.

"Oh, I'm so glad!" said Betty. "And let me whisper a secret: I always loved Charles more than Harrington. Charles is a dear!"

Dawn's eyes shone with her deep joy.

"Oh, do you?" was all she could say, but she wished she dared tell Betty that she was a dear also.

Then her little sister-in-law went away and left her to wash her hands and smooth her hair for supper, and in a moment Charles came in.

Dawn stood in the middle of the room, looking about, her eyes shining, the firelight glimmering over her dark hair and bringing out the green lights in the silk frock she wore. She looked so young and sweet and dear as she stood there alone, taking in the picture of her new home, that Charles paused to watch her, and then came softly up and folded his arms reverently about her, drawing her close. It was a long, beautiful moment of perfect bliss, the memory of which stayed with the two through all that came afterward. Then their lips met and sealed the sacredness of their union.

But Betty's voice broke in upon the joy:

"Charles, the supper is getting cold, and you know I told you to bring her down at once. Come quick!"

Reluctantly they prepared to go.

"One minute, Betty!" Charles called. "I must wash my hands first!"

"Charles, you know you are just admiring your wife, and not hurrying a bit," called back saucy Betty. "Do make haste. I want to admire her myself."

"Before we go down, Dawn, I must say one word. Don't let them know anything about your not knowing. They think that you understood it all and were willing. I can't see how it happened. Mrs. Van Rensselaer went upstairs last night to tell you all about Harrington, and to take my offer to you, and when she came down she said you wanted to think it over."

The deep color came in Dawn's cheeks, and the flash into her eyes.

"She did not speak to me last night after you came," she said.

"But in the morning, after I saw you in the garden—did she tell you nothing then?"

"She only talked to me about the wedding, and told me I must not look up during the ceremony, that it was not nice. That seemed to be the only thing she cared about."

"Didn't she tell you at all about Harrington?"

"Not a word, except that I ought to go down and talk with him before the ceremony? Was he asking for me?"

The dark eyes took on their frightened look.

Charles frowned heavily behind the big damask towel with which he was drying his face.

"Never mind, dear. Harrington has behaved outrageously, but we will not talk about it now. I'm ashamed to call him my brother."

"Oh! He is your brother, isn't he?" said Dawn, suddenly perceiving the fact. "Of course!"

"Didn't you know even that? What could the woman have been thinking about? What object could your mother possibly have had in not telling you everything?"

"Charles!" Betty's voice was insistent now.

"Yes, Betty. Just ready," answered Charles impatiently.

"She is not my mother, you know, and she never liked me," said Dawn, in a low voice, as if she were ashamed of it all.

"Never mind, dear; let's forget it now, and be happy.

He stooped and drew her face against his for just an instant, and then they went out to the impatient Betty.

Downstairs it was all gaiety and brightness. Once Charles said with a soft light in his eyes, "I'm sorry Mother couldn't be down to-night. How is she feeling now?" and Dawn looked at him in awe and love, and thought how beautiful it was to have a mother that one longed to have about.

"Your mother will be all right in the morning, I think," answered his father, with just a tinge of sadness in his voice; and a quietness settled over them all for a moment. Dawn thought it was because they loved her so much and were sorry she was sick.

"We didn't ask any of the neighbors in to-night, because we thought you would be so tired, and it would be better to wait till you were rested, so we could have a real party and do things up nicely, not in such a hurry. They don't even know yet that Charles is married, you know."

Betty's voice gushed into the pause that had come in the conversation, as if she wished to fill it quickly, no matter with what.

"Yes, that's right," approved Charles. "We don't want a lot of folks around. We just want you folks for a while."

After supper Cordelia took Dawn up to their mother's room.

Dawn's heart beat high with hope. She had caught but a glimpse of Charles's mother that morning, and did not remember clearly how she looked. The young bride's heart went out to her with a double love, because her own lost mother had been so dear.

Mrs. Winthrop was lying in a great bed with a rose-colored canopy. The bed-curtains were of white starched dimity, and the white linen all about her made her look like some delicate flower in an elaborate vase. The canopy threw sea-shell tints on the delicate complexion that had not darkened in spite of years, and the rosy light from the open fire on the other side of the room played over her beautiful white hair that was carefully arranged in curls on her cheeks. The bed-gown she wore was of homespun linen, fine and elaborate in make; her small, patrician hands were glowing with rare jewels. The delicate face was that of a beautiful woman; beautiful yet, in spite of the fact that she had grown old; beautiful and proud, yet lovable. She looked like some rare bit of Dresden china, perfect of its kind, and perfectly cared for. Dawn paused on the threshold shyly and admired her. Then she came forward at Cordelia's introduction, but, instead of taking the delicate hand that was held out coldly to greet her, she stooped over impulsively and kissed her new mother. She had never done such a thing to any one since her own mother died, but she wanted to give her best to Charles's mother, she was so glad to-night.

"Sit down," the high-bred voice commanded politely. "Yes, there in the chair where I can see you. Cordelia, you need not remain."

Dawn sat down, and there was a pause until the door closed after Cordelia. Somehow, the young wife's heart began to sink a little. The room looked so very large, the bed was so high and big, the beautiful old lady so small and far away, and her smile was so like a picture.

Madam Winthrop turned her handsome eyes with an uncordial coolness upon her new daughter-in-law, and looked her through. She was a loving and lovable woman at times, but she did not seem so now.

"I have sent for you"—she spoke the words with

deliberation and incisiveness—"to tell you that I forgive you."

Dawn gasped, and looked at her in amazement; but the lady paid no heed to her, only further to fix her with her eyes, and went on:

"I did not think it would be possible at first, but I have conquered my feelings, and am now willing to forgive you."

Dawn could do nothing but look at the woman in horror. Her tongue seemed tied. At last she stammered out:

"For what?"

"That is an entirely unnecessary question," said the cool voice. "You surely know how much trouble you have made. It is absurd to ignore it, or try to gloss it over. It seems strange that one so young as you should have had the power to make my poor, impulsive boy forget his duty. You should have known—but, then, I have forgiven you, and I will say no more about that. You are very beautiful, I must admit, and Harrington was always one who admired beauty, but I feel sure that of himself he would never have gone as far as he did. However, as I say, we will not talk of that. I have forgiven it, together, of course, with your other offences. And it is of the consequences of those that I feel it my duty to speak to you."

Dawn sat watching her, fascinated as is a bird sometimes when it keeps its eyes on a cat and is unable to move. It seemed to her she would scream if she only had the power, but the power of speech was gone for the time being.

"You know, of course, that Charles is very young. He isn't really a full-grown man yet. He hasn't finished his college course. You ought to understand that you must in no way interfere with his life, to spoil it. It ought to be enough for you that you have accepted his generous offer, when he was sorry for your being jilted by his brother, and kindly offered to take his place so as to save you from the mortification of having no wedding. I haven't an idea that Charles really expected you to think of it for a moment, but he is warm-hearted and always ready to offer help in any distress. It would have been far more seemly in you to decline the offer, and in your people to insist upon your doing so, if you did not know enough to do it yourself. But that is now too late to mend, so we will not speak of it, and, as I have said, I have fully forgiven it. What is unalterable is always best forgiven, if possible. What I wish to say is this:

"Having married my son under these most extraordinary circumstances, it becomes you to be most modest and retiring, and hereafter to put aside every personal consideration, in order that he may not be held back from his natural ambitions. I hope you get my meaning?"

A crimson flush had been stealing up into Dawn's cheeks, and the steel lights were coming into her eyes, but she was unable as yet to make any reply. The cool elder voice went on with the torture:

"I am willing, as I say, to forgive you, but I shall expect from you docility and a willingness to be guided by me in everything. As long as you remain in my house, which will, of course, be at least as long as my son remains in college, and as much longer as he deems wise afterward. I thought it was best for you to understand everything thoroughly at the start. Having robbed one of my sons of his happiness, and robbed me of the other one, it is becoming that you should walk circumspectly in every way. I have, of course, forgiven you. But it is a terrible thing which you have done——"

"Stop!"

Dawn sprang to her feet, her hands clasped, her face white with anger, the lightning in her eyes.

"You are saying things that are not true! You are blaming me for what I have not done. I will not hear another word of it. I did not want to marry your son Harrington. He came after me while I was in school and tormented me to marry him. Afterward, he told my father and made him think it was all fixed between us and Father wrote and gave his consent, and they planned the wedding and everything without asking me a thing about it. I did not want to go home, because I was frightened. I did not want to be married. I knew Father would be angry if I should break it off after everything was arranged. He is very proud, and has a terrible temper. But I dreaded it so that I was almost crazy.

"I don't know yet how it came about that Harrington

didn't come to the wedding. No one has told me, and I hadn't thought to ask, I was so glad to find I wasn't married to him. I didn't know anything about being married to your other son. I thought I was being married just as it was planned to—to Harrington. I don't know how that happened either. I haven't had time to ask Charles yet. I just found out a few minutes ago that he and I had been married."

"That is a highly improbable story," began the astonished woman in the bed. "You will not gain anything by telling me tales like that. Nothing but the strict truth is ever spoken in this family. You will only bring trouble upon yourself by telling what is not true. Besides, you certainly know that I would not believe a thing like that. In the first place, why shouldn't you want to marry Harrington? He certainly is as good as you are. And the very idea that a girl in her senses could be married without her own consent! It would be impossible to be married and not know it."

Dawn stood quite still for a full minute, surveying her antagonist. The beautiful color had flown into her cheeks again at mention of untruth, but, as was her wont in moments of great provocation, she had herself under perfect control. The elder woman acknowledged to herself that the girl was very beautiful, and lay there watching her victim with a degree of satisfaction she would not have felt, could she have known what was passing in the girl's mind.

Dawn's voice was clear and controlled when she spoke again. All excitement seemed to have gone out of it, but every word went straight to the mark like sharp steel:

"You say I have robbed you of your son. You may have him back again at once. I did not ask him to marry me, and I cannot stay in your house if you doubt my word. I shall never trouble either of you again."

She turned swiftly and silently and went out of the room, closing the door noiselessly behind her. The old lady lay still in blank astonishment. For any one to speak to her in that manner was unprecedented. To disappear and leave no opportunity for rebuke was outrageous. She felt helpless and outgeneraled. Not in years had her superiority been so rudely set aside as during this whole affair. For the moment she was bewildered, and lay thinking it over, unable even to make up her mind whether or not she should pull the bell rope and call some of the family, to tell what had happened. Truth to tell she was mortified that her well-laid plan had ended so ignominiously.

Dawn went swiftly across the hall to the door of her own room, which she had left so joyously a short hour before.

The candles had burned low, but the firelight was flickering softly over everything, and made the room look a very haven of comfort. The poor child searched it furtively now, to make sure that no one was there. For just a moment she stood in the middle of the room, looking about, her hands clasped tragically over her heart, her eyes full of unspoken agonies. The whole ugly import of the new mother's words swept over her and seemed as if it would overwhelm her. Then she girded herself to carry out the resolution she had formed, her proud nature stung to the quick.

On the big white bed lay her bonnet and mantle. It was the work of but a moment to put them on, though her fingers trembled so that she could scarcely tie the ribbons under her chin.

Charles had unfastened her trunk before he went down to supper, and set it open for her. There on the top, where she had slipped it in after her step-mother had shut the trunk and gone downstairs, lay the sombre gray frock she had worn at Friend Ruth's school. She had put it in with sudden impulse, as being the only thing she had left of her girlhood. Mrs. Van Rensselaer had seen to it that her step-daughter's outfit was perfect, as befitted the daughter of her father. No Winthrop should criticise her for lack of elaborate and costly outfit. But the gray dress which had been cast aside was the one Dawn had worn afternoons at the school, and it reminded her of pleasant days among the girls, with care-free thoughts—a little gray girlhood, which had nevertheless become bright in comparison to the new life. She snatched the gray frock, and in it wrapped a few light articles she felt she might need, taking only necessities, and of those but few. These she rolled tightly in the frock, pinned the bundle firmly, saw that it could be hidden under her mantle, caught up her hand-bag which contained a purse with twenty-five dollars which her father had put into her hands when she left home, and was ready.

She had not stopped to think how she was going to get out of the house without being seen. A glance out of the front window showed a balcony with a wrought-iron railing, which hung inside the white pillared front piazza, but Charles and his father sat just below, talking in low, pleasant voices. She could not get out that way. Equally impossible, of course, would be the front door, even if she could get through the hall without Betty's seeing her.

With one long look down at Charles, she put out a protesting hand toward him, as if bidding him farewell. It wrung her heart to look at him. She turned quickly away, paused an instant in the middle of the room, and swept it with her eyes, then, with a little tragic wave of renunciation, she went swiftly into the room beyond. The open desk caught her attention. She stopped and, taking up a pen, wrote on a sheet of paper:

> *Goodby. I had to go.*
> *—Dawn*

She wrote hurriedly, feeling that she had but a brief respite for her flight. Then, casting down the pen, she went to one of the windows in the room and looked out. There was another balcony here, and she stepped out. It was dark, but the candle-light from the dining-room showed a terrace below. It did not look to be a great distance.

For an ordinary runaway bride, this balcony would have been impossible as a mode of egress; but Dawn and her schoolmates had practised all sorts of gymnastics from the windows and roof of the old barn, and even on the gables of the house itself. She knew how to drop like a cat from a considerable distance. She could swing from the great high limb of the old cherry tree that overlooked the Hudson, longer than any of the other girls, and then drop gracefully in their midst, without ruffling her composure in the least.

But to perform such a feat attired in her first long dress of rustling silk, with a bonnet tied under her chin, and a bundle and hand-bag to look after—to say nothing of doing it in an unknown and almost entirely dark place—was another thing.

Dawn glanced back into the room, but could think of no other way. It wouldn't be pleasant to fall and break her leg at the outset, but she fancied she heard steps coming up the stairs, and to hesitate might bring discovery.

She leaned quickly over the railing of the balcony and dropped her bundle down to the terrace. It fell with a hushed thud among the tall grass, and did not sound as if the distance were great.

Twisting the cords of her hand-bag twice about her wrist, she swung her feet over the railing and stood on the outer edge of the balcony, holding the rail lightly, and shaking out her skirt so that it would not impede her progress. Then she cautiously crept down, holding to the ironwork of the railing, and then to the floor of the balcony, and hung for a moment to get her breath and be sure of herself before she let go. Then, closing her eyes, she dropped to the terrace like a thistledown, in spite of the voluminous skirts.

She paused an instant to pick up her bundle and make sure her hand-bag was safe, then, gathering her skirt and holding it close with one hand, that her feet might be freer, she sped down the terrace and away into the unknown darkness.

## CHAPTER XVI

IT was Charles who had come up the stairs. He had grown impatient of the delay, and come in search of his wife. He paused before his mother's door and listened to hear the pleasant voices of the two who were most dear to him. He had pictured them getting acquainted with each other, and he meant to walk in and say that the time was up and he must not be kept out any longer. He listened, but he heard nothing. He waited a moment longer, but still the silence. What could it mean?

He tapped gently at the door, and called, "Mother, may I come in?" His mother gave a cold assent. She had not yet recovered from the shock she had received.

"Why, where is Dawn?" he asked, pausing on the threshold and looking about the room, as if expecting to find her in hiding, just to tease him, perhaps.

"If you wish to come in, please have the goodness to close the door after you, Charles," said his mother severely. "You are in danger of forgetting everybody else in your sudden and extraordinary infatuation."

The joyous spirit of the young man came down to earth with a thud, and he closed the door and stood looking at his mother blankly, as if to try to fathom the look in her face.

"Your wife left me some minutes ago," his mother answered the question which his eyes repeated. She spoke haughtily, as if the offence had been partly his. "She did not seem to enjoy my company."

"Mother!" said Charles, aghast at his mother's tone even more than at her words.

"Oh, yes, 'Mother'!" she repeated, angered anew at the reproach in his tone. "I suppose it will be that from now on. She left the room declaring her intention of also leaving my house. I suppose by this time she has seen the impossibility of that, but you will find you have married no angel, I can tell you. Whatever possessed you, I cannot understand. Such a little spitfire! You should have seen her great eyes flash."

"Mother, what had you been saying to her?" Charles tried to speak gently. He saw that here was something that needed careful handling. He blamed himself inwardly that he had not had more forethought than to prevent a meeting between the two while his mother was still wrought up over his brother Harrington.

"What had *I* been saying to *her?* Indeed, Charles,

you forget yourself! You would better ask what had *she* been saying to *me*." In her indignation, Madam Winthrop rose on one elbow and faced her son. "I had been most kind and patient and forgiving. I had made up my mind for your sake to put everything by, and I sent for her to tell her so. I told her I would forgive her all she had done to spoil your brother's life and yours——"

"Mother! You never told her that!"

Charles towered above the little woman in the bed, every inch of his manhood roused in honest indignation.

"I certainly did," said the mother, her own anger rising anew. "I explained the whole matter to her, and told her I would forgive her entirely. And then just because I suggested some things she might do to help you who are so young and inexperienced, and who had so generously given up all your own ambitions just to save her from a few hours' mortification, she got very angry. She turned perfectly white, and her eyes looked like two devils. You wouldn't have known your pretty little angel if you had seen her. I will admit, of course, that she is pretty, but 'handsome is that handsome does' is a very true adage. You will find it out yet. She was most insulting —told me that I was lying, or words to that effect—and then she got off the most extraordinary yarn about not knowing she had married you. I told her she must know I couldn't believe such a story as that, and, now that I think it over, I don't see how she can be quite right in her mind. Perhaps Harrington had suspected as much and took this way of getting out of a most unfortunate union, and you were so blind that you just jumped in head-foremost, without ever waiting to make an inquiry——"

"Mother, stop!" Charles's face was white, and his voice was trembling with suppressed horror. "Remember you are talking about my wife!"

"Yes, your wife!" exclaimed his mother, beginning to cry. "That's the way it goes. A child forgets all his mother has ever done, the minute he sees a pretty, silly face."

Then she sat up with sudden resolution.

"Well, *take* your wife and go *out of my house,* then, if you and she are going to combine against me, and dictate to me how I shall talk!"

Then with a moan she threw herself back upon her pillows and lost consciousness again.

Charles stood looking down miserably at her for an instant, his mind in such a whirl of emotions that he scarcely knew which was strongest. Then, with a remembrance of Dawn, he turned, half-distracted, and pulled the bell-cord that hung by the head of his mother's bed. These fainting spells were frequent and not alarming, he knew. Stepping to the head of the stairs, he called:

"Betty, tell Aunt Martha to come to Mother at once. She has fainted again."

He waited only to hear Aunt Martha's quick, excited step upon the stair, and then he went to find Dawn.

Opening the door of the sitting-room, it startled him to feel the emptiness that pervaded the place. He had expected to find Dawn weeping in the big chair, or perhaps huddled upon the bed. That would have been Betty's way. He had often acted as comforter to Betty during her childish woes. Even in his anger and trouble, he was thrilling at the thought of how he would comfort Dawn, his own little girl. He was the only one in all the world now to whom she had a right to look for comfort.

He strode through the rooms hurriedly, looking in every possible place for her, and unwilling to accept the conclusion his mind had instantly jumped to, that she was not there at all.

He even pushed aside the curtains and stepped out upon first the front balcony and then the side one, thinking that she had taken refuge there from intrusion by Betty or the other girls. But there was no sign of her recent step, and in the darkness the tall grass down below on the terrace told no tales of a little crushed place where her bundle had fallen and where her feet had rested lightly when she dropped. Next morning, before any one would think to look, the grass would be standing tall as ever, and they would never know how she went.

Stepping back into the room again, Charles at once saw the writing on the sheet of paper lying on the desk. When he had read it, he caught it hastily in his hand as if it could give him some clue to her whereabouts, and started down the stairs and out of the front door to find her. He knew only one thing then, and that was that he must find her and bring her back before any one else discovered her flight. She could not be far away yet. Charles hurried out into the darkness. The family were attending to the mother, who had recovered consciousness. He could hear her moaning, and a sudden bitterness came over his soul, that her blindness and selfishness should make them all so much trouble. He had never thought of her in any but a gentle, loving way before, and it shocked his spirit to have to think differently now; but his indignation at her treatment of his young and blameless wife was roused beyond his present control.

He searched the grounds and garden carefully, going over every possible hiding-place twice. As he did so, he reflected that she could not have known where to go to hide, and he felt sure he would find her in a minute or two. The minutes grew into thirty, and he had found no trace of her. He went down the street quite a distance in one direction, only to be sure she would have chosen the other, and to hurry back. An hour passed with no trace of her, and then he began systematically to go over the grounds again, calling her name softly; but a screech owl mocked him, and the night wind only echoed back his voice emptily.

Once he drew near the house and under the balcony where Dawn had escaped. He heard his sister calling him, "Charles, Charles! Mother wants you!" and his heart grew bitter. Then Betty's head came out of the window, and she called again:

"Charles, where are you and Dawn? Mother has been moaning and crying for half an hour. She wants you, and nothing else will stop her but the sight of you."

Then, out of the darkness, Charles answers his sister, and the tone of his voice frightened her:

"Betty, I cannot come. There is something more important than even Mother just now. I'm sorry for Mother, but I'm afraid it's all her fault. She has been saying things to Dawn, and Dawn has gone!"

"Gone!" Betty's horrified voice seemed like a fresh recognition of the awful truth that his young wife was beyond his easy reach, and a dreadful foreboding entered his soul.

"Oh, Charles!" Betty gasped. "But she can't be gone. Her things are here, aren't they? Wait—I'll look."

Betty disappeared, and in a moment more her white, scared face reappeared on the balcony, and she was holding a candle high above her head.

"No, they are not there. I've even looked in the closet, thinking she might have hung them up. Her bonnet and mantle were on the bed before supper, but they are gone from the room. I found her gloves, though—one on the bed, and one on the floor. Here they are." She tossed them to him as if they were an important clue, and Charles caught at them as if they were something most precious.

"What shall we do?" she asked. "Hadn't I better call Father? We ought to find her at once, poor little thing! She'll be frightened out in the night all alone. How could Mother! But then she was so upset with Harrington, I don't believe she understood things fully, do you?"

But Charles had no time to listen to Betty's sympathetic chatter. His heart was wrung with the thought of the girl he loved out in the night alone, afraid perhaps of the unknown perils about her. He must hurry to her aid.

"Yes, tell Father to come to the front door, quick! There's no time to lose. And, Betty, don't rouse the neighbors. Let's keep this quiet."

"Of course," said his little sister. "How fortunate they don't know yet that it was you who was married." Then Betty flew to call her father, telling him excitedly all the way to the front door what had happened.

"Poor child! Poor child!" said the father tenderly, as he listened to the tale. "And poor Mother, too; she just didn't understand."

Charles made no response. He did not feel like pitying his mother yet.

"What do you think I had better do, Father?" he asked. "I've gone everywhere about the place; and down the road a good way in each direction."

"She will have started home, I suppose—it is a girl's natural refuge," said the old man thoughtfully. "There's only one road if you don't take the train. She wouldn't likely go all that way around."

"But, Father, she doesn't know the way. It was all quite new to her."

"Oh, that's easy. She will ask, and of course anybody will direct her. She's probably asked somebody quite near the house here. If you only knew whom, you could easily trace her, but, as you say, it's best not to say anything about it, for it would get out to the neighbors. We'll soon trace her. There are only two ways by which she could reach the main stage-road. You go down to the stable and saddle the two sorrel mares. The blacks are tired with the long drive to-day, so you'd better take the sorrels. The men are all gone to bed by this time, so you'll have to do it yourself. You take one horse and go the road by the sawmill, and I'll take the other and go around by Applebee's farm, and then if she should have taken it into her head to go back by the way you came, I couldn't miss her, for she couldn't have gone further than that by this time. Had she any money with her?"

"I don't know," answered Charles miserably.

"Cheer up, lad, we'll find her inside of two hours, never fear. Hurry up, and I'll be with you in half a minute."

Five minutes later, the two horses and their riders parted company at the cross corners, and started on the search.

## CHAPTER XVII

DAWN fled through the dark grass, straight from the house, not knowing or thinking where she was going, only to get away. In a moment she reached a high hedge of dense growth, and, not daring more than to glance toward the house, she crept swiftly along toward the street. A few rods from the sidewalk she found a small opening and slipped through into another great yard. Keeping close to the hedge, she soon reached the front, and slid

out at the gate like a wraith, wondering what she would
do if some one in the neighbor's house should accost her.
But no one was near. She could hear footsteps coming,
and gay voices, so she turned and hurried the other way,
though it carried her past the house she had just left. It
would not do, she thought, to meet any one just yet.

It was this little circumstance that determined the
direction of her flight, and carried her away from the
road her kindly pursuers expected her to take.

She presently reached a lane and turned into it. It
happened to be a private lane leading to a farm-house
set far back from the street, and as she approached the
house the deep bay of hounds heralded her coming. Her
heart stood still with fright, for she had read much about
the horror of being pursued by bloodhounds. In those
days there was much talk of the pursuit of escaped slaves,
and the girl's imagination suddenly saw herself surrounded by a great pack of hounds sent to bring her back.
She paused and crouched beside the fence. Presently she
heard a man's voice not far away, and saw a speck of
light moving and bobbing here and there near the dark
outline of the house. Then her senses came back. This
was not a dog sent after her, but a man, who had heard
her, an intruder, near the house. Perhaps he would come
and search her out. She must get over that fence as fast
as possible.

The silk skirts rustled horribly, and cold chills of
apprehension crept down Dawn's back, as she found how
much harder it was to climb a fence encumbered by long
skirts and a bundle, than when dressed as a care-free
school-girl. That gave her an idea. She ought to get off
that silk dress as soon as possible, for its noise would at-
tract attention.

Another howl of the dog startled her just as she
cleared the fence, so she began to run. Fortunately, the
house was between her and the town, and she had not to
turn back upon her way. She discovered by the humps and
hillocks that she was in a meadow, and she struck out as
far away from the house as possible, though the way was
rough, and several times she fell. But the dog's howling
was more distant now, and she concluded he had been
chained. Ahead of her, she could see a dark line of trees,

and she hurried toward them. At least, she could pause there a minute and arrange her clothing.

She crept within the edge of the woods, and dared not look around, so easily her imagination could people it with evil spirits. She was naturally of a courageous nature, and at school had always been ready to dare anything just for fun, but it was a different matter to be running away into the great night world of a place you had never seen.

With trembling fingers, she unfastened her bundle, being careful to stick the pins on the corner of her handkerchief in her hand-bag, where she could find them in the dark. It was a work of time and care to extricate the little gray frock from the bundle and be sure to lose nothing in the darkness. She unrolled it cautiously, gathering the other things within the largest garment she had brought, and then slipped the dress out from underneath, first taking the precaution to pin the smaller bundle together. Then she took off her mantle, slipped out of her silk frock and into the gray one, all the time nervously staring into the darkness of the fields through which she had just come. What if some one should catch her now?

The blood pounded through her heart, and poured up into her face, as though it were on a mad race to strangle her. Her hair was wet with perspiration and clinging to her forehead, yet she felt a chill. It seemed as if her fingers were growing wooden and clumsy as she turned the silk frock inside out and folded it carefully, pinning it over the other bundle, so that it would show only a gray cotton lining. The silk mantle she put on again, and, feeling carefully about to see that she had left nothing behind, she turned to face the blackness of the woods.

It was only a maple sugar grove on the edge of a prosperous farm, but it looked inky black, and might have been filled with all sorts of wild animals, for aught she knew. Yet she pressed on. She felt as if the woods were a friend, at least. She had been used to walking among the trees and telling her troubles there to the birds and breezes, and now it seemed a natural refuge, in spite of its blackness. If only it were the old woods she knew at the school, she would not be afraid at all. But fear henceforth must have no part in her life. She had herself to look out for, and she would never, never go again where any one could talk to her as that dreadful woman had talked. She shuddered as she remembered the cold, cultured voice, and the scorn that had pierced her soul with a shame that she knew was unjust. Her rising anger helped her to go on and put down any timidity that she might have felt, and presently, through feeilng from tree to tree, she came out to the other side of the maple grove. Far away to the east she could see a pale moon rising. She started toward it, keeping close to the maple groove, as if it were a friend. The way led over two or three more meadows, and now in her little gray frock she found it much easier to climb the fences.

At last she came to a straight, white road in the country, with the slender moon hanging low over it. With relief, she climbed the intervening fence and took her way along the beaten path. Her light prunella slippers had found it hard travelling in the meadows.

The day had been a long one, and filled with excitement, beginning with fear and trouble, and preceded by a sleepless night. Dawn was very weary now that she felt herself safe from the terror that possessed her, yet she must walk all night, for it would not be safe to lie down, she knew. She had heard of wild beasts lurking on the edges of towns, and a wolf or a bear would not be a pleasant companion.

On she went through the sweet summer night, slackening not her pace, even though there was now no longer need for haste. It seemed to her tired spirit that she must go on and on thus, throughout ages, always alone and misunderstood and pursued. The thought of her husband and their beautiful day together seemed like some tantalizing dream, that hovered on her memory and sickened her with its impossibility. Such joy as his love offered her was too great for her ever to have hoped to attain. Yet in her secret soul she knew she was glad to have had it, even if only to have it snatched from her.

As she thought over her own hasty action in leaving her husband's home forever, she could not feel she had done wrong. Never, never could she have lived with others taunting her that she had been married out of pity —for that was what his mother's words had meant.

Charles had not married her for love, but for pity, because, for some unexplained reason, Harrington had chosen to desert her at the last minute. Her exhausted spirit did not care to know the reason. She could but be thankful that he had. Anything, *anything* was better than to have been married to *him*.

All at once a wild fear possessed her that perhaps by leaving the refuge of his brother's home she had again put herself in danger of Harrington. Perhaps he would find her out, follow her, and compel her to come with him.

As the night went on, all sorts of curious fancies took possession of her excited brain, until she started at her own shadow, and thought some one was following her when all was still in the empty road behind.

Once or twice she sat down by the roadside to rest, but the awful desire for sleep which crept over her frightened her, and she staggered to her feet again.

The road wound into a lonesome wood of tall forest trees, so high that the moon's faint glimmer served only to make the path look blacker. But now she was too dead with weariness to have any fear, and she walked on and on into the blackness of the forest, with no care save to keep going. At last, under a group of pines that huddled together as if they were of one family, she stumbled over a great root that obtruded among the slippery pine needles and fell headlong. She lay still for a moment, dazed, and then the sense of relief and exhaustion became so great that, without a thought of wild beasts, she drew her bundle up under her head and continued to lie still on the soft, sweet bed of needles.

The great pines bent their feathery heads over her, and the wind crept into the branches and softly sang a lullaby over the lonely little pilgrim. Regardless of dangers that might be stalking about her, she slept.

Quite early in the morning, before the first faint streaks of day had penetrated the cool retreat where Dawn lay asleep, there came a soft murmur of gentle music from the trees all about; and soon a sleepy twitter brightened and grew into a chorus of melody, bird answering to bird from tree to tree. Up and down and around, in and out and over, the threads of song spun themselves in-

to a lovely golden web of harmony that seemed to shut
the vaulted forest in loftily from all the world, and in
the midst of it all Dawn awoke.

It was quite gradual, her return to consciousness, as
if the atmosphere of sweetness and melody pervaded her
soul, and stirred it from its slumber in spite of itself,
bringing new life and a great peace.

At first she did not open her eyes, nor think where
she was. It was enough that she smelled the pines and
felt the soft lap of nature where she lay. It seemed still,
very still and restful; cool and sweet and dark. That she
knew with her eyes closed. Up above, where the birds
sang, she seemed to feel a golden light coming, coming,
and knew that it would soon grow into morning. But now
she might just allow herself this little time to lie still and
listen and wait. There came to her consciousness a thrill
of freedom that in her fright and hurry the night before
she had not realized. For months now she had been
half-planning to run away from the things that were sad-
dening her life, and now she had done it. She was free!
Free to order her small life for herself.

Down deep in her heart tugged the agony of a great
loss, yet it was as of the loss of something she had never
really had—only dreamed of briefly. She would not let
herself think of Charles now. She wanted to keep his
memory as something sweet to take out and look at
sometimes when she was lonely, but that could not be
until the first bitterness of the shame of her union to him
was past. She wanted to forget the scene in his mother's
room, her terrible helplessness before the onslaught of the
woman's tongue; and just rest and feel that she was free.

Freedom meant getting away from Harrington Winthrop and from her step-mother, and from her father's
wrath, or his possible efforts to shape her life. What else
it meant, she had yet to learn. She supposed there was
some place in the world where she might work for what
she needed. The thought of her livelihood did not trouble
her. Youth feels equal to its own support always, if it
has any spirit at all. Dawn had plenty of spirit, and felt
sure she could earn her "board and keep." At present, she
was concerned only in getting rested and getting away as

far as possible from all the evil things which seemed to have combined to crush her.

The light came on, and the morning entered the forest. A saucy little squirrel ran up the tree beneath which the girl lay, and, poised on a high twig, looked down and chattered at her noisily. Down fell a bit of bark upon Dawn's face, and, laughing involuntarily, she sat up and looked about her. The dim aisles of the forest were lit with golden lights now, and the birds, their matins almost finished, were hurrying about with breakfast preparations. A wood-thrust spilled his liquid notes out now and then, like a silver spoon dropped into a glass. A robin called his mate, and a blackbird whistled forth a silken melody. Dawn laughed aloud again at the squirrel, and tossed back the curls that had come loose from the confining comb during her sleep. It was good just to be here and to be free.

The squirrel chattered back at her and ran up the tree. Dawn unpinned her bundle and made her simple toilet. There was no brook near, where she could wash her face, but perhaps she would come to one by and by. She combed out her hair as well as she could with only a back-comb, and did it up on her head, for she must have dignity now if she were going out in the world to shift for herself. Then she looked over her small possessions carefully, as a shipwrecked mariner might take account of the wreckage he had saved. She took a kind of fierce joy in the thought that she had brought none of the elaborate garments which her step-mother had prepared for her trousseau. They were all the simple school garments that had been put at the bottom of her trunk.

She rolled up the bundle again and pinned it closely, then tied her bonnet on demurely, straightened her frock, and was ready for the day.

A soft little pathway of light beckoned her through the woods, and she followed it, her bundle tucked under her cape, her hand-bag with its cords safely twisted about her wrist.

The bar of light grew brighter and broader, and led her to another road. Unwittingly, she had come a way that would take her far from the place where she started more directly than any other she could have chosen. The sight of the white road in the dewy morning light gave her new zest for her journey. Her sleep, short though it had been, had rested her wonderfully, and she was eager to get on her way.

She climbed the fence and fairly flew down the road. It was very early, and she would be far on her way before people were up and stirring. There were mile-posts on this road, and guide-boards sometimes at cross-roads. That meant that a stage-route came that way. She studied the next guide-board carefully, and decided that she was on the direct route to New York, and that the miles might mean from New York to somewhere else. Not Albany, of course, for she must be far to the west of that. Perhaps she could find out later, as she went on. What if she should go as far as New York? How long would it take her? She could not go all at once, probably; but gradually she might work her way down. Why not? The world was before her. She would watch the mile-posts and see how long it took her to go a mile.

Thus dreaming, she flew along like a bird.

Here and there she passed a farm, and soon she began to see signs of life about. The men were coming from the barns with brimming pails of milk. As she passed one house somewhat nearer to the road than the rest, she caught the fragrance of frying ham and the aroma of coffee. It made her hungry.

A mile further she came to a small white house not far from the roadside. Outside the door a woman who wore a sunbonnet and a big apron sat on a three-legged stool, milking a mild old cow. As Dawn came near, the woman gave the last scientific squeeze, and moved the pail from its position under the cow, then, taking the stool in one hand and the pail in the other, started for the house. The face she showed beneath the deep sunbonnet was a kindly one.

Following an impulse, Dawn turned in at the front gate, and the old woman paused to see what she wanted:

"Could you let me have a glass of milk?" Dawn's voice was sweet, and she held her purse in her hand. "I would be glad to pay for it. I started early this morning, and am hungry. I'm on my way to the next village."

The woman's face lit up at the sight of the girl's smile.

"A glass of milk?" she said. " 'Course I can, but I don't want no pay for it. Just you keep your pennies for a new ribbon to wear under that pretty chin. Set down under the tree there on the bench, an' I'll bring a cup."

She put down her pail on a large flat stone, and hurried in, coming out in a moment with a plate of steaming johnny-cake and a flowered cup of delicate china. The woman strained the milk into the cup and stood watching her while she ate the delicious breakfast.

"Come fur?" asked the hostess, eying the sweet young tramp appreciatively.

"From beyond Schoharie," she answered quickly, remembering the name on the last cross-road signboard she had passed.

"H'm! Right smart way fer a little slip of a thing like you to come alone. You must 'a' started 'fore light."

"Soon after," laughed Dawn. She felt as if she were playing a game. Then, perceiving that the old lady was curious and would ask questions that she did not care to answer she launched into a description of the morning sky and the early bird songs. The old woman watched her as if she were drinking in a picture that did her good.

"Bless me!" she said. "That sounds like poetry verses. How do you think it up?"

Then she whisked into the house again and came out with a paper of doughnuts.

"You might get hungry again 'fore you get to the village, and these doughnuts was extra good this time. Just take 'em an' eat 'em to pass the time as you go. If you feel hungry when you come along back, just stop in. I'll be glad to see your pretty face. It does a body good. Goin' back before sundown?"

"No," said Dawn; "I may stay some time. I'm not sure. But I thank you very much for your kind invitation, and I know I shall enjoy the doughnuts. I love doughnuts. We used to have them in school once a week in the winter, but only one apiece."

"So you've been to boardin'-school!"

The old woman would fain have detained her, but Dawn edged away toward the gate, thanking her sweetly all the while, and saying she must hasten, for the sun was getting high. She hurried down the road at last, pretending not to hear the old woman's question about who were her friends in Schoharie, and where she was going to visit in the village.

Her cheeks were bright with the excitement of the little episode, and she trilled a gay song as she fled on her unknown way. For the time being, all sadness was put away, and she was gay and free as a lark. Just a happy child.

A farmer's boy on a hay-wagon crawling along to the village stopped his whistling and stared at her; and the hired man on top of the load called out to him some remark about her that made the color grow brighter in her cheeks and her heart flutter wildly in her breast. She could not hear what words the man had spoken, but his tone had been contemptuous and familiar. She fairly flew by the team, and fled on down the road.

By noon the johnny-cake and milk were dreams of the past, and she was exceedingly hungry, yet she had not come to a place where she cared to ask for dinner. Every farm-house she came to seemed to have plenty of farm-hands about, coming in to their dinner, and she dreaded their eyes upon her. So she sat down under a tree by the roadside and ate her fat, sugary doughnuts, rested a few minutes, and plodded on.

The afternoon was more wearisome. Her slippers hurt her feet, and she had to stop often to rest. About five o'clock she came to a neat-looking inn by the roadside, where a decent woman sat knitting by the door, and Dawn decided to sacrifice something from her small store of money and stop overnight.

The woman eyed her curiously when she asked for a room and supper. Not many pilgrims so young or so beautiful passed her way unattended. Dawn explained that she was on her way to another town, to look for something to do.

"I suppose you're expecting to teach school," said the woman disapprovingly. "They all do nowadays, when they better be home, helping their mothers make bread and pies."

"My mother is dead," said Dawn quietly, "and I must earn my own living now."

The woman was silenced, and gave the young traveller a pleasant little whitewashed room, where she slept soundly. But an idea had come to her. A teacher! Of course, she could be a teacher. Had she not led her classes, and always been successful in showing the girls at school how to do their sums? She would enjoy playing the part of Friend Ruth, and putting a class through its paces. It quite interested her to think how she would do it. But how would she get her school? Should she go to New York and try, or begin in a country one first?

This thought interested her all through the day, which was Saturday, and kept away the undertone of consciousness of a deep loss. But once, toward evening, she passed a shiny new carryall in which rode a young man and a girl, and a sharp pang shot through her heart as it brought back vividly to her memory the beautiful day which she and Charles had spent together. And then her mind went back to the first time she had seen him, that day when she was standing on the hilltop with her small audience before her, and had looked up and seen the shining of his eyes. It came to her then that she had a certain right of possession in him, as if that day had given her to him and him to her in a bond that could never be broken, no matter how far they might be separated. Quiet joy settled down upon her with the thought that, whatever might come, whether she ever saw him again or not, she was his wife, and nobody, nobody could ever take the thought of it from her.

The sun was setting, and evening bells were ringing in the spire of a little white church, as she came into a small village nestled at the foot of a circle of hills. It reminded her that the next day was the Sabbath.

That day had no sweet associaton for her since her mother's death, but, though she had been only a little child, she could remember walking by her mother's side to church, with her little starched skirts swinging, and her mitted hands folded demurely over the pocket handkerchief, while the bells rang a cheery call to prayer.

There had been no bells on the meeting-house to which
the scholars of Friend Ruth's school were taken every
First Day, and nothing about the service to remind her
of the church where she had sat by her mother's side in
the high-backed pew and heard the hymns lined out, trying to follow the singing of the congregation with her
wee sweet voice, but now the bells harked back over the
years and brought an aching memory of her almost forgotten little girlhood. A sudden longing to go to church
as she used to do came over her, and she decided to find
a place in the village to stay over Sunday and go to service in the little white-spired church. Besides, it was
against the law in those days for any one to travel
unnecessarily on the Sabbath day. Dawn never thought
of doing so, any more than she would have contemplated
the possibility of stealing.

It chanced that she arrived at the village tavern
about the same time as the stage-coach from the opposite direction, and no one noticed that she had not
come on the stage, for there were a number of travellers
who stopped off here for the Sabbath. Seeing them de-
scending from the coach, she went in haste to the landlady and begged that she might have a tiny room to herself. She was a little frightened at the thought of paying
a whole dollar out of her small hoard for the lodging
and her meals until after breakfast Monday morning, but
she shut her eyes to the thought of it and took the
room. It was only a tiny one over a shed that was given
her, but everything was clean and sweet, and the supper
smells came richly up through the open window to her
hungry senses. On the whole, she was quite content when
she lay down to rest in her own little room that night
and dreamed of churchbells, and weddings, and sweet
fields of clover and new-mown hay.

## CHAPTER XVIII

THE next morning the roosters crowing under her window awakened her, and for the moment she thought she was back in school, with the barn-yard not far away; but other and unfamiliar sounds and odors brought her back to realities, and she rememberred she was a lone traveller putting up at an inn.

She lay still for some time, thinking over the strangeness of it all, and the tragic happenings of the last few days. The thought of Charles brought tears to her eyes. The dearness and loss of him came over her as it had not had time to do while she was hurrying on her way. But this morning, for the first time, she felt that she was far from every one who knew her, and hidden securely so that she could never be found, and that she might look her life in the face and know what it all meant. It was inevitable that in reviewing her life the first and largest part of all should be Charles and her brief but sweet acquaintance with him. That she was his wife thrilled her with unspeakable joy. The fact that she had deliberately renounced him took away to some extent the sting of the manner in which she had been married.

As she thought it all over, she realized that the only real shame in the whole affair was that she had been about to marry Harrington Winthrop when her heart was full of fear and hatred for him. She seemed to see many things in a new light. In fact, the child had become a woman in the space of a few days, and she understood life better, though it was still one vast perplexity.

One thing remained of all the past, and that was the memory of the love of Charles. Even the remembrance of her dear mother was dimmed by it. It seemed to be the one eternal fact which stood out clearly, and in the light of which she must hereafter live. That he had been generous and kind enough to marry her for the sake of relieving her from humiliation, as his mother had intimated, only made Dawn love him the more. But because of the generosity of that act, she must never trouble him again. She had renounced him. It was the least she could do for him, under the circumstances, in return for his great kindness. But whatever happened, she must be true to his memory, and be such that he would always be proud of her if he should chance ever to hear of her, though she meant to take care that he did not.

If she had been a little older and wiser, if she had understood the ways of the world better, she would not have been so sure that she was taking the most direct way to reward Charles for his kindness to her. But she did not understand, and so was sincere and earnest in her mistaken way of being loyal to him. One thing, however, made her glad. She felt that no matter how far apart they might be during the rest of their lives, they had understood each other, and their souls had met in a deep, sweet joy. As she thought of the moment before supper at his home, when he had held her in that close embrace, and laid his face upon hers and kissed her, the sweetness and pain of it were too much for her, and with a sharp cry she hid her face in her pillow and wept bitterly.

It never occurred to her, poor little pilgrim, that he might be grieving just as deeply over her absence and the mystery of her whereabouts as was she for him, or she would have flown to him in spite of all mothers-in-law, and made him glad.

The tempest of her grief swept over her like a summer storm, and was gone. At her age she could not grieve long over what had been hers so briefly that it had scarcely become tangible. But as it had been the dearest happening of her life, and the only bright thing in her girlhood, it took the form of a mount of vision from which ever after she was to draw her inspiration for the doing of the monotonous tasks of life.

She arose and washed away the marks of the tears, and dressed herself carefully in her green silk for church, arranging her hair demurely on the top of her head, with the curls as little in evidence as possible. She wished to look old and dignified, as befitted a person travelling by herself, and looking for a chance to teach school.

The village was a pretty one, and as she walked down the street to the church her heart went out to it. As she sat in the tall pew where the beadle placed her, she glanced shyly around at the people who came in, and wished she might stop here and get something to do. Yet her heart shrank from any attempt to speak to them or beg their help.

A lady came in leading a little girl by the hand, a sweet-faced child with a chubby face, and ringlets in clusters on either cheek, held there by her fine white, dunstable straw bonnet, with its moss-rosebuds and face-ruche of soft lace. After they were seated, across the aisle, the little girl leaned over her mother and stared at Dawn, then smiled shyly, and the young wanderer felt that she had one friend in this strange place.

A sudden loneliness gripped her heart, and she wished she were a little girl again, sitting by her mother's side. How many, many times she had wished that the last few months! The thought made her heart ache, it was so old a hurt. She felt the smart of tears that wanted to swim out and blind her vision, but she straightened up and tried to look dignified, remembering that she was a woman now—a married woman. She wondered, would it be wrong to pretend, as she used to do at school sometimes? She wanted to pretend that Charles sat by her side, they two going to their first church service together. She decided there would be no harm in that, and moved a little nearer the corner to make room for her dear companion. It gave her a happy sense of not being alone, and she glanced up now and then as if he were there and she were watching him proudly. It was not hard to imagine him. She was good at such things. It thrilled her to think how his arm would be close to hers, his sleeve touching her hand, perhaps, as he held the hymn-book for her to sing with him. And to think that if only her marriage had been like others, she would in all probability have been singing beside him in his home church at this very minute! The thought of it almost brought the tears.

There were no hymn-books in the little village

church, but the minister lined the hymn out, and Dawn
stood up to sing with the rest, her clear voice lifting the
tune till people near her turned to look at the sweet face.
She tried to think that Charles was singing by her side,
but when they came to the stanza:

When we asunder part, it gives us inward pain,
But we shall still be joined in heart, and hope to meet again.

it was almost too much for her, and she had to wink
hard to keep back the tears, for it came over her that
she could not hope to meet Charles again, but must go
on with the being asunder always.

The minister had gray hair and a kindly face. He
preached about comfort, and Dawn felt as if it were
meant for her. As she listened, an idea came to her.
She would go to the minister and ask him to help her
find a school. Ministers knew about such things.

She went to the afternoon service also, and after it
was over two or three women shook hands with her,
looked curiously, admiringly at her rich silk gown, and
asked her if she were a stranger.

She smiled and nodded shyly. Then the minister
came and shook hands with her, and brought his tired-
looking wife to speak to her. She watched them go across
the churchyard together, and up the steps of the old
parsonage. The minister seemed tired, too, but there was
sympathy between the two that seemed to rest them both
when they looked at each other and smiled. It touched
the girl-wife. Here were two who had walked together,
yet who seemed to be agreed, and to be happy in each
other's company. She felt instinctively, from the minister's
face, that *he* would not have sent his wife away from
his home, no matter what she had done. He would not
have thought she had done anything wrong in the first
place. It came to Dawn that perhaps it had been her father's quick temper and hasty judgment that had made
all the trouble for her mother. She remembered lately an
unutterably sad expression about his eyes. Perhaps he
was feeling sorry about it, and ashamed. It made the girl
have a tenderer feeling for the father she had never really
loved. She pitied him that he must live with her step-

mother. She had not as yet connected Mrs. Van Rensselaer with her own present predicament. Her main sensations were dislike for her father's second wife, and thankfulness that she was out of her jurisdiction. It remained for deeper reflection to tell Dawn just how much her step-mother was to blame for her having been married to one man, supposing all the time that he was another.

The next morning quite early, Dawn attired herself in her little gray frock and tied her bonnet neatly, then, leaving her bundle in her room, ready to move in case her mission failed, she presented herself at the parsonage and asked to see the minister.

She was shown into the study, where the good man sat in a big hair-cloth chair by the open window, reading.

He received her kindly and gave her a chair.

"I've come to see whether you can help me to find something to do," she began shyly. "My mother is dead, and I must earn my own living. I have relatives to whom I should be a burden, and I have come away so that they will not be troubled with me."

She had thought out during the night watches just what to say.

The minister looked at her keenly and kindly through his spectacles. Long experience had made him a good judge of character. He saw nothing but guileless innocence in the sweet young face.

"What is your name?" he asked, by way of preliminary.

Dawn's face flushed slightly, but she had anticipated this question.

"I should like to be called Mary Montgomery," she said shyly. "It is not my real name, but my relatives might be mortified if they should hear of my being at work. They are very proud, and would not like to have their name mixed up with one who works. Besides, if they should hear of my being here this way, they would think that they must come after me and take care of me, and I don't wish them to. I want to be independent." She gave the minister a most engaging smile, which put a well rounded period to her plea.

"How do I know that you have not run away?" he asked her, half smiling himself.

"Oh, I have run away," answered Dawn frankly. "I knew they would try to keep me if I told them, but I left word I had gone, and they will not worry. They do not love me. They wanted me to stay only because they felt it a duty to care for me, and they will be greatly relieved to be rid of me without any trouble. That is why I came. You see, they told me as much, and it was very uncomfortable. You would not want to stay where you knew you were in the way, would you?"

Dawn looked into the old minister's eyes with her own wide, lovely ones, and won his heart. She reminded him of his little girl who had died.

"I suppose not," he said in a half amused tone. "But don't you think it would be better for you to confide in me? Just tell me your real name, and where you come from, and all about it, and then I can help you better. I shall be able to recommend you, you know."

"Thank you, no," said Dawn decidedly, getting up as if that ended the matter. "If I told you that, and then you were asked if I were here, you would have to say yes. Then, too, if you knew, you might think it was your duty to let my friends know where I am. Now you have no responsibility about it at all, don't you see? But I don't want to make you any trouble. If you don't know of some work I might do here, I will go elsewhere. I can surely find something to do without telling my real name. I know I am doing right. You were so kind when you spoke to me yesterday, that I thought I would come and ask you, though I had intended going on this morning."

"Wait," said the minister. "Sit down. What do you want to do? What kind of work are you fitted for?"

"I have been educated at a good school," said Dawn, sitting down and putting on a quaint little business-like air which made the minister smile.

"Did you ever teach school?" There was much hesitation in the minister's voice. He was not altogether sure he was doing right to suggest the idea, she was such a child in looks.

"No, but I could," replied Dawn confidently. "And,

oh, I should like it! It is just what I want. I love to show people how to do things, and make them learn correctly. I used to help the girls at school." There was great eagerness in her face. The minister thought how lovely she was, and again that fleeting likeness to his dead child gripped his heart.

"You are very young," he mused, watching the changing expression on her face, and thinking that his child would have been about this girl's age.

"I am almost seventeen," said Dawn, drawing herself up gravely.

"Our village schoolmaster left very suddenly last week, to go to his invalid mother's bedside, and it may be some months before his return. Indeed, it is possible that he will not come back at all. He intimated as much before he left. We have not had opportunity as yet to find another teacher, and the school has been dismissed for a few days until we can look about for a substitute."

"Oh, will you let me try?" Dawn sat on the edge of her chair, her hands clasped, her lovely eyes pleading eagerly.

"But some of the scholars are larger than you are."

"That will not matter," responded Dawn, undaunted. "I could always make the girls at school do what I wanted."

"There are some big boys who might make you a good deal of trouble," went on the minister. "Our school has the name of being a hard one to discipline. We have always had a man at its head."

"I am not afraid," said Dawn, fire in her eyes. "I should like to try, if you will let me. You cannot tell whether I can do it unless you let me try."

"That is true," agreed the minister gravely. "I suppose there would be no harm in your trying. I could talk with the trustees about it, though the matter has been practically left to me."

"Oh, then, please, *please,* try me! I am sure I can do it," Dawn pleaded, and the look of his dead child's eyes in her face conquered the minister's scruples.

"Very well, I will try you," he said, after a thoughtful pause. "I will see the trustees and have the notices put up at once. School will open to-morrow morning. But

I warn you it will be no easy task. I feel that it will be an extremely doubtful experiment."

"Oh, thank you!" cried Dawn, her eyes bright with anticipation. "I am not afraid, and I shall do my best. I am sure I can teach a school."

"Poor child!" thought the minister. "Am I doing right to send her into such a trial?"

Aloud, he only said:

"You will receive sixteen dollars a month, and will board around, Miss Montgomery."

Dawn looked up at the new name she had chosen, and saw a twinkle in his eye. She smiled in recognition of his acceptance of it.

"Where are you stopping?" he asked.

"I am at the Golden Swan," she answered. "I can stay there a little while yet. I have a little money, though it will not last many weeks."

She wrinkled her sweet face into dimples and smiled at him, as if having no money were a matter of little consequence.

He admired her courage, and, bending upon her a look of benediction, said kindly:

"We will arrange the matter of boarding as soon as possible. I will see Mrs. Gillette, the wife of the proprietor of the Golden Swan. They have a daughter in school, and possibly their two boys will attend also, though sometimes at this time of year they are both out working on the farm. But the Gillettes always take the teacher for their share of the term."

Dawn went smiling down the parsonage path. It seemed to her the larkspurs had grown bluer and the verbenas pinker since she came up a few minutes before, and her feet fairly danced down the street, she was so happy over her good fortune. It was like a beautiful story, the way it was turning out. She had no apprehensions about her ability to handle the village school, for she had had no experience of what bad boys could be; so there was nothing to cloud her bright day, save now and then a brief pang of longing for Charles. For the most part, her mind was too much filled with anticipation of the morrow to have room for thoughts of the past. She went to the Golden Swan, and told Mrs. Gillette that she was to remain there for a few days at least, then she found the village store and made a few simple purchases, among them needles, thread, and a thimble. Then she chose material for an apron, and hurried home to make it. The school-teachers she had known had always worn aprons. They were a badge of office. But the apron she made was not like Friend Ruth's. It was small and coquettish, and edged with a tiny ruffle.

Dawn knew how to sew beautifully, for that had been one of the accomplishments Friend Ruth required of all her pupils. With a pair of borrowed scissors, the young girl fashioned the garment, and cut the tiny ruffles, rolling the hems as she had been taught to do, and scratching the gathers scientifically. By night she had a dainty little apron ready to wear to school. It was a frivolous bit of a thing, but it filled her with delight, for it was such an apron as she had always desired, but had not been allowed to have while in school. Simplicity held sway where Friend Ruth ruled.

At the supper table it was whispered around that a new school-teacher had come to town. There were notices up at the corners and all the cross-roads. School was to "take up" on the morrow. Some of the people at the table looked suspiciously at the pretty young stranger sitting demurely by herself at the end of the table, and wondered if she were the new teacher, but others said no, she was entirely too young.

After supper Dawn went to the big book wherein were registered the names of the guests, and wrote down "Mary Montgomery" in a clear, round hand. Mr. Gillette watched her carefully out of the corner of his eye. As he saw her about to turn away, he said gruffly:

"Put down the place. We like to know where our folks belongs."

"Oh!" said Dawn, a pink flush stealing into her cheek. What should she put? Then, quick as a flash, she thought, "I have adopted a name—why should I not adopt a home, too? I am on my way to New York. If I do not remain here, I shall go there—if I can get there. I will choose New York for my home. It is a large place, and no one will expect me to know every one there. Besides, it will also stand for New York State."

So, without another word, she wrote "New York" beside her name. She might as well have written "Heaven," for it stood to her as a kind of final destination, far away and pleasant, the only place now that she could look to for a real home.

"You ain't the new schoolmarm, be you?" inquired the worthy proprietor of the Golden Swan cautiously.

"Why, yes," said Dawn, happily conscious, and laughing merrily to think of the word "schoolmarm" as applied to her who but yesterday was a scholar.

"Now, you don't say!" said the proprietor, settling back in his chair and putting his feet on the office table in front of him, while he shoved up his spectacles to get a better view of her. "Some said as how you was, but I couldn't think it. You look so young."

"Oh, I'm quite old," said Dawn anxiously. "I'm far older than I look." And she hurried away, lest she should be questioned further.

It was soon noised abroad that the new teacher was stopping at the Golden Swan, and many a villager dropped in to have a look at her. But she was nowhere in evidence. Up in the little whitewashed chamber, with her candle lighted and the shades drawn, she was standing before her tiny looking-glass, arrayed in her new, beruffled apron, and trying to look grave and dignified, and as much like Friend Ruth as possible.

If Charles could have seen her all absorbed, his heart would have been sadly cast down to see how little she seemed to miss him. But later, when she had put out her candle and crept into her bed, she sobbed a long time into her pillow with loneliness and excitement.

# CHAPTER XIX

THERE was much curiosity in the village concerning the new teacher, who was reported to have come from

New York, and to be exceedingly young. Some thought the minister had made a great mistake to hire a woman, for the school was a hard one to manage, and even a master found it difficult to control the big boys. There was so much talk about it that the scholars themselves were quite excited. Even the big boys, who usually preferred to get out of the summer session although it meant hard work in the hayfields, decided to go to school and see for themselves.

Quite early the scholars might have been seen wending their way toward the old red school-house. They huddled in groups about the steps or under the great elm tree which grew in front and spread its branches far on every side, making a lovely leafy bower for the playground. Peggy Gillette was among the first to arrive. From her point of vantage at the Golden Swan, she was in a position to give accurate information concerning the new teacher, so she knew that she would be most popular this morning. She had, therefore, packed her little dinner-pail hastily and departed soon after breakfast, after making sure that Dawn had gone up to her room to make ready for school.

"She's awful pretty," Peggy told the first knot of eager listeners, "and she's got a lot of real curls on top what ain't tied on. I know, fer I peeked through the crack of the door when she was fixin' her hair last night, and it was down and reached ever so far below her waist. An' she's got dimples when she laughs, and twinkles in her eyes like the stars make, an' she ain't much bigger'n I am. She looks just like a little girl."

"H'm! We'll soon do her up!" remarked Daniel Butterworth, the tallest and strongest boy in the school.

Daniel had a shock of yellow hair that was roughly curly, big blue eyes with curly yellow lashes, and an irresponsible wide mouth, always on a defiant grin. Peggy looked up at him in terror.

"Now, Dan Butterworth," she began, "ef you boys go to playin' pranks on her, it'll be just pur'ly mean. She's jest a girl, an' she's so pretty an' don't look like she was used to rough boys like you."

"We don't want no sissy-baby to teach us," declared 'Liakim Morse, a bold, black-eyed boy, who always

followed Daniel's lead in everything and then went a step
further. "We want a *man* to teach us. The selectmen'll
soon find out they can't put no baby teachers off on us,
fer we won't stand it."

Peggy made a face at them and turned her back,
but Daniel only grinned. He had his plan, and he knew
it would be carried out. He did not need to say much to
his followers. The program was well understood by them.

One of the selectmen, who lived near the school-
house, came over with the key, and stayed about the
place, opening the windows and setting the teacher's desk
in order.

The scholars were all seated demurely with books
before them when the minister came walking in with
Dawn, shy and smiling, by his side. Not one of them
seemed to be looking her over curiously, for it was done
from the side of their eyes; but a kind of groan went
softly over the back rows, where the bigger boys sat,
as much as to say, "This job is too easy. It's scarcely
worth our attention. Why didn't you send us some one
worthy of our valor?"

Dawn looked them over, bright-eyed, her heart beating a trifle fast, but her face on the whole quite confident
and happy. They noted the confidence in the tilt of her
chin, and it gave them intense pleasure to think how
soon they could dispel it. They failed, however, to note
the firmness of that chin, or the determination in the line
of the softly curving red lips. They looked at their victim
warily and rejoiced in her youth and beauty. They had
vanquished many before, but never one so lovely, so
child-like, or so confident. It was an insult to their manhood that the selectmen should have thought she could
teach them.

The minister introduced Miss Montgomery to the
selectman, who shook hands with her, wished her
well, and departed. Then the good old man made a few
gentle remarks to the effect that they should reflect on the
goodness of the new teacher, to whom he referred as "our
young friend," in coming to teach them and guide them
into the devious ways of knowledge, and that they should
refrain from all annoying conduct during her stay, and
behave as model scholars should.

The minister had spent much thought upon this speech, and felt that he had worded it in such a way as to appeal to the sympathy of all the children. In all his mild and reasonable life, he had never been able to comprehend the sinful workings of the unregenerate heart of a boy. He could conceive of no reason why a boy or a girl would be mischievous in school, if the matter were presented rightly to their minds. He felt that he had put it before them as it should be made to appear, and, looking into the demure faces, he hoped that he had accomplished his end, and that the sweet young stranger would have opportunity to prove that she was capable of teaching that school. Though exceedingly doubtful of the experiment, he wanted her to have a fair chance.

After giving one long, lingering look toward the back row of scholars whose studious appearance was almost portentous in its gravity, the old clergyman sighed with relief and turned with a smile of farewell toward the new teacher.

"Miss Montgomery, I will leave you with your school," he said. "I'm sure that they all appreciate how hard is the first day in a new school, and that they will do their best to make it easy for you."

He bowed and went out. His last glance had shown him a vision of serious faces bent upon open books; yet he felt a strange and apparently most uncalled for foreboding.

Dawn surveyed the whole quiet room with a smile, then she untied her bonnet, took off her cape, and carried them to the hook in the corner, obviously used for that purpose by other teachers.

How did the boys on the back seat time the minister exactly, so as to know just the instant he reached the corner beyond the blacksmith's and was out of hearing?

Dawn had turned from a room full of model scholars, to hang up her mantle and bonnet. Turning back, she beheld pandemonium let loose. Something struck her on the cheek, something else stung her forehead. The whole room seemed white with hard little flying objects. Some of them were of paper, wet and soft, some were bits of chalk. It was like a summer snow-storm, and there seemed to be no end to it.

The bewildered young teacher surveyed the scene for an instant, surprise growing into indignation at the outrage. She was young enough to like fun as well as any one, and for an instant she felt like laughing at the sight. then she realized that it was intended as an insult, and as an open rebellion against her authority. It hurt her sharply that they thus arrayed themselves against her at the outset, without giving her a chance to show them what she was. Well, if they would be enemies, she would show them she could fight. The crucial test of which she had been warned was upon her. She must make good now if she would hope to at all. This critical moment would tell whether she could ever teach that school or any other. In her imagination she saw the regretful look in the kindly minister's eyes, and the line of his mouth which would say, "I told you so," and she did not mean he should be disappointed. Or, rather, she meant that he should be happily disappointed.

In an instant she was on the alert again, her senses collected. As ever in a crisis, she was cool and able to move deliberately.

It took but a second for her to find out who was the leader of the unruly scholars. The tall form of Daniel Butterworth towered above the rest in the back line, and the grin on his impudent face showed he was enjoying the affair immensely. Without an effort, he was evidently directing the whole thing.

A great indignation came into Dawn's eyes, and the soft lips set in determination. Like a flash she dashed across the room, dodging the missiles that pelted through the air from every side.

Straight at Daniel Butterworth she came, the bully and the leader. He was the tallest and strongest boy in the school, and no teacher had ever dared make a direct attack upon him. Usually, the teachers punished the smaller boys for the sins that were really Daniel's. Dawn, with her quick perception, located the cause of the trouble, and impulsively went straight to the mark with her discipline.

The scholars paused in their entertainment to see

what would happen next, and little Peggy Gillette began to cry: "Oh, Teacher, Teacher, don't ye! don't ye! He won't stand it, he won't."

But Peggy's voice was drowned in the general hubbub, which subsided suddenly into ominous silence as Dawn took hold of Daniel Butterworth's arm and jerked him into the seat.

Daniel, of course, did not expect the attack, or he would not have been so easily thrown off his balance; but coming down on the seat so unexpectedly bewildered him, and before he could understand what had happened blows began to rain upon his head and face and ears. Not that they hurt him much, for Dawn had no ruler or switch or any of the time-honored implements wherewith to exercise discipline. She used her hands, her small, soft, pink palms, that were daintily shaped and delicately cared for, and had never seen any hard labor, but yet were strong and supple.

As he sat still and allowed the new teacher to administer justice, Daniel resembled a kitten backing off, with flattened ears and ruffled fur, and submitting to a severe slapping for some misdemeanor.

Nothing so soft and wonderful as Dawn's hands had ever touched the boy's face before. He sat and took the experience in a dazed delight, subsiding and shrinking at every blow which yet gave him a delicious sense of pleasure as if it were some kind of attention she was offering him. Probably in no other way could she have ever won this boy's admiration.

After the chastisement was over he sat still, blushing and smiling sheepishly, as if he were glad of her victory, while all the rest of the school stood gaping in amazement. Their hero had fallen! He had been conquered by a woman, a woman who was only a *girl!* How could any of them ever again hope to stand against a teacher, if the heart of the strong Dan Butterworth melted like wax in her hands?

Dawn whirled upon them all.

"You may sit down," she commanded grandly, and they sat.

"What is your name?" she asked, turning back to Daniel.

"He'th Dan Butterwuth," volunteered an A-B-C from the front of the room.

Dawn looked Daniel straight in the eye, with a long, burning, scathing scorn.

"You great big baby!" she said at last, her cheeks a beautiful red, her eyes bright with the excitement of the encounter. "Aren't you ashamed?"

The rich red stole up into the boy's face, mantling cheek and brow, and seeming to bring a glow even into the rough, tawny hair and yellow, curling lashes, as he dropped his eyes in a kind of happy shame. It was the first shame, perhaps, that he had ever been made to feel, and it was real shame, yet it was so mixed with wholesome admiration of the small, beautiful creature who had brought it upon him, that it left him unable to understand himself. So he grew redder, though there was no look of anger about him, and soon his habitual smile was growing again, although this time it was tinged with reverence and quite lacked its usual impudence.

The scholars marvelled at him as the new teacher left him with the brand of baby, sealed with her beautiful scorn.

Dawn went back to her seat on the platform, behind the big desk, and Daniel sat still, only lifting his curly lashes to get another glimpse of the loveliness and daring which had attacked and conquered him. Bug Higginson, a small, round imp, who adored Daniel, seemed to feel that the erstwhile leader would expect something of his followers, so he delivered himself of a fiendish grimace toward the teacher, which set the girls near him to giggling, and of which Dawn had the full benefit just as she sat down.

"You may come here," commanded Dawn, pointing straight at Bug with a ruler she found on the desk. "Come here and sit on this stool."

She placed a stool near her own chair and waited for him to obey.

Bug made another grimace, and responded pertly, "I won't!"

It was very quietly and swiftly done, and no one in the school saw the beginning, because they were watching Bug and the teacher; but somehow an instant after

Bug had declined to obey he was taken by the nape of his neck and the seat of his trousers, and deposited on the required stool, while Daniel Butterworth was making his way back to his seat, with a look of unconcern upon his face. Bug was too astonished and too much afraid of Daniel to make a sound or move a muscle.

Dawn looked at the long, lank boy as he sprawled back into his seat and raised his curly eyelashes, to see how she would take his action, and there flashed into her eyes a kindling of surprise, gratitude, and understanding. The school sat in mild dismay. The fun had vanished, and before their halting eyes stretched a monotonous vista of uninteresting school days. For they saw plainly that the leader had gone over to the enemy, and they must surrender.

At intervals during the day some boy would attempt to bring about another insurrection, but he would be promptly silenced by Daniel, who every time received as reward a look of gratitude from Dawn's expressive eyes; and every time the beautiful glance gave him a new thrill of pleasure. He sat docile as a lamb and let her make him study, a thing he had never done before in his whole life. Now and then he raised his eyes, dumb, submissive, and met hers, and the shock of a great revolution reverberated through his nature. He did not know what it meant; he did not know why he was enjoying the morning so keenly; but he entered into the new state of things as in a dream of bliss.

At recess time the boys who had always followed his lead in everything began to jeer at him about the way he had given in to a girl and let her whip him. He did not turn red nor look embarrassed. He promptly settled the boldest of them with a few blows from his loosely hung arms, and the others considered it wise to desist. It was plain that the former bully of the school had fallen in the new teacher's snare, and as it was well known to be unsafe to arouse his fiery temper, the other boys had no choice but to follow in his lead.

"If you fellers say a word about her"—he nodded toward the school-house—"I'll lick every last one of yeh, an' I mean it, too!" he threatened, and then he walked away and sat down under the big elm to whittle.

He always sat down to whittle after he had presented an ultimatum to the other boys.

At her desk opposite the schoolroom door, Dawn heard this deliverance, as he intended she should, and her eyes grew bright. She understood that Daniel Butterworth was her champion, and felt her courage grow stronger at the thought. In a moment more she stood at the schoolhouse door, looking out. Daniel looked up from his whittling and met her gaze. She was smiling, and he felt that she no longer considered him a baby. The diminutive had rankled in his heart, and henceforth his purpose was to prove to her that it was undeserved. If good behavior and hard study alone could do that, then he would behave and study, though it was a new mode of procedure for him.

The most interesting fact of the morning was that Daniel Butterworth had given in to the new "schoolmarm," and all the school knew it.

"Teatcher, thshe licked Dan Butterwuth," announced the precocious A-B-C scholar that evening, as she devoured her supper of mush and milk. "Thshe licked him real hard—jetht thlapped hith fathe an' eyeth an' earth eth hard eth ever thshe could."

Her father dropped his knife and fork on his plate resoundingly. He was the selectman who had unlocked the school-house. He felt in a measure responsible for the new teacher.

"The teacher whipped Daniel Butterwoth!" he exclaimed. "Well, that settles her hash, I s'pose. I didn't much think she'd do, such a little whiffet tryin' to manage great lunkin boys. It ain't in conscience to expect it. We need a *man*. I told Parson so, but he insisted we try her, an' this is how it comes out. Well, it's no more'n I expected. Of course Dan'l's father'll never stand that."

"What did Dan do?" inquired the A-B-C.'s mother practically. She knew how to get at the root of the matter.

"He jeth thet thtill an' took it."

"Dan'l Butterwuth set still an' took a whippin' off'n a girl-teacher!" exclaimed the mother. "Are you sure you're tellin' the truth?"

"Yeth, an' then teatcher, thshe thaid he wath a *great big baby,* an' he jeth thet thtill an' got red, an' then he took Bug Higginthon an' thet him down *hard* where teacher thaid, when he'd thaid, 'I won't' to her. An' then he filled the water-pail fer her, an' licked all the other boyth."

"Well, I snum!" said the selectman gravely. "Mebbe she'll do, after all. If Dan'l's took up fer her, there's a chance."

## CHAPTER XX

DAWN went back to the Golden Swan that evening tired but triumphant. She had had a most successful session of school, and she knew it. She felt the victor's blood running wildly through her veins, and longed to have the minister know how well she had succeeded.

The teaching part had not troubled her in the least. Fresh from school-books, blest with a love of study and a gift for imparting knowledge, she entered into the work with a zest. The problem of discipline, which had bade fair in the morning to shipwreck her hopes, had resolved itself into a very simple matter since she had conquered the school leader. It puzzled her a little to know just how she had done it, and why he had succumbed so easily, yet she felt a pleasant elation in recognizing the power she had over him. As she lay in her little room, after the candle was out that night, she pondered it, and resolved to try to help Daniel to be a fine fellow. Perhaps some day he would grow to be something like Charles. He never could be as fine and noble, of course, for he was a rough boy, uncultured and ignorant; but he had nice eyes, and he might develop good qualities if he were helped. Dawn would have been horrified if she could have known that instead of loafing with the men at the grocery, where he usually spent his evenings, Daniel was at that moment standing in the dark of the kitchen porch of his home, behind the cool morning-glory vines, looking out at the stars and thinking with wonder of the delight it had been to have her soft hands strike his face, and her dainty personality flash down upon him, even in her beautiful wrath.

Daniel Butterworth was only a boy yet, but new thoughts were stirring in his heart, and an absorbing admiration for her had entered into his soul to stay. Hitherto he had been a big, good-natured, rollicking animal. His mind had been upon either fun or practical matters, never upon books. He had not been taught to think. His surroundings had been rough, easy-going, and practical. Nothing beautiful had ever touched him before, yet his soul had responded quickly now that it had come, and in one brief day Daniel seemed to have grown beyond his seventeen years and to have come suddenly face to face with manhood.

And the cause of his sudden awakening had been the new teacher's hands, so small and soft, and yet so strong. As he thought about them, they seemed to have been made of finer stuff than most women's hands; to have been tinted like the inner leaf of a half-blown rose, and to have borne a subtle perfume upon his senses. How he could have seen their color when the "rose-leaves" were smiting stinging blows upon his closed eyes, he did not stop to reason. He leaned his face against a great morning-glory leaf in the darkness, and its coolness against his fevered cheeks reminded him of her hands, and thrilled him in a way he did not understand. He looked up at the stars, between the strings on which the morning-glories twined, and wondered at himself, and thrilled again with a solemn joy. But all he knew was that he liked the new teacher, and meant to study hard, if that would please her, and that he would lick any boy that dared molest her or disturb her gentle rule. So much the little hands had accomplished in their first quick, decisive battle.

Then Daniel kicked off his boots noisily and tiptoed up the creaking stairs to his attic chamber, to make his mother think he had been at the village store, as usual. Not for the world would he have her know he had spent the evening among the kitchen morning-glories, thinking about a girl! And she a schoolmarm at that! He blushed deeply in the darkness at the thought.

After that first day of getting acquainted with her scholars, and finding out who were in the various classes, Dawn fashioned her school on the model of Friend Ruth's as nearly as was consistent with existing circumstances. The rules she laid down were stricter than the village school had ever known before, and went more into detail. A code of ethics was gradually formed among the scholars, who followed the lead of Daniel Butterworth and succumbed to the leadership of the new teacher. Her beauty and her youth combined to make both boys and girl fall victims to her charm. They fairly worshipped at her shrine, and went long pilgrimages after berries or rare flowers and ferns, that they might be rewarded with the flash of gratitude in her lovely eyes. They suffered torments in refraining from their usual mischief, that they might escape the flash of steel from those same eyes, for once that was felt, they had no desire to re-experience it. It became the fashion to treat her as a sort of queen, and Dawn was very gracious to her subjects, though always masterful. She smiled upon their offerings impartially, even upon Bug Higginson's small sister's donation of moistly withered dandelions. Yet when she discovered some deviation from the laws she had laid down, she was severity itself, almost flying into a passion with them, outraged goodness in her eyes, and impulsive intensity in her every motion. At such times she seemed to have a special gift of speech, coming directly to the point and saying the things that would most cut the culprit.

Once behind a stump fence in the woods she came upon a row of her boys placidly smoking corn-cob pipes, in imitation of the village loafers—or of their respected fathers, each of whom had threatened dire things to his offspring if he was ever caught at the practice. Her horror and disgust quickly blazed into words, until every boy wished that a hole would open in the ground wide enough to swallow him for a little while.

Dawn had no convictions or principles about the matter. She was moved by an innate dislike of the practice, intensified by the fact that Harrington Winthrop had once smoked in her company while walking with her in the woods, and had never even asked permission. The smell of tobacco smoke ever after gave her a sickening sense of dislike.

The boys threw their pipes away, and Daniel Butterworth, rising from the root of the tree on which he had been seated, commanded:

"Fellers, if she don't like it, we quit! D'ye understand? We quit entirely. I'll thrash any boy that breaks the rule."

The pipes were thrown away, and seven boys with very red cheeks and downcast eyes entered school a trifle late that noon and sheepishly slunk to their desks.

The next morning Daniel Butterworth was found tacking up on the blackboard a clipping from a newspaper, in which was set forth how a certain Eliphalet Howe, a guest at the Tremont House in Boston, had been arrested for breaking the law which declared that there should be no smoking on the streets. The said Eliphalet had been found guilty and fined twenty-five dollars for the offense, though he had pleaded in defense that the sidewalk where he stood to smoke was in front of the Fremont House, and that therefore, as he was on the premises of the house where he was stopping, he was not breaking the law.

At recess the scholars filed solemnly around and read the item, and looked with awe at Daniel, who read the papers and knew so much about affairs. Dawn smiled to herself to see how Daniel was helping her.

But Dawn knew nothing of the thrashings her champion gave to the smokers whose habits were not easily broken up, nor how they were forced to find other quarters for their secret meetings, or scatter by themselves in hiding to pursue the practice. Public opinion had turned, and it was no longer popular to do anything the teacher disliked. Daniel was even known to send two boys home one day as they entered the school yard, because they smelled of smoke and he had told them the teacher did not like it.

It was not to be supposed that in so large a school everything would always be pleasant and easy, nor that the scholars would always be angels. They had their noisy days, and their mischievous days, and their stupid days, and now and then Dawn felt disheartened and discouraged. But matters were made far easier for her than she perhaps fully realized, because of Daniel Butterworth and his devotion to her.

Dawn was grateful to the boy, and in return for his championship she let him carry her books home, walking a little way behind with some of his devoted boy followers, while she was escorted by an eager group of little girls.

At first there was a sort of jealousy of her among the older girls, who were inclined to toss their heads, and whisper among themselves that she was no older than they, so why should she put on so many airs? They suspected her of taking the attention of the boys away from them; but as the days went by, and Dawn entered into her work with enthusiasm, planning debates and plays and readings for them, and making even the dullest lessons glow with interest because she really seemed to like them herself, opposition melted away and they succumbed to her charm.

For one so young and inexperienced, it was wonderful what she could do with those girls and boys. The parents began to talk about it, the minister saw it with gratification, and pleased himself by thinking his child might have been like that if she had lived. Presently the whole town was proud to own her as a kind of public institution, like the doctor and the minister.

There were a few old ladies who shook their heads and wondered how it was that she had come so far, from that wicked city of New York, to teach their school, without there being a single relative in the vicinity. The village seamstress, with half a dozen pins in one corner of her mouth, would talk about it wherever she went to work, and say, "What I'd like to know is, who knows anything about her? What is she? Why doesn't she tell about herself?"

But in spite of all, Dawn walked calmly back and forth to her school, and managed the scholars with a degree of dignity and skill that would have done credit to a far older teacher. The whole town gradually began to love her. It was a nine days' wonder that Daniel Butterworth had been so changed by her influence. His mother never could get done thanking the new teacher, sometimes with

tears running down her cheeks. Often she would send to
her by Daniel a paper of fresh doughnuts or a soft ginger-
bread, or even a juicy apple-pie, as a token of her thankfulness.

Dawn was "boarding round," and the days she spent
at the Butterworths' comfortable, weather-beaten old
farm-house were one continual jubilee for the family, and
a season of triumph for the teacher. The best dishes and
the finest table-cloth were got out, and a fire was built
in the solemn front room. There, after the supper, which
was composed of all the nicest things Mrs. Butterworth
knew how to concoct, the family would gather around
the teacher to listen while she talked or read to them.

And Dawn, because she wanted to help Daniel, and
also because she thoroughly enjoyed the admiration and
attention she was receiving, entered into it all, and hunted
out stories to read to them, and finally gave them a taste
of Shakespeare, which she read with remarkable understanding and dramatic power, considering that she had
never had any interpreter but herself.

A new world was open to the house of Butterworth.
Even the old farmer sat open-mouthed and listened,
watching the wonderful change of expression on the beautiful girlish face.

There were flowers in a tumbler on the dinner-table,
stiffly arranged by Daniel's oldest sister, Rachel. Daniel
wet and combed his tawny hair before he came to meals.
It was unusual, and the smaller children noticed and followed suit.

It was one day when Dawn sat at the table, talking
and laughing and making them all forget the common-
placeness of life, with her cheeks as red as the late pink
aster tucked in among her curls, that Daniel's mother
noticed with a heart of satisfaction the look on her boy's
face. That Daniel should take to a girl like that was all
and more than her mother heart could wish. And why
not? Were not the Butterworths well off? Was not their
farm the largest and most flourishing in the whole country? True, they had not painted their house in a long
time, and didn't go in much for fancy dressing, but that
was easily changed; and the barns had always been kept
in fine repair, which was a good test of prosperity. Thus

Mrs. Butterworth meditated in the watches of the night, but she never mentioned the matter, even to the boy's father, for John was "turrible easy upset of an idea, an' it was just as well to let things take their own way, 'long's it was sech a good way for once."

But Dawn had no idea that any such notion had entered the good woman's head, and enjoyed her stay at the Butterworths' heartily, going on to the next place with regret.

There were places where boarding round was not altogether agreeable; where the rooms were small and cold and had to be shared with younger members of the family; where the blankets were thin, or the feather-beds odorous; where the morning's ham sizzling in the spider on the kitchen stove below came up through wide cracks in unappetizing smoke; where the master of the house was gruff, and her welcome was grudgingly given. Many a night she cried herself to sleep in these places, and wondered why she had been born to suffer so, and to be so lonely.

The thought of Charles, and of the day of her wedding, was growing to be like a dim and misty dream. She still hugged it to her heart, as a most precious treasure, but day by day it was becoming more unreal to her.

However, take it all in all, Dawn was perhaps happier than she had been since she was a tiny child with her mother. She was interested in her work, enjoyed the companionship of many of the children, and was pleased to feel that she was independent and self-supporting. Of her own private fortune she never thought. She had been told that there was money left to her by her mother's father, but it made little impression, and she had never cared to ask how much. It was just a part of the world she had left behind her when she ran away in her attempt to undo mischief she had never meant to do. She kept herself much more strictly than Friend Ruth had ever succeeded in doing, feeling as she did her responsibility, now that she was a real teacher. But she allowed herself many a playtime as the winter drew on and the snow-falls made coasting and skating possible. There was a hill behind the school-house where at noon she coasted

with her scholars, shouting and laughing with the rest.
Each boy strove to have the honor of her company upon
his sled, but she distributed her favors impartially.

It was only when she went home with "Bug" Higginson, to spend her week, and discovered to her dismay
where he got his nickname, that her heart failed her entirely, and she felt she had met with something she could
not bear. However, that experience did not last forever
and Dawn went cheerily on her way, brightening the
whole town with her presence, which, now that she was
set free from the confines and oppression that had always been about her, seemed to grow and glow with a
beautiful inner life.

The school-children were not the only ones who
admired the new teacher, and sought her society. There
was not a young man in town who did not gaze after her
as she went down the street, and wish himself a scholar
again in the old red school-house.

About Christmas time, a new annoyance loomed up
and threatened to spoil Dawn's bright prospects. Suddenly, without warning, the youngest of the selectmen,
Silas Dobson, took a violent interest in the school. He
would drop in at all hours, and stay the session out, taking occasion to walk home with the teacher, if possible.

Daniel, who had never presumed to walk beside
her alone, frowned heavily and grew almost morose as
the thing was repeated.

Dawn was very polite and a little frightened at first.
It spoiled the cosy feeling of her school to have visitors.
The presence of this particular selectman stirred up the
latent mischief in the scholars. As his visits were repeated, the teacher was filled with a growing consterna-
tion.

Silas was a long, thin man about thirty years old, a
widower with five children, and an angular mother, who
kept them in order. He was the editor of the village paper, and as a literary man he claimed that he felt a deep
responsibility toward the school. Daniel heard him say
this one day, and told the boys he'd knock Silas's responsibility into a cocked hat if he bothered the teacher much
more.

Daniel's opportunity arrived one night when there was a quilting bee out the old turnpike road, and everybody was invited to the supper. The quilting began in the afternoon, and Dawn closed school early, so that she and the older girls might attend. The young men were coming to supper, and they were all to ride home in the moonlight.

With her thimble in her pocket and her eyes shining, Dawn hurried off from the school-house in company with the older girls who could sew. They looked back once to wave their hands toward the group of boys who lingered wistfully behind, keeping watch of them. The older boys were to come to the quilting bee later, but they felt— some of them—that the afternoon was a long blank in spite of good skating and the half-holiday. Somehow, the coming of the new teacher had made them more anxious to have the girls along and to have a good time all together. But they consoled themselves with the anticipation of the evening. The teacher had promised to ride home with them, and they were planning a big sleighload, all huddled happily on the straw, with songs and shoutings and a good time generally. Dawn was looking forward to the ride as much as any of them.

But Silas Dobson had other plans. He brought his own horse and cutter, and, having arranged that his mother should return home with a neighbor, he himself planned to monopolize the teacher. To this end, soon after supper he edged over to where she sat among the girls, and conferred the honor of his company upon her for the ride home; at least, that was the impression he gave as he told her that he wished her to go home with him.

"Oh, thank you," said Dawn politely, "but I've already promised to go with my pupils. Daniel Butterworth is to bring a big sleigh, and we are all going home together."

Silas's face darkened and his back stiffened.

"That will be quite uncomfortable for you," he said decidedly, as if it were not to be thought of. Dawn wondered why it was that people were always taking her affairs out of her hands so confidently, without asking her leave. But she was no longer the child she had been at home or school. She was feeling the strength of independence. She sat up with dignity.

"Oh. I shall enjoy it," she answered, sparkling at the thought.

"My cutter is here, and you'd better go with me," said Silas. "I'll speak to Dan about it and make it all right, so he won't expect you."

"Oh, please don't do that!" cried Dawn anxiously. (Why was it he reminded her so much of Harrington Winthrop?) "I promised Daniel and the children. I wouldn't disappoint them for anything. Thank you just the same."

Some one else came up then, and Silas turned away, but Dawn watched him uneasily. From the look on his face, one would have thought she had accepted his attention with delight. He did not act like a man who had received a rebuff.

Later, when Dan drove his horses with a flourish to the old horse-block in front of the house, Silas was waiting for him.

"You needn't wait for Miss Montgomery, Dan," said the selectman in a patronizing tone. "She's going with me."

"She's not any such a thing," growled Dan. "She promised us she'd go in our team."

"Yes, she was afraid you'd be disappointed, but I told her I'd make it right with you," said Silas, in a soothing tone. "Hurry, now, and load up and drive out of the way. Don't you see the other folks are waiting? You wouldn't stand in the way of a lady's comfort, would you, especially when she doesn't want to go with you?"

Dan glared at his adversary in speechless wrath for an instant, while the girls and boys were climbing in, then gave a cut to his horses with the whip and drove the long sleigh with its merry load out into the white mist of the moonlit road and round a curve to the fence, where he flung the reins to another boy, telling him to wait and keep quiet. Then he stole back around the house and stood in the shadow of a great wood-pile, near enough to hear all that went on, but not to be seen.

The guests merrily trooped forth in the path of candlelight that shone from the open house door, and Dawn's musical laugh rang over them all; but when she came out to the horse-block and saw Silas standing alone beside his cutter, she drew back and looked around in dismay.

"Why, where is Daniel?" she asked anxiously. "They told me he wanted me to come now."

"Daniel has gone," said Silas pleasantly. "I explained to him how much more comfortable it would be for you in my sleigh, and, besides, he was crowded as it was. He hadn't room enough for you. Just get right in, and I'll show you what my mare can do in getting you over the snow."

"Daniel is gone!" Dawn echoed in a troubled voice. "Oh, no, thank you"—drawing back timidly and looking toward the door. "I will see if Mrs. Butterworth is inside yet. I can go with her. I will not trouble you."

But Silas was not to be thus set aside.

"Don't think of such a thing," he commanded. "Just get right in." He reached out to grasp her arm and detain her from her purpose, but just as he touched the sleeve of her coat his arm was grasped from behind, and a skilful thrust of Daniel Butterworth's long arm sent him spinning backward into a big snowbank.

When Silas Dobson arose, disconcerted and spluttering, from the snow-bank, Dawn had vanished, whisked around the wood-pile in a jiffy by Daniel, lifted for an instant in his strong arms, carried across a broad expanse of unbroken snow, and tucked neatly into the sleigh among the girls and boys.

The whole sleigh-load had divined Dan's purpose, and they kept silent until she was safe among them, and Dan in the front seat had gathered up his reins again. Then they gave a united shout which rang through the moonlit air and struck sharply on the ears of the disconcerted Silas as he climbed hastily into his lone sleigh and turned his horse's head in the opposite direction.

The next time Silas Dobson came to visit the school he stayed after hours and said he wished to talk with the teacher.

With lowering brow, Daniel lingered in the back of

the room, phenomenally busy with his books. Dawn cast a frightened look around, and her eyes rested on him with appeal. His eyes seemed to give back comfortable assurance of help as he sat down with a thump and began to figure vigorously at a sum he had not finished in the arithmetic class. Silas eyed his youthful enemy, and finally requested that he be sent home, as he wished to have a little private conversation.

"Oh!" laughed Dawn, loud enough for Daniel to hear. "Daniel has to stay to-night to finish his sums. It would not do for me to let him go. I might lose my school if I did not act fairly, you know."

Daniel figured away vigorously, putting down any numerals that entered his head. There was a warm feeling around his heart. It was as exhilarating as scoring a point in a ball-game. He was apparently deaf to what was going on about him, and frowned over his sum in feigned perplexity.

"Sit down Mr. Dobson," went on Dawn, summoning all her dignity. "We can talk with entire freedom here. Daniel is busy and will not notice." She spoke in a low, distant tone, and seated herself at the desk.

"I'm one of the principal selectmen," frowned Dobson, as he sat down at her bidding. "You needn't be afraid to send him home."

"It isn't in the least necessary," said Dawn, thankful to Daniel from the depths of her heart for his presence.

Silas Dobson lowered his voice and, drawing gradually nearer to the teacher, launched into a flowery paragraph which he had prepared and rehearsed before his mirror. It contained phases about Miss Montgomery's starry eyes, raven locks, pearly teeth, and rosy cheeks, and was calculated to convey his admiration in a delicate editorial manner. Noting the drooping eyelashes and deepened color of the girl before him, he proceeded from this preamble to make her understand that his interest in the school had not been altogether for the school's sake, and that he was offering her honorable attentions, which, if all went well, would mean a proposal of marriage later.

If he could have seen the steel flash under the drooping eyelashes, he would not have gone on to impress her with the value of such an offer, nor told its advantages in half so complacent a tone.

As usual Dawn had control of herself in this unpleasant crisis, and while his words filled her with dismay and repulsion her tone was cool, low, deliberate:

"I have no doubt you mean to be kind, Mr. Dobson——" she began.

"Not at all, not at all, it is my pleasure and my will," he interrupted effusively.

"But," she went on, ignoring his interruption, "I have no desire for attention from any one, and will have to ask you to excuse me from accepting it."

He looked at her in astonishment, and thought she must be coquetting; but his most earnest solicitations failed to get anything further from her than the fact that she would rather not receive his attentions.

"Do you know," he asked angrily, "that I am a man of importance in this town? I have influence enough with the selectmen to take this school away from you if I choose. Take care how you treat me!"

"I suppose there are schools in other places, then," answered Dawn coolly, looking him in the eye now, though she felt every fibre of her being in a tremor.

"Are you aware, Miss Montgomery, that I am an editor, and that a very slight word from my pen would go abroad through the land and ruin your reputation so that you could not get any school anywhere?"

"I cannot see why you should want to do such an unkind thing as that, after what you have said about liking me, but if you do, you need not stop on my account. I can find something else to do. I certainly could never have anything more to do with a man that threatened such things."

"I did not say I would do any such thing, Miss Montgomery," began Silas, eager now to retract his angry words. "I was merely trying to show you what risks you were taking in talking to me as you did. I mean well by you, and I think you ought to appreciate it. If I were to offer these attentions to any other girl in the village, she would feel flattered."

"Daniel"—Dawn's voice rang clear and without a trace of the excitement she was under—"if you need help with those sums now, I can give it. Bring them up here, please."

Daniel lost no time in getting to his feet and gathering up his scattered papers, but the selectman arose in protest and put out his hand toward the teacher.

"Don't call that boy up here yet," he commanded, and dared to lay his hand upon the girl's arm as he did so, bringing his smug countenance quite near, that he might speak so the approaching boy would not hear.

But the words on his lips were never uttered. Without an instant's hesitation, Dawn sprang away from him, crying, "Don't you dare to touch me, sir!" and with catlike agility Daniel glided up the aisle and struck the selectman full in the face. Silas reeled backward off the platform, and staggered ignominiously against the wall, clutching at the blackboard rail for support, his hat rolling at his feet and his general appearance undignified, to say the least. Daniel stood in a combative attitude, looking at him contemptuously. He would have enjoyed nothing better than to give Silas Dobson a good thrashing.

"You shall answer for this, you young rascal," threatened Silas, shaking his fist at Daniel, as he recovered his balance and began to brush the chalk dust from his best coat. "This is the second offense, remember!"

Silas was no match for Daniel in a fight, and he knew it.

"All right," said Daniel, unconcerned. "We'll see who does the answering, but don't you dare touch Teacher again, d'ye hear?"

"I shall have a talk with Mr. Butterworth, who is also a selectman, and with the minister," said Dawn, with dignity. "If they wish me to give up the school, I will do so, and thus save you the trouble of doing what you have threatened, Mr. Dobson."

"You make a great mistake, Miss Montgomery," said Silas, thoroughly alarmed now. "I have no desire to have you give up the school."

"Well, I guess you better not have," said Daniel threateningly—"not unless you want a good coat of tar and feathers." There was a look of wrath in the boy's blue eyes that boded no good for the discomfited selectman.

"You have not understood me," repeated Silas lamely, glaring with helpless anger at Daniel, and then casting a wistful appeal at the teacher.

But Dawn had taken up the arithmetic, and was figuring rapidly. She only raised her head to say coldly, "Good afternoon, Mr. Dobson. You will do me a favor if you won't come to visit the school any more. You hinder my work, and I do not like it." Then she turned to Daniel and began to explain the sum.

"You have not understood me," murmured Silas again.

"I guess you've been understood all right," said Daniel grimly over his shoulder.

With a last angry glare at Dawn's protector, and a threat he would never dare to carry out, Silas Dobson took himself off the scene of action.

The next week there appeared a prominent editorial about the public school and its brilliant young teacher, who was doing so much for the youth of the village, and should be encouraged in every way by the parents.

Daniel read it to a group of the boys in the school yard, and then cut it out with his penknife and pinned it to the blackboard, as an expression of the sentiments of the whole school.

After that little episode, there was a closer bond than ever between Daniel and his teacher. They never talked it over, nor even mentioned it, except that Dawn, as Silas's footsteps died away that afternoon, had put her little hand on the boy's rough one for just an instant, and said:

"Thank you so much, Daniel. I do not know what I should have done if you had not stayed."

Daniel had turned away with a sudden feeling as if he was going to choke, while the blood in his heart pounded up into his face. But aloud he only said in a bashful tone:

"Aw, that's nothin'. He needs a good lickin', an' I'd like to be the one to give it to him."

Afterward, Dawn wondered that she had dared to speak as she had to Silas Dobson, a selectman, and the editor of the paper. And if she had it in her to do so

now, how was it that she had allowed Harrington Winthrop to lead her on to a hated marriage, when she might
have easily stopped it by being decided? Had her brief
months of independence given her courage? It seemed
strange to her now that she had been so afraid to tell her
father what she felt about it until matters had gone so
far that it was almost impossible to stop it. Her heart
burned within her sometimes to go back and tell Harrington Winthrop just what she felt about him. She had been
weak, she decided, terribly weak, in yielding in the beginning to her desire for a home of her own, and for
freedom from any possibility of having to stay in the
house with her father's wife. Yet, were not all women
weak and helpless sometimes, when it came to a testing of
their strength against men? Her mother had not been able
to cope with her father's will. It was all a mixed-up
world, and full of trouble. She turned on her scanty
cornhusk pillow and wished for the dawn of a day that
would have no sorrow.

Just why it was that her experience with Silas Dobson made the thought of Charles and her marriage so
much more vivid than before, Dawn could not understand, and she thought about it a great deal in the watches
of the night, when she should have been sleeping. A new
phase of her position was forced upon her: she was in a
measure deceiving other people about herself. Silas Dobson, disagreeable as he was, had no idea that his attentions were an insult to her because she was already married. Of course she could refuse to accept attentions
from any one, but if Silas Dobson had been a pleasant
and agreeable man, it might have been difficult to explain to him without telling him the truth why she could
not ride nor walk with him. It was all a terrible problem,
and night after night she cried herself to sleep.

Sometimes she stayed in unpleasant quarters, where
she had perhaps to climb a ladder, and share the loft
above the lean-to kitchen with two of the small children
of the family. Often the cracks would be so wide that
the snow would blow in, drift across her bed, and even
blow into her face. Then as she dropped off to sleep,
lulled by the roar of the wind outside, she would wish

that the snow might come softly and cover her out of sight, that she might sleep forever.

At other times, the thought of Charles brought a great longing to see him, and to hear his voice whisper, "My darling," once more, as he had that night when they stood for one blissful moment together in their room, before Betty called them. Then Dawn would go over all the happenings of the evening: the scene at the supper table, and every syllable that Madam Winthrop had uttered, up to the awful moment when the mother had hurled her accusations, and the truth had burst upon the young bride's heart in all its nakedness: that she was married out of generosity! Bitterness toward this woman was changing slowly into understanding. How was the mother to blame for what she had said? It was all true, except that she, Dawn, had not known it, and was therefore not to blame.

Then she began to wonder how it was that she could have been so deceived. She could not blame her mother-in-law for doubting her word, for would not she also doubt that a girl could be married to a man and think he was some other? Whose fault had it been? Not Charles's, for he had fully vindicated himself. She would sooner doubt herself than him. Could her father have known about it? Could he have wished her to be married to one whom she did not know, without even telling her? It was believable that he might have thought it of little importance to her, if he, her father, willed it so; yet while often treating her as if she were a chattel, without will of her own, he had ever been perfectly frank with her. She felt that he would have informed her of the change of bridegrooms, and not merely carried out his wishes without announcing it to her. She could scarcely believe he could think it would not matter to her. But after careful thought she was inclined to lay the deception at her stepmother's door, and she was not long in fathoming the true reason for it. Mrs. Van Rensselaer knew her unhappy state of mind, and probably feared that Dawn would rebel against being married. To have her remain at home was the worst possible thing that could happen to her step-mother, Dawn knew, for from

childhood she had been hated by the woman who had
taken her outraged mother's place. It was all quite plain
—all but one thing: how had Harrington Winthrop been
turned aside from his purpose of marrying her? Had he
done it of himself, or had her father found out something
about him that he did not like, or had Charles managed
it for her? And where was Harrington? Would she ever
meet him again? The thought took such hold upon her
that it visited her in dreams and made her cry out in
alarm as she sought to hide from his pursuing phantom.

After her experience with Silas Dobson, Daniel was
ever vigilant, attending her to and from school, albeit
seldom alone with her. He seemed to be entirely willing
that his favorite followers should share his privileges of
her company; and often there were several tiny girls, or
older ones, in the triumphal procession going to and
from the red school-house, taking "teacher" home. Daniel
showed himself a gentle giant toward the little ones, too,
picking them up when they fell down, wiping off the
mud, and carrying them if they were tired. Dawn saw
him daily growing more manly and kindly, and she felt
proud of him. Perhaps, some day, he might become something like Charles, though never quite so cultured, for he
lacked the refined home training. But she realized more
and more that he was a good boy and a great comfort
to her. As for herself, she felt years older than he, and
far beyond him in experience. She never dreamed how
it was with him toward her. If she had, she might have
given up in despair, and cried out that there was nothing
good for her in the world.

So Daniel continued to guard her, and to watch the
movements of Silas Dobson as a cat watches a mouse.
If Silas had wished, he would have had no opportunity
to repeat his troublesome attentions, for whenever he
found himself in the neighborhood of where the teacher
happened to be boarding, he was likely to notice Daniel
in the immediate foreground.

So the long winter went pleasantly by. There were
husking bees, quiltings, singing-school, and Lyceum
nights. Dawn became a prominent participant at all. In
singing-school, no voice was so clear as hers, and she
could take the high notes to the envy of every other

soprano in the village. At the Lyceum her readings were more popular than any others.

In spite of her frequent loneliness, and her feeling of being cast off by all who should naturally protect her —though it was her own fault, of course, that she had run away, and she blamed no one—Dawn had never been quite so happy in her life. Her hours were pleasantly employed, she had friends who admired her, and she might do as she pleased. It opened a wide and interesting life before her. If only there had not been that ache as of something lost, that memory of her one beautiful day of love, which remained as a haunting vision, she would have felt herself blest beyond most girls. But all the time there was that sense of something wrong, that could not be set right; of a great mistake that might not ever be mended.

And then, one morning when a hint of spring was in the air, and the snow was all gone save lingering patches in dark corners and in shady hollows, and the sunshine was making everybody feel glad, she came face to face with Harrington Winthrop!

## CHAPTER XXI

IT was in front of the Golden Swan that she met Harrington. He was just coming down the steps, and must have arrived the night before.

He stopped suddenly, with the look in his eyes like a cat's when she spies a bird and, crouching, steals slowly nearer.

Dawn paused for just an instant, too, in wild dismay, having the instinct to flee, yet realizing that she must not, because the whole town would think it strange. She wished to have the power to pass him unrecognized, yet with sudden sinking of soul she knew that she had not. His eyes had met hers with recognition, and she must hold her position courageously. She wished she knew all the circumstances of his giving her up, and it flashed across her that she must not let him know that she was ignorant of them. He must have no advantage, for his strange power over her might crush her in spite of herself. Something tightened round her heart and gripped it like a vise as his cold calculating glance looked her over, and a cruel satisfaction settled about his hateful mouth.

Dawn gave a sort of gasp and started on, summoning all the spirit with which she had vanquished Silas Dobson, and wondering why she could not be as haughty and as brave now. The sight of Daniel's butter-nut clad shoulders in the distance, waiting at the corner with a group of other boys, gave her courage, but her face was white, and she felt her limbs trembling beneath her.

But Harrington Winthrop did not intend to let her slip through his fingers thus easily, now that he had found her, apparently far from her natural guardians. He of course knew nothing of her marriage with his brother.

He hastened down the steps with effusive manner and smiling countenance, and extended his hand in a warm greeting—if anything he ever did could be said to be actually warm.

"I did not expect this pleasure," he said in an oily voice, and with an impressive glance intended to convey deep emotion.

She drew back from the hand he offered, and wished she could take her eyes from his hateful ones, but she could not.

"Poor child!" he murmured in mock pity. "They have told you terrible untruths about me, and you have suffered and find it hard to forgive. But, indeed, it was none of my fault. I will explain the whole matter, and we can still evade the enemies who are trying to part us, and be happy togeher."

Dawn shuddered!"

"Where can we go that we shall not be interrupted? Suppose we walk in the woods?"

Dawn was filled with terror. She looked about wildly, and saw to her relief that Daniel, with his special body-guard in the rear, was sauntering slowly toward her. His attitude of protection gave her courage. He was watching the stranger with a curious suspicion. Had his intuition told him that she needed help? Daniel was but a few steps away.

She drew her breath in quickly, and spoke in a clear voice:

"I have no time to talk with any one at present. I am on my way to school, and shall be busy until late in the afternoon. I am a teacher."

She drew herself up with dignity, and he realized that she was not the simple child he had seen last, but a woman with an independence of her own.

"Dismiss your school," he said in the voice he was used to having obeyed. "I cannot possibly wait until this afternoon. I must talk with you at once. I don't intend to let you slip through my fingers so easily, now that I have found you, my pretty lady." He smiled, but there was a sinister menace in his voice.

"It is impossible to dismiss school," said Dawn decidedly. "I should lose my position if I did a thing like that. Besides, I do not wish to talk with you. There is nothing to talk about."

"There is everything to talk about," said the man, a fierce light coming into his eyes. "They have told you lies about me, and taken you away from me, but I mean to have you in spite of them. I will explain to you all about that poor woman. She was never my wife at all. Come, let the school take care of itself. You will have no further need of it. You belong to me, and I will take care of you. Come with me!"

The last word was a command, and with it he took hold of her shoulder almost roughly and attempted to turn her round.

At once there was a low growl behind his heels, and Daniel Butterworth's dog took hold of the calf of his leg as if he too would say, "Come with me!"

Harrington promptly let go of Dawn, who took advantage of her freedom and fairly flew down the street, leaving Daniel to settle up matters between his dog and the stranger, in whose frightened antics the boy was secretly taking deep delight. When Dawn had turned the corner and was out of sight, Dan called the dog off. Then Harrington Winthrop discovered that his lady had departed. Before that time he had been otherwise occupied.

Angry, baffled, and exhausted, he was in nowise attractive. An interested group of boys and one or two little girls who had torn themselves away from the teacher's side encircled him. Dan looked at him in quiet amusement, and then called his dog and betook himself to school. Most of the group followed him, with reluctant glances back at the dishevelled stranger. One little girl lingered, eying him wonderingly, and twisting her apron-strings.

"Where is your school-house, little girl?" asked Harrington sharply.

The child felt compelled to answer.

"Round that there corner over there, and down the road a good piece."

Harrington glanced after the boys and the dog uncertainly. Did the dog go to school also?

"Where does your teacher board?" he asked again.

"She's boardin' round, an' it's Ann Peabody's turn this week. She's got a boy what's blind in one eye."

"Ah! Indeed! That's a pity. Where does Ann Peabody live?"

"Next door but one to the church. The house with Johnny-jump-ups by the gate, an' a laylock bush by the stoop."

"Thank you. Now tell me what time your school lets out, that's a little lady."

"It don't let out till four o'clock—but it'll be took up 'fore I get there if I don't hurry."

She took to her heels forthwith, and Harrington Winthrop limped up the steps of the Golden Swan to repair damages and consider his next line of procedure.

When Dawn arrived at the school-house she was almost too frightened to stop. It was late, and most of the scholars were there. They trooped gladly in after her. She had made school for them a kind of all-day picnic, and they were eager to begin it. Even after she had hung up her bonnet and cape, and opened the high lid of her desk, her heart was beating like a trip-hammer. Now and then she looked apprehensively toward the door, and was reassured when at last she saw Daniel saunter in with a comfortable smile on his face, while the dog took up his station on the door-step. Rags often came to school. It was a part of his privilege to guard the teacher, and he felt he had earned a morning session by his gallantry in defending her against the rude stranger who had dared to lay hands upon her. He sat down comfortably just inside the school-room door, his forepaws hanging over the step, but he kept his head erect. With his nose on his paws and one eye closed, not once during the morning did he relax. He felt that there was further trouble to be expected, and he must be ready.

Dawn smiled, albeit with trembling lips, and set about the morning's routine; but her mind was troubled, and she kept starting and glancing uneasily toward the door. Daniel saw this, and grew grave with apprehension. What had the stranger to do with the teacher, and why did she seem to be so uneasy? Had he some power over her? She certainly did not look happy when he had laid his hand upon her arm, just before, he, Dan, had given that low signal to Rags. She couldn't have liked the stranger to be there, or she would not have run away when she got the chance.

At recess she made Daniel happy by calling him to the desk and in a low tone thanking him for helping her. She did not explain further than to say that the man was an old acquaintance whom she did not like. Daniel understood him to be in the same class with Silas Dobson.

During the morning session of school Dawn's mind was in a whirl, trying to think what she should do. She dreaded the coming of the afternoon, when school would close, and she must go back to Mrs. Peabody's house. Winthrop would certainly search her out. It had been a great mistake to let him know she was the school-teacher, for though he did not know her assumed name he could easily find her now. She dreaded any encounter with him. A frenzy of fear had taken possession of her.

As the morning went on, she tried to make some plan for escape. No longer was it safe in this vicinity. She must get away and hide from him. Where? Could she ever hope to evade a man who spent his entire time travelling over the earth? He had the assurance of the devil himself, and it was almost hopeless to try to get beyond his grasp. Nevertheless, she must go.

The reading class which recited just before the noon-hour stumbled on its way for once without correction, while Dawn planned her next pitiful move.

At noon she sent one of the older girls to Mrs. Peabody's, to get her bag and a few little things that were lying about the room. She usually kept everything neatly packed in a large bag she had made—everything except her silk dress, which was hung on a nail. This the girl promised to fold nicely and put into the bag. She was to tell Mrs. Peabody that Dawn had decided to go a day before the time was up, and to thank the lady for all her kindness, and say Dawn was sorry she could not very well leave to explain it herself. The girl felt honored by the commission, and performed it to the letter, wishing the while that she knew where Teacher was going a day ahead of time, and resolving to ask her mother to invite the teacher to come to their house ahead of time, too.

Rags took up his station on the school-house steps again for the afternoon session, having been abundantly fed from the generous dinner-pails, on apple-pie, doughnuts, and chicken bones. Rags felt it in the air that something was going to happen, but nothing did, and four o'clock came at last.

Dawn had made the scholars write in their copybooks during the last hour of the afternoon. "Command you may your mind from play," straggled up and down a whole page in many of the books, while blots grew thick among the words, but no teacher wandered alertly up and down the aisles to watch and to correct; sometimes —oh, blessed honor!—to sit down and hold the quill pen, or, better still, take the dirty little fist of the writer into her own pink hand and guide the writing. The teacher sat behind a raised desk-lid, diligently writing, and took no heed of notes, or whittling, or even paper balls. Daniel Butterworth finally took Bug Higginson by the collar and stood him up behind the stove, but still the teacher wrote on.

It was a letter to the minister she was writing, and her young breast heaved with mingled emotions as she wrote. It was hard to have to leave this first school, where she had been so happy, and where she could still be so happy if she only had some one to protect her from the man who would probably haunt her through life. She had felt that she must make some brief explanation of her departure to the kind old man who had trusted her, and upon whom it would fall to explain her absence.

DEAR DR. MERCER [she wrote]:

*You have been so very kind to me that it gives me much sorrow to tell you that I must go away. Something has happened that makes it necessary for me to go away at once. I cannot even wait to say good-by to you or any one else. I am so sorry, for I have been very happy here, and I have tried to do my best; and there is the singing-school this week, and the barn-raising where I promised to read them a story after supper, and my dear school! I love them all! Will you please tell everybody how sorry I am to go away like this? You have all been so good to me, and I shall never find a place I love so much as this, I am sure, but I truly cannot help going. If you knew all about it, you would understand. Please thank Mrs. Mercer for the pretty collar she gave me that belonged to your daughter, and tell her I will keep it always. I am sorry to leave you without a teacher, but there is almost a month's pay due me, and perhaps that will help you to get some one right away. So please forgive me for leaving the school just as it was when I got it. I love it, and wish I could stay.*

*Yours very gratefully,*

*Mary Montgomery*

After folding, addressing, and sealing this letter, she closed her desk; then with sudden thought, as she caught Daniel's troubled eyes upon her, she open it again and wrote hastily:

DEAR DANIEL:

*I am having to go away in a great hurry. I cannot say good-by to anybody, but I must thank you for all you have done for me. I thank you more than words can ever tell. You cannot know how hard it is for me to go away from the school. Please study hard and try to be a good boy and then some day, when I hear of what a great man you are, I shall be so proud to have been your teacher.*

*Go to college, Daniel, and be as great a man as you can, and don't forget that you have helped me very, very much ever since I came here.*

*Your Grateful Teacher*

Her hand trembled as she sealed this other note. She closed the desk hastily and glanced at the clock. It was one minute after closing time. Bug Higginson was decorating the stove with a caricature of one of the selectmen. It all looked so homely and familiar and dear, and she was to see it no more! The tears sprang to her eyes, and she could scarcely control her voice to dismiss the school.

She shook her head and tried to smile when the girls asked if they might wait for her to walk home, telling them she must stay a little while, that she had something to do.

They all filed out save Daniel, who sat quietly in his seat, watching her with sad, puzzled eyes. Daniel had seen the glint of a tear as she looked at them.

"Aren't you going home to-night, Daniel?" she asked. She was dreading momentarily the approach of Harrington Winthrop. She seemed to know he would come to walk home with her. So did Rags, who sat very stiff and straight on the door-step, with bristling ears and eyes alert.

"Don't you want I should stay?" asked Daniel, and his eyes hinted that he understood she was in trouble.

"Oh, no, thank you, Daniel," she said, trying to make her voice sound cheery and natural, but somehow it broke into almost a sob.

Daniel eyed her curiously for a moment, and then got up slowly from his desk and went out. He gave Rags a look as he passed. The boy and the dog thoroughly understood each other. Rags did not stir. Daniel went down the path and out to the road; then down the road a few paces, after which he climbed the fence back into the school-yard. Then he walked over to a log behind the school-house and sat down where he could watch the road to the village.

As soon as he was gone, Dawn looked about her, caught her breath a moment, and seemed to bid good-by to all the childish forms that had but a few minutes before occupied the now empty benches. Then, spying Rags still

sitting in the doorway, she took the note she had written
to Daniel and, going over to the dog, tied it around his
neck with a bit of string. Rags got up and wagged his tail,
glancing eagerly at her, then back to the road again.

Dawn patted him lovingly.

"Take that note to Dan, Rags," she commanded.

Rags barked questioningly. He wanted to tell her
that he had been ordered to stay with her, but she did not
seem to understand. He wagged his tail harder, but he
did not budge.

"Go, Rags, good dog. Take that to Dan." She pointed
out the door.

Rags cast a protesting, anxious bark at her, a furtive
glance down the empty road, and hustled out the door. He
reasoned that Dan was near at hand and must settle the
confliction of duties himself. He could not but obey the
one whom he and his master alike worshipped.

The minute the dog had gone, Dawn put on her bonnet, caught up her cape and bag, and slipped out of the
door and around the school-house on the side farthest
from the village.

She fled through the back yard, crept under the lower
rail of the fence, and proceeded over into the meadow
where they had coasted all winter. In a moment more she
was out of sight down the hill. She had but to cross the
log which formed a bridge across the brook and she would
enter the woods that lay at the foot of Wintergreen Hill.
There she would be safe and could get away without being
seen by any one.

Daniel cut the string which held the note and sent
the dog back to his post, while he slowly unfolded it and
read, his hands trembling at the thought that she had written and sealed it, and that it was for him. A great tumult
of emotions went through his big, immature heart as he
tried to take it in. He had known something would happen, and was glad he had not gone away.

Rags hustled back to the school-house steps, but instantly he knew something was wrong. He looked into the
empty room. She was not there. He smelled his way up
to the desk, but could not bring her into existence. He
snuffed his way out to the steps and down the path in a
hurry, then came back baffled, with short, sharp, worried

barks, to hunt for the scent again. Snuff! Snuff! Snuff! Bark! Rags could not understand it. Yes—but it was— there was the scent! Snuff! Snuff! Snuff! Bark! Bark! He tried it over again to make sure. The scent went around the left of the school-house, through the girl's play-ground. What could she have gone around there for at this time of day? Had the enemy come during his absence and stolen her away?

Rags hurried around the school, snuffing and barking, scuttled under the fence in a hurry, and away down the hill, his bark growing more sure and relieved every minute.

Daniel was not accustomed to receiving letters. He grasped the meaning of that first sentence slowly, having lingered long over the "Dear Daniel." But he got no further than the first sentence: "I am having to go away in a great hurry." He got to his feet rapidly and went around to the school-house door. A great fear was in his heart. The absence of Rags confirmed it. He entered the deserted school-room. No one was there. He stepped up to the teacher's desk. A letter addressed to the minister lay there. Daniel stood still by the teacher's desk, his heart filled with foreboding, and read the remainder of his own letter. As he finished, he heard a step outside the door, and, looking up, saw the stranger of the morning before him.

Instinctively he reached out for the minister's letter on the desk and put it with his own into his coat-pocket. Then he faced the intruder quietly, and something in his steady blue eyes reminded the man of his morning encounter with the dog. He felt that he had an enemy in the boy before him.

Winthrop took off his hat and inquired suavely:

"Is Miss Van Rensselaer here? This is the school-house, isn't it?"

"It's the school-house all right," answered Dan, "but there ain't no Miss Van Rensselaer round. Don't know no such person. You must 'a' ben told wrong."

"Oh, no; I saw her this morning. In fact, she must have expected me. I refer to the teacher of this school."

"The teacher's Miss Montgomery—Miss Mary Montgomery—an' she's gone. She boards this week with the Peabodys', up by the church, second house beyond. She hasn't been gone from here five minutes."

"That is very strange," said the visitor. "I just walked down past the church and did not meet her."

"She sometimes stops a minute to see how the black-smith's little sick girl is, at the corner here. She might 'a' gone there, but she never stays long. You'd best go right up to Peabody's."

Daniel was anxious to get rid of the man, and he was certain that the teacher had not gone in the direction of the Peabodys', for he had watched the road every minute until he came around to the front of the school.

Harrington Winthrop took himself away, with a baffled look on his imperious face. As soon as he had passed from sight, Dan reconnoitered the school-yard.

There was no sign of anybody. He listened, but could not hear the dog. He gave a long, low whistle, and instantly from the distance, toward the woods, he heard a faint, sharp bark in answer. He whistled again, and again came the dog's response.

Daniel was over the fence in a second and down the hill, not whistling again until he reached the log across the brook. Then the dog's bark was nearer, but it ended suddenly, as if some one was holding his muzzle. The boy thought he understood, and bounded rapidly toward the place from which the sound seemed to have come. In a moment more he had plunged into the darkness of the woods.

## CHAPTER XXII

DANIEL found Dawn huddled at the foot of a tree, behind a thicket of laurel, with her bag beside her, and tears on her frightened face.

The dog had broken away from her and met him with a joyous bark, wagging his tail and running back and forth between them, his ragged, hairy body wriggling joyously; for had he not both of them here together, far away from intruding strangers? Why should not all be well now?

"Oh, Daniel!" said Dawn, in a voice that was almost a sob. "Why did you come after me?"

"I had to," said Dan, looking almost sullen. "I couldn't let you come off alone. Besides, you don't need to go. We won't let anybody hurt you. I can knock that fellow into the middle of next week if you say the word."

But the trouble was not lifted from her face.

"You are very good, and I thank you more than I can ever tell," she answered him; "but I must go away. He is a bad man, and he thinks he has some power over me. It would be of no use for you to knock him into next week, for he would be on hand again the next week to deal with. He would tell the minister and everybody that he had a right to take me away, and they would all believe him. He can make wrong things seem right to people. He has done it before. I'm afraid of him. I never expected to meet him here. There is nothing to do but get away where he can't find me. I must get away at once, or he may follow me. Will you please take Rags and go back now, and will you take a letter that I left in the school-house to the minister? I am so sorry to go this way, but it cannot be helped. I must get away from that man."

"Is he—has he any right?" began Daniel lamely and then burst out: "I mean, is he anything to you—any kind of relation, you know?"

"Nothing in the world, I'm thankful to say, and he never shall be as long as I live. But I never could feel safe again, now that he knows where I am."

Dan stood puzzled and troubled.

"Say, don't you know how you're going to make all the school feel bad if you go this way? The little ones'll wait for you to-morrow morning, and they'll go there to the school and you won't be there. We never had a teacher that made everybody like to study before. You oughtn't to go this way. You *can't* go!" He stopped, choking.

Dawn looked at him a moment, the tears gathering anew in her own eyes; then suddenly down went her head in her hands, and she cried as if her heart would break.

"Oh, Daniel," she said, "please don't! I don't want to go. I shall never be as happy again, I know, and you have been so good to me! But I must——"

The big boy went down on his knees beside her then, and put his rough hand reverently on hers.

"Don't," said he. "Don't. I've *got* to tell you something. Perhaps you won't like it—I don't know. I'm not near as good as you, and I don't know as much as you do, but I'll study hard, and go to college, and do anything else you say, just to please you. If you only won't go away. If you'll just stay here and let me take care of you! I love you, and I don't care who knows it! I've been feeling that way about you all winter, only I thought perhaps you'd like me better when I got more education; but now you see I've just got to tell you how it is. Don't you like me enough to stay and let me take care of you? I love you!"

But Dawn interrupted him with a moan.

"Oh, Daniel! You too? Then I haven't got anybody left. Not a friend in all the world!" she sobbed afresh.

Daniel dropped down on the moss beside her in dismay. His heart grew heavy as lead within him, and the world suddenly looked blank.

"Yes, you have," he said. "I'll be your friend if you won't let me be anything else. I was afraid it would make you mad," he spoke hopelessly. "I ain't good enough fer you, I know, but I'm strong, an' I'd study hard and get an education, and I'll take wonderful care of you. You shouldn't ever have to work. You're a lady. That's why I like you. You're the prettiest thing that was ever made, an' I'd like nothing better'n to work hard for you all my life. But I might 'a' known you wouldn't think I was good enough." He broke off helplessly, and she saw that his broad chest was heaving painfully and that his usually smiling lips were quivering.

She put out her hand and laid it gently on his.

"Dear Daniel," she said, "listen! It isn't that at all."

He caught the cool little hand and pressed it against his eyes that were burning hot with boyish tears he was ashamed to shed. It was years since tears had been in those eyes. He had almost forgotten the smart of them. He had scorned the thought of them even in his babyhood, yet here, just when he longed to be a man, they came to make his shame complete.

"Listen, Dan," said Dawn earnestly. "It isn't that at all. You're good and dear enough for anybody, and I do love you, too, for you've been very good to me. I love you for yourself, too, but not in that way, Dan, for I love some one else. I loved him first and shall always love him, and—and—I belong to him. I couldn't belong to any one else, you know, after that. I'm sorry, Dan, so sorry you feel bad about it, but you see how it is. I *belonged* to some one else first."

"Is it *him?*" he blurted out fiercely.

"Oh, no, Dan! Oh, no! I'm very, *very* thankful it isn't that man. If it were, I should die. I couldn't love him. You wouldn't think I could!"

There was silence in the quiet woods for a moment.

"It ain't Silas Dobson?" he asked fearfully at last.

Dawn's laugh burst out softly then.

"Oh, Dan! You know better than that. You knew without asking. How could any one love him? No, Dan; the one I belong to is fine and grand and noble—everything he ought to be."

"Then, why doesn't he take care of you?" burst forth Dan indignantly. "I wouldn't let you teach school if you belonged to me, and I wouldn't let that fellow frighten you. He can't be all you say, or he'd take care of you."

Dawn's cheeks were very red.

"He doesn't know where I am," she said softly. "I went away because—well, it was for a good reason. It was for his sake. I had to go. Things had happened. I can't tell you about it, but it would have made him trouble if I had stayed."

Dan sat looking at her steadily, a great, wistful yearning in his eyes.

"I guess you're wrong 'bout that," he said thoughtfully. "I guess he'd rather have you *an'* the trouble, than to have no trouble without you. Leastways, I would, an' ef he don't love you that way, he ain't much account."

A troubled look came into Dawn's eyes. It was the first time she had questioned, from Charles's standpoint, the wisdom of her running way.

"It would have made a lot of trouble all around," she said, shaking her head doubtfully.

"Say, look here!" said Dan, sitting up suddenly. "You tell me where that fellow is, an' I'll go tell him all about you, and how that other fellow is worrying you, and how you need him to take care o' you; an' then if he don't seem to want to find you and look out for you, why, I won't tell him where you are. I'll come back and take care of you myself, any way. You needn't like me nor anything if you don't want to, but I ain't going to stand having you off running around the world, frightened of that fellow all the time, not if I have to chop him up myself. I tell you, I *love* you!"

Dan's blue eyes were flashing, and his cheeks were red with determination. He had let go of her hand as if it were a gracious favor she had bestowed upon him for the moment in his dire distress, and he had no right to keep it, but Dawn put it out again and laid it on his gently.

"Daniel, you are my dear friend for always, and I am glad to feel that you would take care of me if you could, but truly there is nothing you can do. I would not have you go to him for the world. He must not know where I am, nor be troubled ever by any thought of me. It was for that I came away. You would grieve me more than I can tell you if you did. I want him to forget me, because it could only make him trouble if he found me. He would *have* to come to me. He would *want* to come, I know, if you told him. But I don't want him to come. You don't understand, of course, and I mustn't tell you any more, only there is nothing can be done but for me to go away and find a place somewhere where no one can find me. Then people will forget, and I shall not bring any trouble or disgrace on him—though it wasn't at all my fault," she added. "I want you to know that, Daniel."

"Of course," growled Dan, looking down at the little hand on his as if it were an angel's and might be wafted away with a breath. "But I'm going with you myself, then, and see you to some safe place."

"Oh, but you mustn't, Dan. I couldn't let you. It wouldn't be right, you know. People would think it very strange."

"People needn't know anything about it. I don't need to talk to you. I can keep far enough away to see that no one hurts you, till you get a good, safe place."

"But, Dan, the folks at your home? They would think we had gone away together! I do not want them to think wrong of me, even if I'm not there to bear it."

Dan was baffled. He saw at once that it would not do. He must go back and bear the loneliness and the thought of her fighting her own battles.

"Well, I'll go with you now, any way," he said at last, with determination. "I'll see you safe to some coach somewhere, an' come back in the night. I can get to my room without Mother hearing me. She never worries about me now any more, an' don't stay awake to listen for me. She'll never know when I get in. I'll go back an' tell 'em I helped carry your bag across country to Cherry Valley coach, or somewhere. I've got the parson's letter here in my pocket. That villain came to the school-house after you, an' I picked up the letter so he wouldn't see it."

"Oh, did he come to the school after me? Then perhaps he has followed us. Dan, I must go quickly!"

"Come on," said Dan, as though he were proposing to walk to his death. At least, he was not to leave her yet. He picked up her bag, and helped her to her feet; then, still holding the hand by which he had helped her up, he bent over and kissed it reverently. Then he straightened up with a royal look of manhood in his eyes and turned to her:

"You won't mind that just once, will you? That hand did a whole lot fer me, beginning when it gave me that first licking."

Dawn smiled sadly. Then with sudden impulse she reached up, caught his face between her hands, drew it down to her own, and gently, seriously, kissed him upon the forehead as if it were a sacred rite.

"I love you, Dan," she said. "I'm so sorry it can't be the kind of love you want. But I'll be your dear friend always. I never had a brother. Perhaps I might call you my brother. It would be nice to have a brother like you. You have been very, *very* good to me, and I shall never forget it."

Dan looked at her as if she had laid a benediction

upon him. After all, he was young, and it was much to have her friendship. And if another had her love, at least he, Daniel, was on the spot and might help her now, which went a great way toward making him feel better about the other fellow. The boy had begun to have a lurking pity for him, besides. And who was he, Daniel, that he should hope to hold a girl like this for himself? It was much that he had known her. It was right that she should have a lover such as she had described—"fine and grand and noble." Almost the great heart of the boy-lover felt he could take them both in and care for them, and bring them together, perhaps—who knew?

They hurried through the woods, the boy directing the way now, and she depending upon him. He decided that it would be well for her to take a certain stage line that could be reached only by a good walk of several miles across the country. He knew the way, and she was only too glad to have a guide.

That was Dan's great day of happiness. For years afterward he remembered every little incident. He seemed to know while it was all happening that it was a special gift granted him in view of the sorrow and sacrifice he must pass through. His was no passing love of a boy. He realized that the girl beside him was one in a thousand, and that it was enough for a lifetime just to have known her, and to be able to remember one such perfect afternoon as this.

To Dawn, it was given to understand her power for that brief season, and to use it to its utmost for the boy's good. She talked to him earnestly about himself and his future, and urged him to make the utmost of every opportunity. She made him understand that he had the gift of leading others, and that some day he might take a great stand in the world for some cause of Right against Wrong, when others would flock to his standard and let him lead them to victory. It was an unusual thing that a girl like Dawn should see his possibilities and point him to a great ambition, but Dawn was an unusual girl.

Some girls, even though they might have done no real wrong, would have taken advantage of the boy's confessed love, and have coquetted with him. Dawn treated him with the utmost gentleness, as if she understood the pain she must inflict, and would fain give him something fine to take the place of what he had lost.

When they came to a hill they took hold of hands and raced down. When they came to a brook he helped her gravely across, just as he had helped her ever since she came to teach the school. He said no more about his love. It was understood between them that it was a closed incident, to be put away in the sacred recesses of their hearts. Into the girl's face had come a tender, womanly interest that for the time being almost made up to the boy for the loss of her. It was while they were walking down a long stretch of brown road, straight into a glorious sunset, that the boy asked quite suddenly:

"Has *he* been to college?"

Dawn knew at once whom he meant, and began simply to tell all about Charles. It did her good to speak of him. It seemed to bring him nearer. Her face blossomed into sweetness as she talked. There was not much to say, not much about him that she could tell to a stranger, from her one brief day's acquaintance with her husband, yet she managed to say a good deal. Charles would have been amazed to hear her describe his high ambitions and noble thoughts. He did not dream how well the girl had read him during their one blissful day together. And now she was painting him as an ideal for the rude boy who walked beside her and listened, with his heart filled with patient envy; that presently lost its bitterness in pity for the other one, who might have her great love, yet might not walk beside her as he was doing.

At last Dan broke in upon her words:

" 'Tisn't right he shouldn't know where you are. If he's anything like what you think he is, he's 'most crazy hunting you. I know how he feels."

Dawn shook her head sadly and told him he did not understand, but his words sank into her heart for future meditation, and she could not quite get away from the thought that perhaps she had been wrong, after all, in going away. Perhaps it might have been more heroic to stay and face the hard things right where she had been.

The long spring twilight had almost faded into darkness as they came at last to the inn where the coach would pass. Neither had spoken for some time. There was upon them a sense of their coming separation, and it depressed them. Already Dawn was looking into her lonely future, and dreading to lose this only friend she had. Already Dan was realizing what the going back was to be.

They had arranged it all. Dan was to take the letter to the minister, and explain that he had helped the teacher to catch a cross-country stage. He had taken it upon himself, also, to carry messages to the scholars and to her kind friends—brief messages of good-by, and haste, and sorrow; with the promise, too, at Dan's earnest solicitation, that if she ever could she would return to them.

Then at the end they had no time for parting. The stage was just driving up to the inn as they reached there. There was no time even for supper, though neither of them thought of it at the time.

Dan put her into the coach and arranged her bag comfortably, but he had to get out at once, as others were pressing in. He went outside in the dim light and stood by her window, looking up, trying to keep Rags from breaking away and getting into the coach. Something in his throat choked him. He could not speak.

The people were all in, and the driver was climbing to his place, when Dawn reached out her hand and caught Dan's, giving it a quick little squeeze.

"Dear Dan," she whispered as she leaned out, "don't forget to be the best you can."

He caught the little hand and laid his lips against it in the half-darkness. Rags had broken away and was barking wildly at the coach door, but the horses started and took Dawn away from the boy and the dog, and in a moment more they stood alone in the road, looking down the street at the dim black speck in the distance which was the coach.

Then slowly, silently, the one with downcast head, the other with drooping tail, Daniel and his dog took their way back over the road they had come so happily that afternoon. The dog could not understand, and now and then stopped, looked back, and whined, as if to say they ought to go back and do things over again. At last, when they reached the country roadside where all was still, and there were only the brooding stars to see, Dan sat down on a bank by the roadside upon the cool, wet earth that was just beginning to spring into greenness and buried his face in his hands. Then he gave way to his grief, while Rags, almost beside himself with distress, whined about him, snuffed up and down the road, and then sat down and howled at the late moon, which was just rising over a hill.

By and by Dan got up and called the dog. Together they started on their journey again, a silent, thoughtful pair. But never afterward did the boy Dan return. He was a man. He had suffered and grown. In his face were born resolve and determination. People wondered at the change in the careless, happy boy, and grew proud of his thoughtfulness.

## CHAPTER XXIII

The night that Dawn left her husband's home marked the beginning of an era of sorrow in the history of the Winthrops.

The distracted young husband and his father rode all night long.

Charles reached the Van Rensselaers' home a little sooner than old Mr. Winthrop, who had further to go. The young man's white, drawn face startled Mrs. Van Rensselaer as he stood to greet her in the gloomy parlor, where the scent of the wedding roses still lingered.

She was in workaday attire, to set her house in order and prepare for what she hoped was to be a season of peace in her hitherto tempestuous life. Dawn was off her hands finally, she felt, and she had no serious forebodings concerning her share in the matter. The hard part had been to get the girl off without her finding out the trick that had been played on her. It had amazed the step-mother that her plan had worked so well. She had been prepared for the discovery to be made soon after the ceremony, but she had trusted to Dawn's fear of publicity, and Charles's evident infatuation, to hush the matter up. Mrs.

Van Rensselaer had been reasonably sure that she could even keep it from her husband's knowledge, though she was prepared with a plausible story in case he remonstrated. His sense of pride would make him readily persuadable to almost any plan that would hide their mortification from curious friends. She had been sure that she could make him see that the whole thing had been done for his daughter's good. And now that the step-mother had succeeded even better than she had hoped, in getting the couple off on their wedding trip without either one discovering her duplicity, she had been at rest about the matter. Charles was enough in love to be able to make everything all right, and he would never blame her for having furthered his plans, even though not quite in the way he had arranged. Dawn could not fail to be pleased with the husband her step-mother had secured for her, and even would thank her in later life, perhaps, for having helped her to him.

And so Mrs. Van Rensselaer had gone placidly about the house, putting things to rights, and enjoying the prospect of a comfortable future without the fear of an unloved step-daughter's presence haunting her.

But when she saw Charles's face a pang of fear shot through her and left her trembling with apprehension. His voice sounded hollow and accusatory when he spoke:

"Is Dawn here, Mrs. Van Rensselaer?"

A thousand possibilities rushed through the woman's brain at once, and she felt herself brought suddenly before an awful judgment bar. What had she done? How had she dared? How swift was retribution! Not even one whole day of satisfaction, after all her trouble!

She tried to summon a natural voice, but it would not come. Her throat felt dry, and as if it did not belong to her, as she answered:

"Here? No. How could she be here? Didn't you take her away?"

The young man sat down suddenly in the nearest chair with a groan, and dropped his head into his hands. The woman stood silent, frightened, before him.

"Mrs. Van Rensselaer, what have you done? Why did you do it?"

"Well, really, what have I done?" The sharp voice of

the woman returned to combat as soon as the accusation pricked her into anger. "I'm sure I helped you to get a wife you seemed to want bad enough and never would have got if I hadn't managed affairs. You haven't any idea how hard she was to manage or you'd understand. It was a very trying situation, and it isn't every woman could have made things go as well as I did—not to have a soul outside your family know there had been a change of bridegrooms. You see, none of our friends had ever seen your brother, and as the name was the same there were no explanations necessary."

"Mrs. Van Rensselaer, I would never have married Dawn against her will. It was not right for you to deceive her. She ought to have been told just how things stood, and what my brother had done."

"H'm! And had a pretty mess, with her crying and saying she wouldn't marry anybody, and all the wedding guests coming? Young man, you don't know what you're talking about. That girl isn't easy to manage, and I guess you've found it out already. She's like a flea: when you think you have her, she's somewhere else. I knew something desperate would have to be done before she ever settled down and accepted life as it had to be, and I did it, that's all. Well, what's the matter, any way? Have you got tired of your bargain already and turned her out of your house?"

Mrs. Van Rensselaer was exasperated and frightened. She scarcely knew what she was saying. Any moment her husband might come into the house. If she could only get the interview over before he came, and perhaps hide at least a part of the story from him! She dreaded his terrible temper. She had always had an innate presentiment that some time that temper would be let loose against her, and she knew now the moment was come.

Charles looked up with his handsome and usually kindly eyes blazing with amazement and indignation:

"Mrs. Van Rensselaer, my wife has gone away. We have searched all night and cannot find her. I was sure she had come home. Oh, what shall I do?"

"Well, I'm sure I don't see how I'm to blame for her having left you," snapped out Mrs. Van Rensselaer. "I did my part and made sure you got her. You ought to have been able to keep her after you had her. How'd she come to leave you?"

"I cannot tell exactly. She went up to see Mother a few minutes after supper, and then——"

"Oh!" said Mrs. Van Rensselaer, with disagreeable significance.

"And then we could not find her," went on Charles, unheeding. "She left a note with good-by. That was all. I have no clue."

The front door opened, and Mr. Van Rensselaer walked in. His face was white, for he had not slept well. In a dream his dead wife had stood before him and seemed to be taking him to task about her child, the daughter who left her father's house but a few hours before. He had gone out for the morning mail, hoping to get rid of the phantoms that pursued his steps, but his head was throbbing.

How much he had heard of what they had been saying, they did not know. He stood before them white and stern-looking, glancing from one to the other of the two in the dim parlor.

"Where is my daughter?" he asked.

"She is gone, Mr. Van Rensselaer," answered Charles pitifully. "I have searched for her all night long. I hoped she was here."

"Gone?" repeated the father in a strange, far-away voice; then he wavered for an instant, and fell at their feet, as if dead. The accusations of his own heart had reached their mark. The iron will yielded at last to the finger of God.

They carried him to his bed and called the doctor. Confusion reigned in the house. The old doctor shook his head and called it apoplexy. Mr. Van Rensselaer was still living, and might linger for some time, but it would be a living death.

And so, while he lay upon his bed, breathing, but dead to the world about him, they made what plans they could to find his daughter. Charles's father came in sadly, reporting no success in the search. They started out once more after a brief rest.

Mrs. Van Rensselaer was in no condition to help them now. She had her hands full, poor woman. One thing had been spared her: her husband did not know her part in the disappearance of his daughter. Perhaps he might never need to know; yet as she went about ministering to that silent, living dead, whom she had loved beyond anything earthly, her heart was full of bitterness and fear.

The months that followed were terrible to Charles. After a few days of keeping the matter quiet and hoping they would find her by themselves, they made the disappearance public, and the whole countryside joined in the search.

The greatest drawback to success was that so few people had seen Dawn since she grew up. The servants in her father's house had seen her during the week she had been home from school, but scarcely any one else except for a passing glance on the street. All searching was in vain. There were notices put in the papers of that region. They sent to her old school for knowledge of her; they left no stone unturned. And the wonder of it is that Dawn's friend, the minister, or some of the selectmen, especially Silas Dobson, did not see the notices that appeared in New York papers and in those of smaller towns, and connect the mysterious disappearance with the new teacher that had come to their village. But the old clergyman had vouched for her, and there was apparently no mystery about her. This good man did not often have opportunity to read papers of other towns, save his regular weekly religious sheet. Then, too, the place where Dawn had found refuge was small and insignificant, and not on the line of most travel. She could not have been better sheltered from the searchers.

It was the day after Charles had been to see the body of a young woman who had been found in the river some fifty miles distant from his home, that he became ill with typhoid fever.

Not for a day had he rested or given up his search. When one clue failed, he went to the next with restless, feverish energy, and a haunted look in his eyes. The boy had become a man, and the man was bearing a heavy burden. His father saw it, and grieved for him. His mother saw it, and accused herself. His sisters saw it, and did their best to help him. Betty was constantly thinking up new plans for the search, and saying comforting, cheering things to her brother. Charles loved her dearly for it, but nothing brought relief. His affection for Dawn had been such as rarely grows in a human heart, even after years of acquaintance. It had sprung full-bloomed into being, and filled his whole soul. It is said that to the average man love is but an incident, while to a woman it is the whole of life. If that be so, there are exceptions, and Charles was one of them. He kept his love for his girl-wife as the greatest thing life had for him, and thought of nothing else day or night but to find her.

No one dared to suggest his going back to college. That would be to admit that the search was hopeless, and that might prove fatal to Charles. The neighbors had begun to shake their heads and pity him. It was even whispered that the girl might have run away with another man, though no one ventured to say such a thing in the hearing of the family.

If it had been in these days of telegraphs and telephones, railroads and detectives, it would have been put a matter of days until they had found her, but in those times travel and search were long and hard. There seemed little hope. It was the third dead face which Charles had searched for likeness to the girl he loved. He came home worn and exhausted, his spirit utterly discouraged and weary, and he was an easy prey to the disease which gripped him from the first in its most violent form.

Silence and sadness settled down upon the Winthrop household while the life of Charles was held in the balance. The father carried on the search for the lost wife more vigorously than ever, believing that the sight of her might bring his boy back even from the grave; but nothing developed.

News from the Van Rensselaers gave no hope of the paralyzed man's recovery. He was lying like a thing of stone, unable to move. He could not even make a sound. Only his eyes followed his tormented wife, like haunting spirits sent to condemn her. The face was set in its stern expression, like a fallen statue of his proud, imperious self.

It was mid-winter before Charles began slowly to creep back to life, and there was still no clue to Dawn. They dreaded to have him ask about her; though they had noticed how he had searched their faces every morning after consciousness returned to him. He knew as well as they that nothing had been accomplished toward finding her.

One day he seemed more cheerful and a little stronger, and called old Mr. Winthrop to his side.

"Father," said he, "I've been thinking that perhaps she'd not like to come back here, the way she feels about it. There was a little white house on the hills beyond Albany that we noticed as we came along on the train. We both said we should like to live there among the trees. Would you be willing that I should take the money Grandfather left to me and buy that little house for her to come to? Then I could put a notice in the papers telling her it was ready, and perhaps she would see it and understand."

The old man's heart was heavy, for he had begun to believe that Dawn was no longer in the land of the living; but he would have consented to any plan that would comfort his boy and give him a new interest in life, and so as soon as Charles was able to travel they went together to purchase the small farm and little white house. The next day there appeared in the New York papers this notice, which was printed many weeks and copied into numerous village papers:

*Dawn, the little white house we saw near Albany is ready for us. Write and tell me where to find you.*
                                                    *Charles*

But nothing ever came in answer, though Charles watched every mail with feverish anxiety; and he still kept up his search in other directions. So the spring crept on, and almost it was a year since Dawn had left him.


## CHAPTER XXIV


DAWN had been in New York two months, after various trying experiences in getting there, and all that time she had been unable to find anything to do by which she could earn her living.

The miserable little boarding place, the best she could afford, was growing more and more uncomfortable as the hot weather came on. Dawn was thin and worn and sad. Her money which she had earned during the winter, and which she had always carried sewed inside her garments, was fast melting away. A few more weeks, and she would be penniless. She began to wonder what would come next, and to question whether it would not have been better to stay with the school, and trust the old minister and Daniel to protect her from Harrington Winthrop. But always, after thinking it over, she decided that she could not have been safe when he knew her whereabouts.

There was one other thing which troubled her constantly now. It was that sentence of Daniel's: "He'd rather have you *and* the trouble, than to have no trouble without you." Was it true? Did Charles love her that way? Was she giving him trouble by staying away? "If he's anything like you say he is, he's most crazy hunting you," Daniel had said. Was *that* true, too? Could he be hunting her yet? Had she been wrong in coming away? Gradually she came to admit to herself that there might have been a better way. She might have made a mistake. But it was too late now to remedy it. She could not go back on her promise that she would trouble him no more. She could not bring added disgrace to him now that she had stayed away all these months and everybody must know it. Oh, how long and hard life was! And then she once more went wearily at her task of hunting a position.

Slowly, stealthily, up from the south; strangely, unexpectedly, down from the Canadian border, there crept a grim spectre of death. Heard of from afar with indifference at first, it gradually grew more terrifying as it drew nearer. Now and then the death of a well-known victim caused uneasiness to become more manifest.

Hotter grew the sun, and nearer drew the spectre. The daily papers contained advice for protection against it. The cities cleaned their streets and warned their citizens. The temperance societies called attention to the fact that hard drinkers were in more danger than others. Meat and milk and vegetables were carefully inspected. Water was boiled. Cheerfulness was put on like a garment, and assurance was flaunted everywhere. People were told to keep up a good heart and keep clean, and there was little danger. Still the spectre crept nearer, laying hands upon its victims, and daily the reports grew more alarming. It was near the end of June when the ministers met in New York and petitioned the President to appoint a general day of fasting and prayer to avert the oncoming pestilence.

Andrew Jackson replied that it was in their line, not his, to decide whether this matter was important enough to bring to the notice of the Almighty, and he left it in their hands. The days went by, and the spectre crept on. The Governors of the States began to appoint days of prayer. At last the cholera was a recognized fact. It had come to do its worst. The newspapers abandoned their talk of its impossibility, and set about making the best of things, describing the precautions to be taken, the preliminary symptoms, and the best method of treatment. For a time, during the latter part of June and the early part of July, it was hoped that by vigilance and care it could be kept out of New York City. The worst of the pestilence was in the Southern States, though it had made great ravages as far north as Cincinnati. And from Canada it was spreading south into New York State. Here and there a little town would have a single case, which would send terror throughout the county, and daily the number grew greater.

Charles was looking worn and thin. He had bought the little house, and had had it renovated. It was furnished now, and waiting for the bride who did not come. His heart grew sick with the great fear that was growing within him, the fear that he should never find her on this earth.

Of late, a new worry had come to him. A letter had come to his father from Harrington's wife, saying that she was destitute, as her husband had deserted her again. He had stayed with her but a week after he brought her home, though he had promised many things.

In spite of himself, Charles could not get it out of his mind that Harrington had spirited Dawn away somewhere. He did not doubt her for an instant. He would not let himself think that she might still have some lurking love for the man who had not scrupled to do her a wrong. He laid all blame, if blame there was, upon his brother. Harrington had sometimes appropriated his younger brother's boyish treasures to his own use when they were both younger, and Charles had no doubt he would not hesitate to do thus even with his brother's wife, were such a thing possible.

Sometimes the remembrance of the terror in Dawn's eyes when she asked about Harrington and where she would have to meet him, made Charles fairly writhe, and he felt that he must fly somewhere, to the ends of the earth if need be, and find her.

He lay on the couch in the library one warm evening in early July. Betty sat beside him, reading the New York paper which had just been brought by the evening coach. She was trying to distract his mind from the ever-present sorrow over which he seemed to brood every minute when he was not in actual motion trying to find his wife. This evening there was a deeper gloom over them on account of having received that morning news of the death of Mr. Van Rensselaer.

Charles lay still, with his face shaded from the candlelight, and let Betty read. He was paying little heed, but it made Betty happier to think that she was helping him to bear his pain. The little sister's sympathy was a great comfort, and so if she could think she was helping him, he was glad. He was occupied in trying to think out a plan for finding Harrington, just to make sure that he knew nothing about Dawn.

"Here's something about the new railroad, Charles. Shall I read that, or would you rather have me read *Parley's Magazine* than the *Commercial-Advertiser?*"

"Oh, read the *Commercial-Advertiser,* by all means," said Charles, trying to rouse himself to take an interest for Betty's sake. His head was aching, and he was weary in both body and soul.

"Well, listen to this, Charles. Isn't this wonderful? They've completed the railroad from Saratoga to Ballston. They can go eight miles in twenty-eight minutes! Think of that beside the stage-coach travelling! It takes only an hour and five minutes to go from Ballston to Schenectady, and you can go from Albany to Saratoga in three hours. Who would ever have believed it true? Do you suppose it is true, or have they exaggerated?"

"Oh, I guess they can do it," said Charles, with a sigh. The new railroad made him think of his wedding journey. Oh, to take it over again and never let his bride out of his sight!

Betty read on:

*"Governor Howard, of Maryland, has set July 4th as a day of prayer that the cholera may decline. Governor Cass says——"*

but a low moan from Charles made her fly to another column to distract his mind:

"Here's the report of the meeting of the Foreign Mission Board in New York. Would you like to hear that? It looks interesting. The evening address was made by the Honorable Stephen Van Rensselaer. Why——" Betty stopped in dismay, but Charles answered the wonder in her tone quietly:

"Yes, Betty, Stephen Van Rensselaer is a cousin of Mr. Van Rensselaer. He is a fine speaker. Read about it."

But Charles did not attend, though Betty rattled off a lot of statistics glibly, inwardly blaming herself for constantly coming upon things that would remind Charles of his loss.

*"There are twelve missions now, with fifty-five stations, under the Board. Seven are in India, two in Asia, four in the Mediterranean, seven in the Sandwich Islands, twenty-seven among the southwestern Indians, four among the northeastern Indians, and four among the Indians of New York State. There are seventy-five missionaries, four physicians, four printers, eighteen teachers, twenty farmers and mechanics, and one hundred and thirty-one females, married and single, sent out from this country."*

My! Isn't that a lot!" commented Betty.

Just below the report of the missionary meeting was a brief paragraph. She plunged into it without stopping to glance it over.

"DISAPPEARED. *A female dressed in a white straw bonnet trimmed with white satin ribbon, a black silk gown, white crêpe shawl with flowered border, black silk stockings, and chocolate-colored parasol.*"

"Oh!" cried Betty in dismay, and then went wildly on to the next column, not daring to look at her brother:

"*The Honorable William Wort has purchased a plantation in Florida, and is going to work it with hired hands. This will do more toward opening the eyes of the slaveholders than all the declamatory efforts of the free States since the adoption of the Constitution.*"

"That is quoted from the *United States Gazette*, Charles, and the editor of this paper has a long, drylooking comment on it. Do you want to hear it?"

Betty looked uneasily at her brother, but his white face was turned toward the wall.

"Here's an article about Barnabas Bidwell, and something about General Prosper Wetmore. Doesn't father know General Wetmore, Charles?" Betty felt she was not getting on well at all.

"I believe he does," answered her brother patiently, and then the knocker sounded insistently through the house, and Charles came to an upright position in an instant. He seemed ever to be thus on the alert for something to happen. And this time something did happen.

A negro boy stood at the door with a note scrawled on a leaf from a memorandum-book. He said he was to give it to Mr. Winthrop at once. As his father was out, Charles read it. Betty held the candle for him to see. It was badly written, with pale ink. Betty's hand trembled and made the candle waver. She felt that something momentous was in the air.

"Come to me at once. I'm desperately ill.—Harrington," read the note. It was like the writer to command and expect to be obeyed.

Charles pressed the note into Betty's hand, saying, "Give it to Father as soon as he comes, and don't let Mother or Aunt Martha know." Then he seized his hat and sprang out into the night, urging his escort into a run, and demanding an explanation as he went.

But the boy could tell little of what was the matter. He knew only that he had been sent in great haste, and that the gentleman was very sick.

The night was still and warm. There was a yellow haze over the world, and a sultry feeling in the air. People had been remarking all day how warm it was for the season of year.

Charles plunged through the night with only one thought in mind. He was to see his brother in a few minutes, and he must take every means to find out whether he had any knowledge of Dawn. His whole soul was bent on the purpose that had been his main object in life during the past year.

It occurred to him that Harrington might be in need of medical attendance, though that was a sort of secondary consideration at the time. So he sent the negro boy after their family physician. He himself went on alone to the inn, some two miles from the village, where the boy said his brother was stopping.

When Charles reached the inn he found a group of excited people gathered near the steps, and the word "cholera" floated to his ears, but it meant little to him.

In a moment he was standing by his brother's bedside.

Harrington turned away from him with a groan.

"Is it only you?" he muttered angrily. "I sent for Father."

"Father was not in. He will come as soon as he returns. I will do anything you want done. I have sent for the doctor. But before I do anything, you must answer me one question. Do you know where Dawn is? Have you seen her since the day of the wedding?"

Harrington turned bloodshot eyes upon his brother. "Who is Dawn?" he sneered. "Oh, I see! You mean Miss Van Rensselaer. Yes, I remember you were smitten with her the only time you ever saw her. I believe in my soul it was you who cheated me out of my little game, and not Alberta at all. Well, it doesn't matter. I've got something better on the string now, if I ever get out of this cursed hole. Let the doll-faced baby go. She wasn't worth all the trouble it took to keep track of her."

Then suddenly he was seized in the vise of an awful agony, and cried out with oaths and curses.

Down below his window a group of huddled negroes heard, and a shudder went through them. They drew away, and whispered in sepulchral tones.

Charles stood over his brother in helpless horror until the agony was passed, and Harrington gasped out:

"Go for the doctor, you fool! Do you want to see me die before your eyes?"

Charles's voice was grave and commanding as he stood over his brother and demanded once more:

"Answer me, Harrington. Have you seen her since the day of the wedding? Answer me quickly. I will help you just as soon as I know all. I shall not do a thing until you tell me."

A groan and a curse were all the answer he got, and a cold frenzy seized him, lest he should never get Harrington to tell what he knew. He understood that his brother was a very sick man. Great beads of perspiration stood upon his forehead.

"Get me some whiskey, you brute!" cried out the stricken man. "That awful agony is coming again. Well, if you must know, she's teaching school in a little forsaken village over beyond Schoharie—Butternuts, they call it. At least, she was till I appeared on the scene. Then she made away with herself somehow. I stayed three days, waiting for her, but she didn't come back. I stopped off last week, and the people said she'd never returned. No one knew anything about her but a tow-headed boy who called himself Daniel and said he helped carry her bag to the stage-coach. Now get me that whiskey quick. I feel the pain coming again."

Charles turned without a word and dashed downstairs to the landlady, demanding hot water and blankets. He knew little about illness, save what his mother's semi-invalid state had taught him, but he had read enough in the papers lately to make him sure that Harrington had the cholera, and he knew that whiskey was not a remedy. Before he could return to his brother the doctor arrived, and together they went up to the sick man, who was writhing in agony, and again demanding whiskey.

The old doctor shook his head when he saw the patient.

"He has indulged in that article far too much already," he said.

Then began a night of horror, followed by a day of stupor on the part of the patient. The doctor had said from the start that it was cholera, and that the disease was almost always fatal to persons of intemperate habits.

Charles held himself steadily to the task of the moment, and tried to still the calling of his heart to fly at once and find Dawn. Not another word had he been able to get from his brother. The pain had been so intolerable that Harrington had been unable to speak, and little by little he grew delirious until he did not recognize any of them. At times he cried out as if in wild carouse. Once or twice he called "Alberta!" in an angry tone, then muttered Mr. Van Rensselaer's name. Never once did he speak the name of Dawn. This fact gave Charles unspeakable relief.

All through the night and day the doctor, the brother, and the father worked side by side, but each knew from the first that there was no hope, and at evening he died.

They buried Harrington Winthrop in the old lot where rested the mortal remains of other more worthy members of the family; and the father turned away with bowed head and broken heart for such an ending to his elder son's misspent life, and kept saying over to himself, "Has it been my fault? Has it been my fault?"

They were almost home when Charles, who had been silent and thoughtful, touched the older man on the shoulder.

"Father, shall you mind my going away at once?" he asked. "I have a clue, and must follow it."

Mr. Winthrop lifted his grief-stricken head, and, looking at his son tenderly, said:

"Go, my boy, and may you gain your heart's desire!"

# CHAPTER XXV

THE next evening at sunset Charles stood beside the Butterworth gate, about to enter, when Daniel came out. The boy had finished his early supper, and was going to the village on an errand. His face was grave and thoughtful, as always since the teacher's departure.

Charles watched him coming down to the gate, and liked his broad shoulders, and the blue eyes under his curly yellow lashes as he looked up.

"Are you Daniel Butterworth?" asked Charles.

"I am," said Dan, eying him keenly.

"Are you the one"—Charles was going to say "boy," but that did not seem to apply exactly to this grave young fellow—"are you the one who carried the teacher's baggage to the stage-coach when she went away so suddenly?"

Charles had studied the question carefully. He did not know by what name Dawn had gone, whether she had used his or kept her own maiden name, or had assumed still another. He would not cast a shadow of reflection upon her, or risk his chance of finding her by using the wrong name, therefore he called her "the teacher." On inquiring about her at the inn where the stage-coach stopped, he had been referred at once to Peggy Gillette, who immediately guided him to the point in the road where he could see the Butterworth house.

Daniel started, and looked the stranger over suspiciously. There was a something about this clean-faced, long, strong fellow that reminded him a little, just a very little, of the scoundrel who had frightened the teacher away; yet he instinctively liked this man, and felt that he was to be trusted. Rags, too, generally suspicious of strangers, had been smelling and snuffing about this man, and now stood wagging his tail with a smile on his homely, shaggy face. Rags's judgment was generally to be trusted.

"I might be," responded Daniel slowly, "and then again I mightn't. Who are you?"

Charles understood that the boy was testing him, and he liked him the better for it. His heart warmed toward the one who had protected Dawn.

"That's all right," responded Charles heartily. "I'm ready to identify myself. I'm one who loves her better than my life, and I've done nothing for a year but search for her."

He let Daniel see the depth of his meaning in his eyes, as the boy looked keenly, wistfully, into his face. Daniel was satisfied, and with a great sigh of renunciation, he said:

"I knew it. I told her so. I knew you would be half crazy, hunting her. You're the one she said she belonged to, aren't you?"

A great light broke over Charles's face, bringing out all the beauty of his soul, all the lines of character that suffering had set upon his youth, and that love had wrought into his fibre.

"Oh, Daniel, bless you! Did she tell you that? Yes, she belongs to me, and I to her, and if you'll only tell me where to find her, you'll make me the happiest man on earth!" He grasped the boy's hand in his firm, smooth one, and they stood as if making a life compact, each glad of the other's touch. "Daniel, I feel as if you were an angel of light!" broke out Charles.

The angel in blue homespun lifted his eyes to the stranger's face, and was glad, since he might not have the one he loved, that she belonged to this other. He had done the best he could do for her, and his was the part of sacrifice.

"I can't tell you just where she is," said Daniel gravely. "I thought mebbe you'd know from this. She's sent me two books since she went away, and they're both postmarked 'New York.' That's all I know."

He pulled out a tattered paper that had wrapped a parcel, and together they studied the marks. Charles's face grew grave. New York was a large place even in those days. Yet it was more definite than the whole United States, which had been his field of action thus far. He would not despair. He would take heart of grace and go forward.

"Daniel," said he, handing back the paper to its owner, with a delicate feeling that the boy had the first right to it, since he was the link between them, "will you go to New York to-night with me and help me to find her?"

Dan's face lit up until he was actually handsome.

"Me?"

Rags wagged his tail hard, and gave a sharp little bark, as if to say: "Me?"

"Yes, both of you," said Charles joyously. He felt as if he were on the right track at last, and his soul could fairly shout for happiness.

"Rags might do a lot toward finding her. He'd track her anywhere. It was all I could do to get him away from her when she got into the stage-coach to go away." Dan looked down at his four-footed companion lovingly, and Rags lifted one ear in recognition of the compliment, meanwhile keeping wistful eyes on the stranger. It almost looked as if he understood.

Charles stooped down and patted him warmly, and the ugly little dog wriggled all over with great happiness.

"Of course he must go with us, then," said Charles.

"Yes, and the way he lit into that dressed-up chap that came and frightened her away was something fine," went on Dan.

"Tell me about it," said Charles.

Dan gave a brief account of Harrington's visit to the village and Dawn's departure.

Charles's face was grave and sad as they spoke of his brother. Harrington's death was too recent and too terrible to admit of bitter memories. He kept his head bent down toward Rags, who was luxuriating in the stranger's fondling, while Daniel was talking. Then he gave the dog a final pat and stood up.

"Daniel," said he, "that man was my brother, and he died of cholera three days ago. He did wrong and made a lot of trouble, and he almost broke my father's heart, but his death was an awful one, and perhaps we'd better not think about his part in this matter any more. He's gone beyond our reach."

"I didn't know," said Dan awkwardly. "I'm sorry I said anything——"

"It's all right," said Charles heartily. "I saw how you felt, and I thought I'd better tell you all about it. I need your help, and it's best to be frank. And now, how about it? Will you go with me to help find her? Will your family object? I'll see to the expense, of course, and will make it as pleasant as I can for you."

"I'll go," said Dan briefly, but his tone meant a great deal. If he had lived in these days, he would have answered "Sure!" with that peculiar inflection that implies whole-souled loyalty. Charles understood the embarrassed heartiness, and took the reply as it was intended.

"How soon can we start?" he asked anxiously. Every moment meant something to him, and he was impatient to be off. He took out his watch. It was quarter to six. "They told me there was a night-coach making connection with the early boat for New York. It starts at seven o'clock. Would that be too soon for you?"

"That's all right," said Daniel, in a voice that was hoarse with excitement. "I just got to change my clothes. Will you come in?"

"Suppose I wait on the front stoop," suggested Charles, seeing the embarrassment in the boy's face.

"All right," said Daniel. "I won't be long."

Mrs. Butterworth looked up anxiously as Dan came into the kitchen. She had been watching the interview from the side window.

"I'm goin' to New York with one of Teacher's friends, ma," he said, in the same tone he would have told her he was going to the village store. "Have I got a clean shirt?"

"To New York!" echoed the woman, who herself had never been outside of the county. "To New York!"—aghast. "Now, you look out, Dan'l. You can't tell 'bout strangers. He may want to get you way from your friends an' rob you."

"What is there to rob, I'd like to know? He's welcome to all he can get."

"You never can tell," said his mother, shaking her head fearfully. "You better take care, Dan'l."

"What's the matter with ye, Ma? Didn't I tell you

he's a friend o' Miss Montgomery? She told me all about him. We're goin' down to New York together to see her. Where's my shirt? He's invited me. You needn't to worry. I may be gone a few days. I'll write you a letter when I get there. I'm goin' to take the dog. We're goin' on the seven o'clock stage an' mebbe I'll find out somethin' about goin' to college. I'm goin' to college this fall if there's any way. I don't know whether he's had any supper. You might give him a doughnut. He's on the front stoop. Say, where *is* my clean shirt, Ma? It's gettin' late."

Daniel had thrown off his coat and was struggling with a refractory buckle of his suspenders as he talked. His mother was roused at last to her duties, and brought the shirt, with which he vanished to the loft. Then the mother, partly to reassure herself about the stranger, filled a plate with cold ham, bread and butter, a generous slice of apple pie, and three or four fat doughnuts, and cautiously opened the front door.

Rags, not having to change his clothes, had remained with Charles, and was enjoying a friendly hand on his head while he sat alert waiting for what was to happen next. When Dan appeared things would move, he knew, and he meant to be in them. He wasn't going to trust any verbal promises. He was going with them if he had to do it on the sly.

Charles arose and received the bountiful supper graciously. When Mrs. Butterworth saw the manner of the stranger who sat on her front settle she was ashamed to be handing him a plate outside, as if he were a tramp.

"Dan'l said you wouldn't come in," she said hospitably, "and I couldn't bear not to give you a bite to eat. You should 'a' happened 'long sooner, while supper was hot. We all thought a lot o' Miss Montgomery. Was you her brother, perhaps?"

While she had prepared the lunch, she had questioned within herself what sort of "friend" this might be with whom Dan was going to visit the teacher. If Dan wanted to "make up" to Teacher, why did he not go alone?

Charles perceived that Daniel had not explained to his mother, and, keeping his own counsel, returned pleasantly:

"Oh, no, not her brother," and he began to tell Mrs. Butterworth how glad he was to have her son's company on his visit to New York. His manner was so reassuring that she decided he was all right, and as Dan came down, his face shining from much soap, and his hair plastered as smoothly as his rough curls would allow, she said pleasantly:

"You'll see my boy don't get into bad company down in New York, won't you? I'm worried, sort of, fer his pa said last night there was cholera round."

Charles's face sobered in an instant.

"We'll take good care of each other, Mrs. Butterworth; don't you worry. I'm much obliged for your letting me have Daniel for company, and I'll try to make him have a pleasant time."

The village people stared at Dan as he got into the stage with the stranger. They wondered where he was going. One of the boys made bold to slide up to the coach and ask him, but he got little satisfaction.

"Just running down to New York for a few days," Dan answered nonchalantly, as if it were a matter of every-day occurrence.

Amid the envious stares of the boys, the coach drove away into the evening, and Daniel sat silently beside his companion, wondering at himself, his heart throbbing greatly that he might within a few hours see the girl who had made such a difference in his life.

About midnight everybody but Charles and Daniel got out of the coach. Comfortably ensconced, the two young men might have slept, but Charles was too nervous and excited to sleep, and Daniel was not far behind him.

"Daniel," said Charles, suddenly breaking the silence that had fallen upon them, though each knew the other was not sleeping, "by what name did she go? Your mother spoke of her as Miss Montgomery. Was that the name she gave?"

"Yes," said Daniel, wondering; "Mary Montgomery."

"It was her mother's name," said Charles reverently. Dawn had talked to him of her mother on their wedding trip.

"Daniel, there is something more that perhaps I

ought to tell you. Did she tell you that she and I are married?"

"No," said Dan. His voice was shaking as he tried to take in the thought. It was as if he were expecting an unbearable pain in a nerve that had already throbbed its life out and was at rest. He was surprised to find how natural it seemed. Then he stammered out:

"I guess I must have known, though. She said she belonged to you, and so nobody else could take care of her."

"Thank you for telling me that," said Charles. He laid his hand warmly on Dan's. The boy liked his touch. Rags, who was sleeping at their feet, nestled closer to them both with a sleepy whine. He was content now that he was really on his way.

"I guess," said Dan chokingly—"I guess I better tell you the whole, because I like you, and you're the right kind. You seem like what she ought to have, and I'm glad it's you—but—it was kind of hard, because, you see, I'd have liked to take care of her myself. I didn't know about you till she told me, and though I knew, of course, I wasn't much to look at beside her, I could have done a lot for her, and I mean to go to college yet, any way, just to show her. You see, I guess it ain't right to go along with you to see her, and not tell you what I said to her. I told her I *loved* her! And it was true, too. I'd have died for her if it was necessary. If that makes any difference to you, Rags and I'll get out and walk back now. I thought I ought to tell you. I couldn't help loving her, could I, when she did so much for me? And, you see, I never knew about you."

It was a long speech for the silent Dan to make, but Charles's warm hand-grasp through it all helped wonderfully, as well as Dan's growing liking for Dawn's husband.

"Bless you, Daniel!" said Charles, throwing his arm about his companion's shoulders, as he used to do with his chums in college. "You just sit right still where you are. It was noble and honest of you to tell me that. I believe in my heart I like you all the better for it. We are brothers, you see, for I love her that way, too, and it gives me a lot of comfort to know you can understand me. But, old fellow—I don't quite know how to say it—I'm deeply sorry that your love has brought you only pain, and I feel all the more warmly toward you that you tried to help her when you knew she belonged to someone else. I never can thank you enough."

"I couldn't have helped it," said Dan gruffly. "If anybody *loved* her, they'd *have* to take care of her, *if it killed 'em.*"

"Dan, old fellow, I love *you,*" said Charles impulsively. "You can't know what this is to me, that you took care of her when I couldn't. I'll love you always, and I shall never forget what you've done for me. Now, begin at the beginning and tell me all you know about her, won't you? I'm hungry to hear."

And Dan found himself telling the whole story of how Dawn had conquered him, the ringleader of mischief in the school, made him her slave, and helped him up to a plane where higher ambitions and nobler standards had changed his whole idea of life.

As he listened to the homely, boyish phrases and read between the lines the pathos of Dawn's struggles, Charles found tears standing in his eyes to think his little girl-wife had been through so much all by herself, without him near to help and comfort. Would he ever, ever, be able to make up to her for it?

He expressed this thought clumsily to Dan, and the boy, all eager now with sympathy, and loving Charles as loyally as Dawn, said royally:

"I calculate one sight of your face'll make her forget it all. Leastways, that's the way it looks to me."

They talked at intervals all night. Charles drew from Daniel his ambition to get an education and be worthy to be the friend of such a teacher as he had had. The boy said it shyly, and then added, "And you too, if you'll let me," and there in the early breaking of the morning light the two young men made a solemn compact of friendship through life. When the sun shone forth and touched the hills, glinting the Hudson in the distance, Daniel sat up and looked about him with a new interest in life, and a happier feeling in his heart than he had had since Dawn went away.

Three days they spent in New York, searching for

Dawn. The paper that had wrapped Dan's book they took to the post-office first, and by careful inquiry were able to discover in what quarter of the city the package was mailed, though, of course, this was very slight information, as she might have been far from her living place when she mailed it. They also discovered the store where the books were bought, for Charles had had the forethought to send Daniel back for them before they started. The clerk who had sold them to her remembered her, and described her as beautiful, with black curls inside a white bonnet, and a dark silk frock. He said she had sad eyes, and looked thin and pale. This troubled Charles more than he was willing to admit to Dan.

Having narrowed their clue to this most indefinite point, they held a consultation and decided that the only thing to do was to walk around that quarter of the city and see if they could get sight of her. Or possibly Rags would get on a scent of her footsteps in some spot less traveled than others. It was almost a hopeless search, yet they started bravely on the hunt, and talked to Rags in a way that would have made an ordinary dog beside himself.

Charles had with him the gloves that Dawn had dropped on the floor beside the bed when she fled from his home. He always carried them with him in his breast-pocket. He took them out and let Rags smell of them. Then Dan said:

"Rags, go find Teacher. Teacher! Rags! Go find Teacher!"

Rags sniffed and looked wistfully in their faces, then barked and started on a sniffing tour all about them, his homely yellow-brown face wearing a look of dog anxiety. He thought he comprehended what they wanted, but was not sure. He had felt a great loss since the teacher went away. Was it possible they expected him to find her?

During the three days, they haunted the streets of the city, both day and evening, and Rags was quite worn out with sniffing. Once or twice he thought he had found a trail, but it came to nothing, and he scurried dejectedly on ahead, hoping his followers had not noticed him bark. On the morning of the fourth day they turned into a narrow street which was almost like a lane compared to other streets. There were only tiny, gloomy houses, and noisy, foreign-looking people stood in the doorways or conversed across the street. It seemed a most unlikely neighborhood for their search, and Charles was half of a mind to turn back and take another street, but almost at the entrance to the street Rags had gone quite wild and nosed his way rapidly down the uneven pavement until he stopped beside a humble doorstep and went nosing about and yelping in great delight. The door was closed, but he tried the steps, and even sniffed under the crack, and then came bounding back to his companions.

"What have you found, Rags, boy?" said Charles halfheartedly. He did not believe they would find any trace of Dawn here.

"He thinks he's found her," said Dan convincingly. "He never acts like that without a reason. Rags, find Teacher! Where is she, Rags?"

"Bow-wow!" answered Rags sharply, as much as to say, "Why don't you open the door and find her yourself?"

An old woman came to the door, and looked sharply at the dog on her clean step. Charles took off his hat.

"We are looking for a friend, madam, who is stopping in this neighborhood somewhere, and we do not know her address. Our dog thinks he has found a trace of her, but he is probably mistaken. You don't happen to have noticed anywhere near here, a young woman with dark eyes and dark, curling hair, lately come to the city— not more than two months ago, perhaps?"

"You wouldn't be meanin' pretty Mary Montgomery—bless her heart!—would ye?" the old woman asked quizzically, surveying the two.

But Rags had stayed not on the order of his going. He had dashed past the old woman and up the stairs to the floor above.

"Och! Look at the little varmint!" said the old woman, forgetting her question and dashing after the dog, thus missing the startled look that came into the faces of both young men.

But after a series of short, sharp barks, Rags returned as quickly as he had gone, almost knocking the old lady down her rickety stairs, in his delight, and bearing in his mouth a fragment of gray cloth which he brought and laid triumphantly at his master's feet.

Dan stooped and picked it up almost reverently and smoothed the frayed edges. It was a bit of Dawn's gray school-dress that she had torn off where the facing was worn and had caught her foot as she walked. Dan recognized the cloth at once. Charles had never seen the gown, but he saw that the bit of cloth had some significance to Dan. He rushed in after the old lady, who had now descended the stairs wrathfully behind the dog.

"Tell me where this Miss Montgomery is, please," he said as quietly as he could. He had followed so many clues and seen them turn into nothing before his eyes, he scarcely could dare hope now. His heart was beating wildly. Was he to see Dawn again at last?

"Och! An' I wish I knew, the darlint!" said the garrulous old woman. "She lift me yistherday marnin', an' it's thrue I miss the sight o' her sweet smile an' her pretty ways. She was a young wummun of quality, was she, an' I sez to me dauther, sez I, 'Kate, mind the ways o' her, the pretty ways o' Mary Montgomery,' sez I, 'fer it's not soon ye'll see such a lady agin.' "

"Has she been here in your house, do you say?" asked Charles anxiously. He felt he must keep very calm or he might lose the clue.

"Yis, sorr, that she was. She ockepied me back siccond floor, an' a swater lady niver walked the earth, if she *was* huntin' work fer her pretty, saft hands to do, what she couldn't get nowhere, sorr, more's the pity. Would yez like to coom up an' tak a luik at the rum? It's as nate a rum as ye'll find in the sthreet, ef I do say so as shouldn't, though a bit small fer two. But there's the frunt siccond floor 'll be vacant to-morry, at only a shillun more the wake."

Daniel held up the fragment of cloth.

"It's the frock she wore to school," he said. He spoke hoarsely and handled it as though it belonged to the dead. It seemed terrible to him to have found where she had been, and not find her.

They followed the old woman upstairs, scarcely

hearing her dissertation, nor realizing that she took them for possible roomers.

The room was neat, as the woman had said, but bare—so bare and gloomy! Nothing but blank walls and chimneys to be seen from the tiny window, where the sun streamed in unhindered across the meagre bed and deal chair and table which were the only furnishings. Charles's heart grew tender with pity, and his eyes filled with tears, as he looked upon it all and realized that his wife had slept there on that hard bed, and had for a time called that dreary spot home. He glanced involuntarily out of the window, noting the garbage in the back yards below, and the unpleasant odors that arose, and remembered the warnings and precautions with which the papers had been filled even before the cholera had come so close to them. He shuddered to think what might have happened to Dawn.

"But where has she gone?" he asked the old woman.

"Yes, that's what we want to know," said Dan.

"Yes, where!" barked Rags behind the old woman's heels, which made her jump and exclaim, "Och, the varmint!" until Dan called the dog to his side.

"She's gone. Lift me, an' no rason at all at all, savin' thet she couldn't find wark, an' her money most gahn. I sez to her as she went out that dor, sez I, 'Yez betther go hum to yer friends ef yez kin find 'em. It's bad times fer a pretty un like you, an' you with yer hands that saft;' but she only smiled at me like a white rose, an' way away, sayin' she'd see, and she thankin' me all the whilst fer the little I'd been able to do fer her—me that's a widder an' meself to kape."

Nothing more could they get from the good woman, though they tried both with money and questions. Dawn had been there for two months, and had gone out every day hunting work. She had come back every night weary and discouraged, but always with a smile. At last she had come home with a newspaper, her face whiter than usual, and, as the old widow had put it, said: "'Mrs. O'Donnell, I'm away in the marn, fer I'm thinkin' it's best;' and away she goes."

The two young men turned away at last, after having made Rags smell all around the room. He insisted upon their taking a folded bit of paper that he found on the floor by the window, as if it were something precious belonging to her. They bade Mrs. O'Donnell good-by, after Charles had given her something to solace her for losing two prospective roomers, and went out to search again.

Rags preceded them down the street, following the scent rapidly until he reached the corner, where he seemed in some perplexity for a time. Finally, he chose the street leading to the river, and going more slowly and crookedly, sometimes zigzagging and sometimes going back to make sure, he brought them at last to the boat-landing.

Perhaps, they thought, she might have followed the advice of the old woman and gone back to her own home region—who knew? With heavy hearts, they set about finding what boats had left the wharf the day before, about the hour the old woman had said that the girl had left her house.

But the morning boat of the day before had just come in and was lying by for repairs. After some questioning, the captain professed to recall such a passenger as they described, but as all the decks had been scrubbed, Rags with his eager nose was unable to corroborate the captain's testimony. Charles and Dan lost no time in securing passage on the boat, which was to sail that evening for Albany, where the captain said he was sure the young lady had gotten off the evening before.

The remainder of the afternoon they spent in making inquiries in every direction, leaving written messages directed to Miss Mary Montgomery, and putting notices in the various city papers. Rags, meantime, was much annoyed and disturbed by their digression. He felt that the boat was the place to stay. He was satisfied they were on the right track. If he had been managing the expedition, he would have had the boat start at once. When it finally did leave the wharf, he sat up on deck with his fore-feet on the railing and barked his satisfaction, then settled down to rest at the feet of the two beloved ones, with a smile of satisfaction on his grizzly face.

# CHAPTER XXVI

THE day before Dawn left New York the city papers officially announced that the cholera had reached the city. Their columns were filled with admonitions, and the symptoms of the disease from start to finish were plainly told. Everybody was ordered to clean up and keep clean.

There seemed to be nothing but cholera news in the paper. A full report was given of every case, and two long columns reported the progress of the disease in other States and cities.

As Dawn passed wearily away from an office where she had spent the entire day waiting for a man who she hoped might use his influence to get her a chance to teach a small school in a country district, but who did not come, she caught the cry of the newsboys.

"New York *Commercial-Advertiser!* All 'bout the cholera!"

It was not often she spent her hoarded pennies for a paper, but a sudden desire to know the truth about the fearful epidemic seized her. She bought a paper, and turned to the general report column. Almost at once her eye caught the name of a town not far from where her father lived, with a report of three cases of cholera. She read on down the column, and suddenly her heart stood still with horror.

SLOANVILLE [she read]. *A man who gave his name as Harrington Winthrop died here last week of cholera. He was in an advanced stage of the disease when he arrived in a hired carriage, and died a few hours later. His father and brother were sent for and arrived before his death. This case has caused a panic among the negroes in the vicinity, and there have been a few suspicious cases of illness which are being carefully watched. Every-*

*thing is being done to prevent a further spread of the disease.*

Dawn felt a sudden weakness, and hurried back to her wretched boarding place to lie down. She did not feel like eating any supper, though the old woman prepared some tea and toast and brought it up to her.

Dawn lay panting on her hard little bed, and the hot breath of the night came in at her window, redolent of all the departed dinners of the neighborhood. A stench of garbage sometimes varied the atmosphere as the faint breeze died away, and the noises of a careless, happy-go-lucky community jangled all about her. She thought of the rules of cleanliness that had been laid down in the papers, and of the probability that they would not be carried out in this street. She pictured herself sick with cholera, with no one but the poor old woman to wait upon her, and no doctor. The smells, the awful smells, would be going on and on, and she would be unable to get up and get away from them. She thought of the hot, hot sun that would stream in at her curtainless window when the day broke again, and wondered why she had come to this terrible city, where there was no work, and no place in the world for a lonely pilgrim whom nobody wanted.

Then over her rolled a deep relief at the thought that Harrington Winthrop would trouble her no more, though it seemed awful to rejoice in what must have been a terrible death. Yet it could not but make life freer for her, for she would have one thing less to fear.

Gradually, as she thought about it, another fear seized her. Charles, his brother, her husband, had been with him when he died. Perhaps he too would take it and die, and she would never know, never see him again in this life. She would be left alone—alone in this awful world where she had no friends, and none to love her, save a poor boy to whose kind heart she had brought only pain.

Why not go back to the neighborhood where Charles was? She need not let herself be known. She could surely find some secluded place where she could earn enough to keep her, yet where she might find out

how he was, and maybe catch a glimpse of him now
and then!

It was strange this idea had not entered her mind
before. It had never seemed to her possible that she
could go back. But now the spectre of death had made
her see things in a different light. She wanted to get back
to the greenness and the coolness of the country, and,
most of all, she wanted to know if Charles was living
and was well. After that, it did not matter what became
of her; but now she knew she was going back, and she
was going at once—in the morning.

She went down to tell the old lady her purpose, and
after that she slept. The next morning she gathered up
her few belongings and took the boat for Albany.

She had no settled purpose of where she would go
after reaching her objective point. She did not know the
name of the town where Charles lived. Strangely enough,
it had never been mentioned in her hearing, and she
had not thought to ask. She was beginning to feel as if
she must have been half asleep when a good many important events in her life happened. Was she half asleep
now also, she wondered idly?

As they passed the old school of Friend Ruth, Dawn
looked out hungrily and longed inexpressibly to be a girl
again, studying her lessons and knowing little of the
hardness of life.

When the boat reached Albany she took the first
stage-coach that appeared, without asking where it went.
Her money was almost gone, but she paid the fare
without a pang. What did anything matter, now that she
was out of New York?

Everywhere the talk was of the cholera, and her
heart grew sick as she heard the details of the dread disease, and long, minute descriptions of how best to nurse
it.

The stage-coach reached a pretty village late in the
afternoon, and Dawn left it, to take a walk and rest
herself from the long sitting.

She had but a few dollars left. Perhaps she ought
not to use any more for fare, but stay where she was if
she liked it, or walk farther.

She did not feel like eating anything, so she grasped her little bundle of well-worn garments, and walked down the village street.

There was a white church with a wide porch, and stairs in front, leading to the gallery. At the side was the graveyard, its wicket gate shaded by a great weeping willow. Just inside was a seat under the tree. Dawn tried the gate and found it unlatched, and she went in and wandered about among the graves, reading here and there a name idly, and wondering how it would seem to lie down and sleep in that quiet resting place.

Deep in the centre, so far from the street that she could not be seen, she sank in the grass at the foot of a green mound, and laid her face down upon the blossoming myrtle. How nice it would be if this were a great, free inn where strangers might come and lie down, and the servants would bring each one a green blanket for covering, and a white stone at the head of his pillow, and let him sleep in peace and quietness forever. She was so weary, so weary, body and soul.

At last she roused herself, and, looking up at the stone above her, traced the name with startled senses:

MARY MONTGOMERY,
Born 1798, Died 1825.
*Blessed are the pure in heart,
for they shall see God*

Now, indeed, Dawn was wide awake! This, then, was her mother's grave. She verified the dates with her own memory. She traced the letters tenderly with her fingers, she took in the significance of the quotation, and read her mother's story as she had never been told it by any one. Her mind, made keen by suffering, could understand and sympathize. Her young heart ached with longing for the mother who was gone from her. How might they have comforted each other if they could only have been permitted to stay together!

A little later she moved her position and saw that there was a smaller mound beyond her mother's grave, and that the white stone read:

CARROLL MONTGOMERY VAN RENSSELAER,
Aged 2 years and 9 months.
*He shall gather the lambs in His arms.*

Before this stone Dawn knelt in wonder. Had she, then, had a brother? And how much more of the story was there? Oh, if she had only asked her father more questions! Perhaps some day she would dare to go to him and find out many things. Not now—not till she was older and had forgotten some of the troubles she had borne. Poor child! She knew not that his body had been resting beneath a stately monument these ten days past!

Beyond her was her grandfather's stone, and beside it her grandmother's, much older and moss-covered. In the same enclosure were many other Montgomerys who had lived and died. Some of their names she thought she remembered. She sighed wearily and, going back to her mother's grave, touched the letters of her name gently, as if she would bid them farewell, picked a spray of the blossoming myrtle, and went sadly out into a lonely world again. She could not stay here; it was too sorrowful.

She walked to the next village that afternoon, and took another coach, the first that came along, going she knew not where. When she reached the end of the route the next morning, she took up her walk again, resolving to spend no more money for riding. She did not realize how long she had walked, but some time in the afternoon she came into a familiar region. She could not tell where she was at first, but as she drew near to the village she recognized it as her native town.

At first she was frightened, and stopped by the roadside to think what to do. Then a great longing to see the garden once more, and creep into the old summer-house came over her. Skirting the woods on the outside of the village, and going around by the saw-mill, she at last came to the hedge at the lower end of her father's garden, and slipped through to the summer-house, as she had wished.

The mansion looked quiet. No one seemed moving about. But, then, it had always seemed that way. She had no fear that any one would discover her, for the hedge was thick and tall, and had not been cut lately. She

crept into her old corner in the greenness and quiet.
The cushions were there as they used to be, but they
looked weather-beaten, as if no one had been there in a
long time. She brushed them off, spread her mantle upon
them, and lay down. It was very still all about, and she
soon slept. Some time in the night she awoke with a
feeling of chill and loneliness. It was night, she knew by
the darkness, and a sense of something strange and sad
brooded in the air. But she was very weary and soon
slept again.

When she awoke again it was late morning. She
knew by the sun that the day was well begun, and she
was impressed almost immediately by the quietness of
her surroundings. There seemed to be no one about. Not
a sound came from the house. The bees and the cicadas
droned and whetted their hot scythes in the burning day,
but otherwise there was a torrid silence.

The little hedged summer-house was not far from
the street. It seemed strange to the girl that she heard no
one passing. She got up and made herself as tidy as the
circumstances allowed, and then stole toward the house,
keeping within hiding of the hedges. She had no mind
to let any one see her, but a strange fascination led her
to look again upon her old home.

The shutters were all staring wide, as if forgotten,
and the front door stood open, but no one was about.
Dawn wondered if the old servants were still there, but
no sound came from the direction of the kitchen. She
stole nearer, though her judgment warned her to go away
if she did not wish to be seen and recognized. A power
stronger than she realized seemed drawing her on.

With sudden impulse, she stepped softly up to the
front door and peeped in. She had no deep love for this
old house, for the memories of her mother there had
been dimmed and marred by later happenings; but Dawn
had been a wanderer so many months now, that even to
look upon a place where she had once had a right to be,
was good.

The hall looked much as ever, though there was no
hat lying on the polished mahogany table, and a coating
of dust showed clearly in the stream of sunshine from
the front door. Her father's walking-sticks were not in

their accustomed place either. She wondered a little, and then was impressed again by the deep stillness that lay over everything. What could it mean? Was no one about? Surely they had not gone off and left the house alone and the front door wide open!

The curious longing for a sight of something familiar which had brought her thus far drew her on. Cautiously she stepped into the hall and peered into this room and that—the parlor, the library, the dining-room, and back through the servants' quarters into the kitchen. All were empty!

The fire was out, and a heap of ashes lay on the hearth, as if no one had made an attempt to put things to rights for hours. There were unwashed dishes on the kitchen table, and on the bread board, beside the knife, lay half a loaf of bread which had moulded in the warm, moist atmosphere. It was all very strange. What could have happened?

With a growing sense that the house was empty now, Dawn went upstairs, looking first into her own old room and the guest rooms, and coming at last to the door of that which had been her step-mother's. It was closed, and she hesitated to open it. What need had she to go in there, any way? It could profit her nothing. If her step-mother was there, Dawn did not wish to see her. The girl paused an instant, then her soft tread turned back again to go downstairs, but a low sound, like a moan, caught her ear, and something made her turn again and open the door, though cold chills were creeping down her spine, and a frenzy of fear had seized upon her.

There upon the high four-poster bed lay her step-mother, her eyes sunken into deep sockets, her cheeks hollow, her nose thin and pointed, her whole face pinched and blue, with lines of agony in her expression.

Dawn felt her heart leap in fear, but she went forward. There seemed nothing else to do.

The sunken eyes turned toward her dully, and the blue lips uttered a low moan, then, suddenly, the sick woman fixed her gaze upon the girl's face in growing horror, and a livid look came into her face.

"Is that you at last?" she asked in a deep, hoarse

voice that sounded strange and unnatural. "Are we both dead?"

A cold perspiration had come out upon the girl, and the awfulness of the situation seemed to be taking her senses away, but she tried to speak coolly, and still the wild beating of her heart.

"Yes, I've come," said Dawn; "but we're not dead. What is the matter? Are you sick? I found the front door open, and no one around."

"They've all gone and left me," moaned the woman, beginning to turn her head with a strange, restless movement from side to side. "They rushed off like frightened cattle. You'll go, too, I suppose, when you know I've got the cholera. Yes, go quick. I don't want to do you any more harm than I have already. Oh!"

The sentence broke in a cry of agony, and the sick woman writhed in terrible contortions, which, passing, left her weak and almost lifeless. The girl's heart was filled with horror, but she took off her bonnet and cape and laid down her bundle.

"No, I'm not going to leave you," she said sadly, almost dully. "I'm not afraid, and, besides, it doesn't matter about me, any way. Have you had the doctor?"

The woman shook her head. The agony was not all passed.

"There wasn't any one to go for him," she murmured weakly, tossing restlessly again. "Oh, I'm so thirsty! Can you get me some water?"

"Where is Father?" asked Dawn, wondering if he too had deserted her.

"Didn't you know he was dead?" asked the sick woman, in that strangely hoarse voice.

"No," said Dawn, shuddering. Everybody seemed to be dying. Would she die, too?

She hurried to the old medicine closet and in a moment returned with the camphor bottle and some lumps of sugar and administered several drops of camphor. The patient's hands were cold and blue. Dawn tucked her up with blankets warmly.

"You lie still," she said in a business-like tone. "I'll get some hot water bottles for your hands and feet, and then I'll call the doctor."

"It isn't worth while for you to stay here and get the cholera," said the woman plaintively. "I'm not going to get over it. I've known it all night. It was coming on yesterday. I tried to straighten up the house, but I was too dizzy and weak. The servants all went away when they heard me say I didn't feel well. There have been several other cases——"

But Dawn did not hear all her step-mother said, for she had hurried down to get a fire started. It was no easy task for her unaccustomed hands to strike the fire from the tinder-box, and after one or two fruitless efforts she decided to waste no more time, but to run to the neighbor's and borrow a kettle of water, at the same time sending a message for the doctor. She was terribly frightened by her step-mother's appearance, and knew she must be very ill indeed. It seemed as if all possible haste was necessary if she would help to save her life.

Upstairs, the sick woman was tossing and moaning. The sudden appearance of the girl who had been the occasion of so much trouble in her life seemed to make the agony all the greater. She knew that she was face to face with death, and now to have the girl she had injured meet her almost on the threshold of the other world, and minister to her, was double torment. If only she could do something to make amends for the wrong she had done, before she left the world and went to meet her just retribution! Her fevered brain tried to think. What was there she could do?

The girl had come, and would probably take the disease and die. Her husband might never know she was here. No one would find it out until she was dead. If only she—Mrs. Van Rensselaer—had some way of letting Charles Winthrop know that his wife had come home. If she could get up and go out into the street and beg some one to take him a message! But her strength was gone, and the agony might come upon her at any moment. She would have to do it at once, or the girl would return and stop her. Could she try?

All her life she had been a woman of iron will. She had made herself and every one except her husband bend to it. She summoned it now. She would try. She would make one supreme effort to right the great wrong of her life. If in the other world to which she knew she was going in a few short hours there was opportunity to meet the husband she had loved as she loved nothing else on earth besides herself, she would like to tell him that she had tried—that at the last hour she had tried to make some amends.

With the extraordinary strength which mind sometimes gives to body at times of great necessity, as in cases of soldiers mortally wounded fighting to the end, the woman crawled out of the bed and dragged herself over to the desk. Her eyes were bright with her great purpose and blazed like sunken fires. Her gray, thin hair straggled down upon the collar of the old dressing-gown she had put on when first taken sick. She seized her quill pen and a sheet of paper that lay there, and with cramped, shaking hand wrote, "Dawn is here," and signed her name, "Maria Van Rensselaer." The scrawl was almost unreadable, but she dared not try to write it over. She dared not add another word. Her time was short. Her strength already was failing. She had yet to get the message into some one's hands. Perhaps even now she would fail. She crushed the folds together with her cold fingers, wrote "Charles Winthrop" and the address, and then tottered across the room to the door. She almost fell as she reached the stair-landing. The dizzy, blinding blackness that seemed pressing upon her almost overwhelmed her. She felt the pain and torment surging back, but she fought it off and would not yield. This was her last chance to make amends—her last chance. She said it over to herself as she clung to the banisters and got down the stairs clumsily. If Dawn had been in the house, she must have heard her.

It looked like miles to the front gate as the sick woman came out on the piazza, but somehow she got there—a queer, ghastly figure of death, clinging to the gate-post, with a letter and a purse in her hand.

In the distance she saw a negro approaching. He was scuttling along with a frightened gait, as if he wished to hurry through the street. She felt her strength going. If she could only stand up till he reached her! It seemed to her hours before he came to the gate. She had kept back out of sight, instinctively feeling he would be scared away if he saw her.

"Take that to the post office or God will punish you!" she said, in the deep, hoarse voice the disease had given her, and thrust the letter and the purse upon him.

The negro stopped with a yell of fright, but her words had the desired effect. She had worked upon the superstition of his race. He dared not disobey her command. Taking the letter and the purse in his thumb and finger, that he might not come in contact with them more than was necessary—for a glance at the face of the woman had warned him of her malady—he ran at top speed to the post-office. His eyes rolled with horror as he told of the old woman who had accosted him. He felt as if his days were numbered and he fled the village immediately, not caring where he went so he got away from the haunting memory of the living dead who had given him the letter.

With almost superhuman effort Mrs. Van Rensselaer turned to go back to the house, but the iron will could carry her no further. Her strength was gone. She had accomplished her errand, and had come to the end. She had done her best to make amends for her sin. She sank unconscious by the gateway.

Meantime, Dawn had hurried through the hedge by a short cut to the nearest neighbor's, but failed to get any response to her urgent knock. She went around the house and perceived that it was closed. The family must be away. She flew to the neighbor just below with the same result, and going on farther down the street to four other houses, found no one in sight. At the fifth, some distance from her home, a woman stepped fearfully out of the kitchen door, and agreed to send word to the doctor, but shook her head at the demand for hot water. She could not spare her kettle. She had sickness in the house herself. No, she didn't think Dawn could get any at the next house either. Everybody that could get away had gone since the cholera struck the town. Then the woman went in and shut the door and with new horror Dawn sped back to try her hand again at making the fire.

The necessity was so strongly upon her now that she fairly *made* that fire burn, and at last had a kettle of hot water to carry upstairs.

Dawn was so intent upon carrying her great steaming kettle up the front stairs without spilling the contents that she failed to hear the wheels of a carriage upon the gravel drive outside. It was not until she had carried the kettle into the bedroom and put it on the hearth and then turned toward the bed that she discovered the bed was empty!

A great horror filled her. Trembling, she knew not why, she quickly glanced into the other rooms on that floor. It seemed almost as if the pestilence had become a living being that could snatch people bodily away from the earth.

She seemed to have no voice with which to call, yet she felt upon her a necessity of great haste. Perhaps her step-mother had gone downstairs in search of her. She hurried down a few steps, then stopped, startled. Some-one was coming into the front door, staggering under the heavy burden of an inert, human form. It looked a vivid blot of darkness against the background of the hot summer sunshine outside.

Dawn hurried down, with white face and horrified eyes, and saw that it was the old family doctor, and that he held her step-mother in his arms. A sudden pang of remorse went through her heart that she had been away from the sick one so long, yet how could she have helped it? Was Mrs. Van Rensselaer perhaps trying to find her, or was she seeking aid, and had fallen by the way?

"Oh, why did she get up!" she exclaimed regretfully. "I came just as soon as I could get the water hot!" Then she caught hold of the heavy form of the unconscious woman and helped with all her young strength to lift and drag her up to her room again.

"She might have been out of her head, child," said the doctor kindly, as if in answer to her exclamation. He was searching in his medicine case for a certain bottle as he spoke. His breath was coming in short, quick gasps from the exertion of carrying the sick woman upstairs, and the perspiration stood in great beads on his forehead. His face looked old and haggard, and his voice was that

of one who had seen much recent sorrow. He walked
rapidly asking a few keen questions and giving brief directions. He nodded approvingly at the kettle of hot water,
sent Dawn for one or two articles he needed, then when
he had done all he could, and the sick woman was breathing more naturally, he turned and looked at Dawn.

She had told him in a few words how she had found
the house when she arrived, and the little she had done.
He looked her through with his kind tired eyes, noted
the sweet, sad face, the dark circles under her eyes, the
pallor of the thin cheeks, and shook his head doubtfully.

"You're young for this sort of thing," he said gruffly.
"It's a hard case, and her only hope is good nursing. I'm
afraid you're not equal to it. You'll break down yourself."

"Oh, no, I'm quite strong," said Dawn, bravely trying to smile.

"Well, I don't know how it can be helped," he
mused. "I don't know of a single person I can get to help
you. It may be Patience Howe could come if she can
get away from the Pettibones. I'll see what I can do.
I'll stop and send a line to Mrs. Van Rensselaer's sister.
She'll likely come down by to-morrow. Do you know she
was here when your father died. Do you think you could
get along to-night alone in case I can't get any one? I'll
try to get back here before dark if I can and bring some
one to stay with you. I haven't had a wink of sleep for
forty-eight hours except what I caught on the road. I'll
get back as soon as I can."

Dawn assured him she would do her best, though
her heart quaked within her at thought of staying alone
with the death-like sleeper upon the bed. The doctor
gave a few directions and cautions, and hurried away.

The house settled into quiet, and the hours stretched
into torturing length. Dawn slipped downstairs to find
some food, for she was growing faint with long fasting.
But there was nothing in the house fit to eat. The bread
was moist and sticky with the damp, warm atmosphere,
and she had no heart to cook anything. She had arranged
the fire to keep the kettle boiling, for hot water was an
essential in the sick-room. Now she caught sight of a

basket of eggs and dropped several into the boiling water. These would keep her alive and be easy to eat.

The afternoon was a long agony. She spent most of the time applying hot cloths, and chafing the skin of her step-mother. From time to time the woman would almost waken or moan and toss in her sleep. As the hot, red sun slipped down in the west and the oppressive darkness settled upon the house, Dawn felt more alone than she had ever been in all of her short, troublous life. She lighted a candle and set it on the floor in the hall, as in the room it seemed to trouble the patient. The long, flickering shadows wavered over the floor in ghostly march, and the nurse sat and watched them till it seemed that they were the shadows of all the troubles that had taken their way through her young life.

It was late in the evening when the doctor finally returned, and he was alone. But Dawn was glad to see his kindly face, for she had almost given up hoping for him that night, and it seemed terrible to her to sit there and feel that the death angel was standing at the other side of the bed, perhaps.

But the doctor's eyes brightened a little as he looked at the patient.

"She's holding her own," he murmured. "You've done pretty well, little girl. Just as well as an experienced nurse. If you can keep it up during the night you may save her life. I'm sorry I couldn't get any one to stay with you to-night, but there wasn't a soul who was not already taking care of two or more cases. I'd stay myself, but there are three cases I must save to-night if possible. Keep up the treatment as before, and if she rouses again try this new medicine."

He was gone as quickly as he had come, and she was alone with her charge once more, but a new spark of interest was in her work. He had said she might save her step-mother's life. She wondered dully why she should care when the woman had done her so much harm, but she did care, and the fact gave her peace.

While she thus thought she was aware that the sick woman's eyes had opened and were gazing at her with a strange, deep wonder, as if they would ask: "Are you here yet? Have you stayed alone to nurse me, when I have always hated you, and done you harm?"

Dawn came quickly over to the bed and stood in the path of light that the candle shed from the hall doorway. She took the patient's hands in her own and noticed they were not so cold as they had been, and she asked gently: "Do you want anything?"

For a moment her step-mother only looked at her, and then her lips stirred as if in an effort to speak, but she uttered only one word, "Forgive?"

Dawn's heart bounded with a sudden, unexpected pleasure, and the tears sprang to her eyes.

"Of course!" she said briskly, "it's all right, but you must lie still and help get well."

A gentler light came into Mrs. Van Rensselaer's anxious eyes. Once more, as if to make sure that she had heard aright, she murmured her question, "Forgive?"

Dawn stooped impulsively and kissed her. Then an actual smile of peace settled into the hard face of the woman on the bed, changing it utterly.

"It's all right," said Dawn again eagerly. "And now you must take your medicine and not talk any more. You are going to get well. The doctor says so, and you must go to sleep at once."

She administered the new medicine, and with another smile like a tired child the sick woman sank away into a gentle, restful sleep.

It was late in the afternoon of the following day that the doctor returned with Mrs. Van Rensselaer's sister, who established herself by the bedside with energy and competence. The doctor, noticing Dawn's wan look and sleep-heavy eyes, ordered her to go to bed at once or there would be two patients instead of one to look after. Mrs. Van Rensselaer he pronounced decidedly better.

Dawn, as she slipped away from the sick room, felt dizzy and faint with weariness. She reflected that she would probably contract the disease herself, and it might come upon her suddenly, She had read of many cases that died almost at once. The thought gave her no alarm. It would be good to go quickly. She went to her own room feeling that she had come almost to the end of things.

Her dress was torn and wet from much working with the hot water and flannels. Her face and hands were blackened with soot from the fire. Tired as she was she must freshen herself a little before going to sleep.

She bathed and dressed in fresh garments that she found hanging in her closet, and put on the little white frock she had worn the day before her marriage, smoothed her hair, and then, taking a pillow and some comfortables from the bed, she went downstairs. The thought had come to her that it would be good to get out to the arbor again, If she were to die, it would be as well there as anywhere.

As she passed down the garden walk, a rose thorn caught her white gown, and in freeing herself she noticed a spray of roses like those Charles had picked for her a year ago. Their fragrance seemed to touch her tired senses like healing balm.

After she had spread her comfortables on the floor of the little summer-house, she stepped back and broke off the spray of roses, and lay down with their cool leaves against her hot cheek. Breathing in their odor, she fell into a deep sleep, in which no dreams came to ruffle her peace.

She had not noticed when she lay down that the long, red rays of the sun were very low. The excitement through which she had lived, the lack of food, the unusual exertion and the sudden release from the necessity of doing anything, made her stupid with weariness. The sun slipped quickly down, and the cool darkness of the garden soothed her. A tiny breeze gave her new life, and she slept as sweetly as the sleeping birds in the trees over her head, while the kind stars looked down and kept watch, and the roses nestled close and spoke of him she loved.

In the village, pestilence stalked abroad and the shadow of death hovered, but in the garden there were quiet and peace and rest. And if the languid winds played a solemn dirge among the pines near the old house, they disturbed her not, safe sheltered among God's flowers with others of his beautiful, dependent creatures.

## CHAPTER XXVII

CHARLES and Dan had stayed in Albany several days, questioning coach drivers and making enquiries at all the inns; but no one seemed to remember Dawn. It happened that the driver with whom she had left Albany had broken his leg the very day after, so he was not there to be questioned. Heartsick and despairing, the two young men did not know what to do. Even Rags was dejected, and whined at having to leave the boat. Somehow he seemed to think it would bring them to her if they but stayed by it long enough. He was for going back to New York when the boat went, and told the others so with a wise bark, but they heeded him not. He went about snuffing helplessly, and spent much time with his nose in his paws, one sad blinking eye open to a disappointing world.

They reached the Winthrop home a few hours before Mrs. Van Rensselaer's letter arrived.

It was Betty who brought the strange, scrawled letter to Charles, and she wore an anxious look. She had half-hesitated whether she would not keep it till morning, he looked so tired and worn. These were troublous times, and no one knew at night but that his dearest friend might be dead by morning. Betty would have spared her brother if she had dared.

Charles noticed the postmark, and tore the envelope open quickly, some premonition quickening his heart-beats.

"Dawn is here!"

He read the significant words, then repeated them aloud, his voice containing a solemn ring of wonder and joy. Could it be true?

"Betty, tell the boy to saddle two horses and have them ready at once. Dan, you'll go with me, of course. . . . No, I've no time for supper. . . . Well, just a cup of hot broth. Or, stay, put some in a bottle, and I'll take it with me. I might need it on the way. . . . Are you ready, Dan? . . . Tell father, Betty. I'll be downstairs in just a minute."

They were off almost immediately, for the willing servant had hastened with the horses, and had ready a lantern for their use when the moon should go down. Betty handed each of them a bottle of hot broth tightly sealed, to put in their pockets. They rode through the night, silent for the most part, each gravely apprehensive of what might be at the end of the journey. It was a strange, abrupt message Charles had received, and he pondered over and over what its purport might be. Was Dawn sick, or dead? Why had not Mrs. Van Rensselaer told him more? Perhaps before he could reach his wife she would be gone again, as before. With this thought, he hurried his horse. Once he caught a glimpse of a sharp abyss within a few feet of where he passed. One misstep and the journey would have ended. Charles marvelled how he was going through unknown dangers without a thought, just because his heart was full of a great purpose.

It was in the early morning that they reached the village where the Van Rensselaers lived.

Rags was tired and splashed with mud. His tail dragged wearily behind him, his head drooped, and his tongue hung out. He wasn't used to being up all night, nor to travelling on foot behind fast horses. He thought his companions must be crazy to come away off here where there was no scent. How could they expect to know what they were doing in the night? Rags wanted a good juicy bone, and a rub in a quiet place.

As the two young men turned their horses in at the great gate, the sound of the hoofs clattered hollowly and echoed back in the empty place.

Rags mounted the steps and sat down, looking disconsolately around. He did not care for this place, fine thought it might be. He was dreadfully tired. The front door was open, but he had no desire to investigate.

Charles dismounted and went into the house. It struck him as strange that the front door should be open so early in the morning. He had noticed the deserted look of this part of the town, and he felt the chill of fear grip his heart. Had the cholera reached her ahead of him? Was it in this town? Even in this house?

As Dawn had done, he looked into the empty rooms.

Rags got up and limped to the door after him, snuffed around, and then suddenly gave a short, sharp bark, and was off with his nose to the ground. He disappeared among the rose-bushes down the garden-path, and his young master sprang off his horse and hastened after him.


## CHAPTER XXVIII


QUICKLY as Dan followed, Rags was before him, with his sharp, peculiar bark, and then a sudden low whine of fear or trouble. The boy's heart stood still, and he hurried the faster. Rags came whining to his feet as he reached the arbor. And then Dan saw her.

She lay sleeping on the pile of comfortables, in her little white frock, with the spray of roses in her hand and a slight tinge of color in her cheek, like the flush on a half-open rosebud. The comb had fallen from her hair, and the beautiful curls lay tumbled out upon the pillow in lovely confusion.

The boy gazed with awe, and then turned his head reverently away. But Rags went whining about her feet again.

Dan signed to the dog to be still, and, bending over with sudden anxiety, watched to see if she were breathing naturally.

Gently as a child she slept, and the roses trembled with her soft breathing. His heart leaped with joy.

"Rags, stay here and guard her!" he commanded. "Sit right there!" He pointed to a spot in the garden walk. "Now be still."

Rags whined softly. He was trembling with excitement.

"Be still!"

The little dog thumped his tail in acquiescence, but looked wistfully after his master as he turned away, and then at the sleeping goddess.

Dan hastened back to the house.

The horses were cropping their breakfast from the lawn at the edge of the gravel driveway. Charles was coming down the steps, his face white and drawn.

"Dan, I cannot find her, and there is cholera here. Mrs. Van Rensselaer is lying desperately ill upstairs! There is another woman caring for her and she says Dawn has gone."

He buried his face in his hands and stood still. Dan thought he was going to fall.

"Don't!" said Dan. "I've found her. Come!" He eagerly drew Charles along the garden walk.

"Oh, do you mean it? Are you sure, Dan?"

"Sure," said the boy. "Rags found her. She's asleep. Walk softly."

"Is there anything the matter with her, Dan?" said Charles apprehensively, yet waited not to hear the answer, for at that instant he reached the arbor, almost stumbling over Rags, who jumped upon him with delight and wagged and wriggled himself joyously—albeit silently.

But Charles stood still and gazed at his beloved. His hungry eyes drank in her loveliness, his anxious heart searched keenly for any sign of illness. He felt himself growing weak with fear and joy.

Dan stood silent behind him, his own face lighting with the other's joy and solemn rejoicing that they had found her.

Not so Rags. He thought the time had come for the princess to awaken and he laid a cold, audacious nose in the open palm of Dawn's pink hand. She at once opened her eyes.

"Dawn! My darling!" murmured Charles, and dropped upon his knees beside her.

Rags was beside himself with joy now. He had brought the teacher to life. But Dan grasped him by the collar and drew him away. He and Rags might rejoice, but it was not for them to intrude at such a time as this.

Charles gathered his young wife into his arms, laying his face gently against hers, and over her stole a thrill of deep, solemn joy. He had come after her! He wanted her! She was loved! In spite of the way she had married him, she was beloved!

She closed her eyes and let the joy flow over her, a sweet, sweet pain, till almost it took her breath away, and brought tears to her happy eyes. He kissed them away, and said over and over, "My darling! My darling! I have found you at last!" and she nestled closer to him and hid her face against his breast.

It seemed a long time to Rags, and finally he broke away from his master with a bound and stood barking joyously at their feet.

"Oh, there is Rags!" exclaimed Dawn, with a happy little laugh. "Dear Rags!"

"Yes!" said Rags in his own way. "Dear *Teacher!* I'm glad I found you!"

"And Dan is here, too," said Charles. "Come here, Dan, and share our joy."

Then came Daniel, his face red with embarrassment, and stood bashfully before her.

"I found him, and he's helped me to find you, dear," said Charles. "He's told me all about everything."

All dishevelled as she was, with her lovely hair about her shoulders, Dawn stood bravely to receive him, and put out both hands to the boy.

"Dear Dan!" she said.

She took his hands in hers for an instant, and Dan bowed his head, but he had nothing to say. He felt that he had received a benediction. Rags saw how he felt about it and tried to help him out.

"Me, too!" he barked, and Dawn, laughing, stooped and patted the dog lovingly, while he wriggled himself half in two in his joy.

"But have you had any breakfast?" asked Charles, with sweet responsibility in his tone, as Dawn shook back her curls and gathered them into a knot on her head, fastening them with her comb quite properly. Dan lowered his eyes deferentially and looked away from the pretty sight, knowing it was not for him.

Dawn's face grew grave.

"Is it morning?" said she. "How could I have slept so long when there was so much to be done! Mrs. Van Rensselaer——"

"I know, dear," Charles stopped her, "but she is being cared for. The woman told me she seemed a little better. I got her letter last evening, and we came at once, Dan and I. We had been down to New York, hunting you, and just missed you. We had gone home utterly discouraged, when this note came, just these words, 'Dawn is here.' We started at once. How long had she been ill?"

"The letter?" said Dawn. "I don't understand. I just came myself yesterday morning. She was very ill when I got here. She couldn't have mailed any letter, unless—— Oh, it must be that she dragged herself out and sent it while I was hunting hot water and a doctor for her? The doctor found her lying at the gate unconscious, and brought her in."

"She had done you a great injury," said Charles, with a grave face.

"But she almost gave her life to make it right again," said Dawn solemnly. "I have heard exertion is usually fatal in cholera. And she asked me twice to forgive her. Think of that! Wasn't it wonderful? But you don't know her and can't understand how unlike her that seems."

Dawn was crying softly now, and Charles soothed her anxiously.

"You must put the thought of it away, dear, or you will be ill, too. Are you sure you feel quite well? It was a terrible experience for you to have to go through alone. Come, we must get you something to eat at once. What did you have last? I hope you ate nothing that had been around the sick-room."

"I ate two boiled eggs," said Dawn, smiling through her tears. "It was all I could find, and I was too tired to make a fire."

"Dear child!" said Charles. "But it was the best thing you could have done, I guess. Dan, there's that broth we brought along. Betty put up enough for a regiment."

"We will go to the kitchen and make a fire," said Dawn. "You must have breakfast, too. You have had a long, hard ride."

"Yes, breakfast!" barked Rags impolitely.

Charles grew grave at once.

"Now, Dawn, you must not go near that house again. You have been sufficiently exposed already. Dan and I will bring you some breakfast. I don't like the idea of your eating anything that comes out of that house. It isn't safe. Couldn't we make a little fire there at the edge of the woods and warm that broth? If we had a tin dish——"

"There's a long-handled saucepan in the kitchen," said Dawn. "I'll go and get it."

"You'll stay right here," said Dan, in his kindly, gruff way. "*I'll* go and get it."

Before they could stop him, he had gone, and in a few minutes he returned with a pail of water, a tea-kettle, a saucepan, and three cups. Then he gathered sticks, and he and Charles made the fire, rigging up a kind of crane to hold the kettle. Soon they had hot water to pour over the dishes and then Dawn heated the broth, and they each had a good cupful. Even Rags had a few spoonfuls, though he sat up quite politely at a word from Dan, with his head cocked sideways, and a knowing look, as much as to say, "Serve yourselves first, and I'll lick the dishes."

After all, it was Dan who did everything for them. He told Charles that it was best he should stay with his wife and guard her. There was no telling but she might get sick or something, and it was not safe for her to be left alone just now. Besides, it was Charles's business to care for her, and for that reason he must keep out of danger himself. What would happen to Dawn if Charles should get the cholera?

"But you might get it yourself, Dan, and we'd never forgive ourselves."

"Aw!" said Dan, turning away in scorn. "Don't you worry 'bout *me*."

So Dan had his way. When the doctor came he agreed with Charles that Dawn should be gotten away at once into a high, healthy region. By this time Mrs. Van Rensselaer's brother had arrived with a faithful family servant. There was no need to stay. Mrs. Van Rensselaer had roused herself to add her voice of urgency that Dawn go at once away from contagion. So they hitched their horses to the big Van Rensselaer carriage and rode away on a second wedding journey, attended by Dan and Rags, two faithful servitors.

Once during the afternoon, when Dan had left them for a few minutes, they had looked after him lovingly:

"Dear Dan!" said Charles. "I don't know what I should have done without him. He must have his college course. How would you like to have us send him to Harvard as a sort of thank-offering for what he has done for us?"

And Dawn smiled happily into her husband's eyes as she answered:

"Oh, how beautiful! Could we?"

They planned it all out briefly then, and that evening, at the setting of the sun, as they rode forth from the plague-stricken village toward the high, cool hills where waited the little white house, Charles broached the subject to Dan.

Charles and Dawn were in the back seat, Dan driving in front, with Rags at his feet, with his head held proudly, as if he had always ridden in a carriage with two gray horses.

"Dan," said Charles, leaning forward a little that he might the better see the boy's face, "when Dawn and I go back to Cambridge in the fall, for my last year at Harvard, we're going to take you with us."

Rags smiled widely. He had heard the talk in the afternoon, and he expected to go to college himself.

Dan turned with a radiant, awed face, and grasped Charles's hand.

"Could I?" he asked eagerly. "*How* could I?"

"You may need some preparations," said Charles. "Wouldn't it be a good idea for you to come up to our house in the hills and let me coach you? How about it, Dawn? We have always room for Dan, haven't we?"

And Dawn, smiling and happy, assured the boy that he would always be welcome.

Later, when Charles drew Dawn's head down upon his shoulder in the darkness, put his arm close about her, and with his free hand held both of hers, there was tender joy and thankfulness.

Dan and Rags, up in front, knew that there were depths of happiness in the back seat not for them, but they were content, for were they not going to college, and in company with the two they loved best of all?

A week later Charles and Dawn stood together on the hillside, in front of their own little house. It was very early in the morning, and off beyond another hill the sun was just flashing into view—a great red disc against a sky of amethyst and opal. Hill, valley, winding river, and every tree and shrub were touched with the glory of the dawn.

They were watching Dan ride away to his home, to gather his belongings, and prepare his family for the new order of his life.

In the afternoon Betty was to arrive by stage-coach. She was to spend the rest of the hot weather in the cool hills with them, until the cholera had disappeared. This was their first time absolutely alone together since they had known each other.

They stood silent, watching the gray figure of horse and man as it proceeded slowly down the hillside and disappeared among the trees in the shadowy road, where night was yet lurking. Slowly, slowly, the sun slipped up, until a great ball of ruby light grew into a brilliant glory their eyes could not look upon. And stretched before them lay the day, with all its radiant possibilities.

" 'And he shall be as the light of the morning when the sun riseth, even a morning without clouds; as the tender grass springing out of the earth by clear shining after rain,' " quoted Charles solemnly.

They involuntarily drew closer together as they looked. Then the husband put his arm about the wife and, looking down upon her, said:

"Dawn of the Morning, do you know that you are like all that to me?"

She hid her happy face on his shoulder, and he bent down and whispered:

"Darling! Dawn of my morning! *My* Dawn!"

Novels of Enduring Romance and Inspiration by

# GRACE LIVINGSTON HILL

| | | | |
|---|---|---|---|
| ☐ | 11762 | **TOMORROW ABOUT THIS TIME** | $1.50 |
| ☐ | 11506 | **THROUGH THESE FIRES** | $1.50 |
| ☐ | 10859 | **BEAUTY FOR ASHES** | $1.50 |
| ☑ | 10891 | **THE ENCHANTED BARN** | $1.50 |
| ☐ | 10947 | **THE FINDING OF JASPER HOLT** | $1.50 |
| ☐ | 2916 | **AMORELLE** | $1.50 |
| ☐ | 2985 | **THE STREET OF THE CITY** | $1.50 |
| ☐ | 10766 | **THE BELOVED STRANGER** | $1.50 |
| ☐ | 10792 | **WHERE TWO WAYS MET** | $1.50 |
| ☐ | 10826 | **THE BEST MAN** | $1.50 |
| ☐ | 10909 | **DAPHNE DEANE** | $1.50 |
| ☐ | 11005 | **STRANGER WITHIN THE GATES** | $1.50 |
| ☐ | 11020 | **SPICE BOX** | $1.50 |
| ☐ | 11028 | **A NEW NAME** | $1.50 |
| ☐ | 11329 | **DAWN OF THE MORNING** | $1.50 |
| ☐ | 11167 | **THE RED SIGNAL** | $1.50 |